I appreciated how vividly the a
with its deceitful beauty of the
deeds. The attitude of Antoinette's compatriots was also
brilliantly portrayed as well as the setting in a Lebensborn—
the subject that not many writers touch upon—was depicted
in great detail. I applaud the author for this wonderful work,
and highly recommend it.

—Amazon Customer

Meticulously-researched and tightly plotted. She covers
all the bases. There's heartache and hilarity, something for
everyone. If you're a serious student of WWII, you'll love the
historical accuracy. If you favor Lifetime movies, Hallmark
cards and silly love songs, you'll love the story line.

—Teri Elders, writer

Next stop . . . a screenplay! Put your seatbelt on . . . here we
go.

—Mona Berglin, San Francisco

Lebensborn Secrets is about the resilience of ordinary people
affected by war, the overzealous believers in a lost cause,
and the healing that is possible after extreme heartache. It
covers everything from the collaboration between the French
Resistance and the British and the strict laws the Nazis put
in place in the occupied countries to Heinrich Himmler's
fascination with the occult and the brutal tactics of the
Gestapo to extract information.

—Anna Horner, *Diary of an Eccentric*

The short, punchy chapters moves along at a rapid clip as
suspense builds on suspense. It's a real page-turner. Plus, the
characters are engaging, and the history, well-researched.

—Steve Rumsey, *North Columbia Monthly*

Antoinette Gauthier is an individual who sees what is happening in her village and wants to do something to help her people. In the process she becomes part of a group of women who give birth to lead Hitler's 1000-year Reich. What happens next shows how situations can affect not only the actions of individuals but how we can look forward to making the most of our lives in the face of challenges and difficulties.

—Cyrus Webb, Conversations Book Club

Drama, fear, realism, fact and humanity make this a book you HAD to finish. And, then you wish for more.

—Readers Favorite

Remarkable.

—Stephen Windwalker, Kindle Daily Nation

I like history books. I have a history major and I married a history fanatic. I especially enjoy historical novels. I tremendously enjoyed reading *Lebensborn Secrets*. For a while I was frustrated with the character of Antoinette, a strong, virgin, mature and level-headed girl who falls so easily for the Major. However, I started comparing her to my own teenage daughter and realized that at that age, the great majority of women are a pendulum of feelings, attitudes, interests, strengths, insecurities and so on. Trying to survive a war certainly could confuse anyone, let alone a young girl who hasn't much experience. At the end, I liked the theme of forgiveness. Forgiveness is the only way to move forward.

—Victoria Broden

LEBENSBORN SECRETS

Lebensborn Secrets

JO ANN BENDER

ISBN-10: 1-882384-04-0
ISBN-13: 978-1-882384-04-4

Book Cover: Graphic Designer, Gloria de los Santos
Interior design: Gray Dog Press, Spokane, WA

For F.C. (Bud) Budinger
. . . and our continuing good times together

A Program of Secrets

At the peak of their power the Nazis did enjoy a period of colossal success due to a number of factors. Persons in 1941 had no way of knowing that there would not be a "Thousand Year Reich."

Lebensborn, and the breeding of children of pure blood for the Führer, was designed especially for women of the upper class and continues to be mysterious, disputed and the most secret of all Nazi programs. Due to its special attributes, put forward with excellent public relations techniques, it was easy for a man to persuade a women to succumb to the idea of being a mother of a child who would be a leader in the New Reich.

The name of the program created by Heinrich Himmler translates as Fount of Life, Source of Life, or Free Born. It provided maternity homes and financial assistance to the wives of SS and Gestapo members at first and then to specially chosen women who were recruited to become impregnated to give birth to genetically superior Aryan children. Fathers were mainly Germans of high class and intelligence who had to support the program financially.

The program also ran orphanages and carried out relocation programs to bring back from other countries biologically fit children to be raised by childless couples in Germany.

Following the war, the children, and often their mothers, led shamed and conflicted lives. The program was so secret that many never really knew their parents. A mother held to her pledge that she would never reveal the name of the father. At war's end, the parental record of each child kept in a big black book at a Lebensborn home was burned.

Lebensborn Secrets

France

Preface

The stone cellar was cold, the light dim. The girl seated on one end of a rough bench shivered, then pressed her arms over a thin blouse. She despised underground places, but the enemy was coming. Soon. Too soon.

Her dark eyes glanced at three men: her brother Leon, and Francois and Maurice from the neighboring village of Cher. They were pouring a hot brew of milk and coffee from a thermos. They began taking places on the bench across from her and were holding the hot mugs tightly in their hands.

They were dressed almost alike in black pants, dark shirts and berets. On their right arm was the same red-and-blue armband as the one she wore. They looked like roosting chickens and she smiled at the thought.

Jacques, her beloved friend and companion since childhood, the one for whom she'd bear any pain, indignity, or effort, even to agree to meet at this dank spot, was studying the map spread between them.

She noticed that Maurice kept flicking his eyes toward a British-Bren thirty-five caliber machine gun on the lopsided shelf behind them. Jacques was focusing so intently upon one section of the map, that he didn't notice Maurice getting up to take down the weapon.

As if knowing how much his sister disliked the chilly, damp cellar, Leon reached over and patted her knee. "This will be the last time, Antoinette. It's been so hot, isn't it good to be a little cold." A year younger than Antoinette, he liked to tease his big sister.

Jacques looked up to speak, his voice blunt. "Can we concentrate."

Antoinette felt the sparkle go out of her brother's eyes as she watched his body stiffen. To soften the rebuke from Jacques, she hastened to make a suggestion.

"I know . . . we must all trust the *same* person. The one point we do agree on is that it be someone who goes in and out of Villepente in the regular course of a day."

Francois repositioned his beret. "Yes, I see. Trains go through Villepente every day. My Paris contact says the baggage man on the late run is one of us. So, we could hand him a suitcase and say, 'My mother's suitcase is falling apart. I am giving it to you for repair, take it to the leathersmith in Villepente.' Then, we go to the leathersmith for any messages."

"Too complicated," put in Maurice. "And, could we trust the leathersmith?" He leaned forward to whisper, "But isn't everything we do is risky, never tried before? Maybe the baggage setup is good as any."

Leon nudged his sister with his foot. "Trust has to be earned. Know anyone who has earned our trust?"

Suddenly Jacques exclaimed, "Hey, remember the little kid—the shoemaker's nephew. The one who found us in the cave and volunteered to help if the Germans came. He's a smart one. Quick on his feet. He surprised us when he showed up and we had traps set for intruders, too. But, he sidestepped those. I've seen him run. I'll bet he could outrun me. He's clever, that one. What do you say to using Gerald to get messages back and forth?"

A stillness fell over the group while they pondered Jacques' suggestion. Then Jacques declared, "Leave that decision for the moment." His hand pointed to various spots on the map. "I say we blow this bridge if we hear they're moving troops to Russia. It's bound to happen. Hitler has to move his men from the coast if he's not taking them across to England."

Jacques continued, his forehead squeezed with concentration. "We'll watch. See how things unfold. Maybe the Brits will have another target for our mischief. Meanwhile, we've got to find out why they're here. Is the day they've come, this day—August 8, 1941, significant?"

His dark eyes looked at Antoinette. "Get to us tomorrow. We'll be by the bridge." He stood up.

"Take care," he said squeezing her shoulder as he passed by, followed by the men. Then he paused to add, "Since there were no objections, we'll ask Gerald to carry our messages."

The men snuck out of the village to head back to another of their hiding places somewhere in the hills surrounding the village.

Antoinette snuffed out the candles, then slipped about the village tacking signs to lamp posts: Vivre dans la defaite c'est mourir tous les jours.

She slashed large "V's" across the words which said, "To live in defeat is to die every day."

Chapter One

Balconies and stairways of houses along the narrow street yielded sweet scents of honeysuckle and bougainvillea. Inside the long, black car leading the convoy, Major Reinhard Hurst, who occupied the sleek vehicle along with three staff officers, was not taken by the pretty appearance of the village. His electric blue eyes seemed focused upon an inward vision, one of glory. In his vision he was seeing mighty throngs of people saluting him and the Führer, "Sig Heil. Sig Heil."

The convoy reached the village square. One of the drivers, so taken with the upper balconies of flowers, ran up a curb by the iron two-tiered ornamental fountain, and stopped so abruptly that the truck immediately following, swerved to avoid a collision and ran over a small brown dog.

"That was Anna's dog!" gasped Gerald, ten-year-old nephew of Monsieur and Madame Gille who was on his way to deliver two pair of mended shoes to Madame Sabrine. Alerted by the noise of squealing brakes, he witnessed the accident out-of-sight alongside a building by another narrow avenue converging upon the town square.

He felt his heart leap in his chest and turned to sprint toward home. "Tanten–Onklen," he called, bursting into the tiny flat above the shoe repair shop, his eyes frantically seeking either his aunt or uncle.

"Shush, Gerald. Onklen is working downstairs." His aunt enfolded him into her round girth, then, pushed his slight figure back. She saw terror in his eyes and knew the Germans had come. "So, finally it has happened," she acknowledged.

"Anna, you know, the butcher's wife, the big one who got so angry at Onklen last week? One of the trucks ran over her dog. Somebody ought to tell her."

"Such a hard thing to see; however, we must let someone else carry the bad news."

"Or, she might blame us."

Gerald vividly recalled the impression the Gilles made upon him when he first came to live with them in Villepente, the little village seventy-five kilometers south of Paris.

He must never call attention to himself or get himself involved in any messy situation. But, he didn't have to be warned. He had learned from an early age that no one liked Jews. In Warsaw, from the age of six, for three years, he had worn a "J" armband and carried an ID card with its addition of the name Israel and his fingerprints. Although his mother tried to reassure him that everything was alright, every day he could see for himself the dangers of being a Jew.

"The soldier kicked the dog off and got blood on his boot, then screamed something nasty. They must be rotten . . . all of them."

"Did anyone see you?" Quivers of fear ran through her voice. He shook his head. She said gently, "Go help Onklen. He needs you. All these shoes piling up."

She watched him run through the door and felt a surge of pride. He'd been through so much for someone his age.

Chapter Two

*D*emanding sounds of the heavy iron lion's head on the Gauthier front door reached Antoinette in the kitchen. CiCi, her fluffy orange cat, startled, then leapt from the soft cushion of a chair, to scurry and hide.

"Attendez, s'il vous plait." Antoinette yelled it out in a stern voice but her heart was pounding as hard as the persistent door-knocker.

She moved quickly to the entry hall, pulled the door latch and flung the door open.

Three Nazi officers clustered together on the steps like statues. She saw their tight jaws and eyes as cold as the bottom of the farm well.

Nazis. And these wore the black Waffen-SS uniform, the uniform of death.

Everyone in the village was well-versed on Nazis. They knew they were the party in power in Germany, the National Socialist Party; the Waffen-SS the military police who guarded Hitler, pledging their souls to the Führer.

Jacques told terrifying things about what Nazis did. The Gilles, neighbors on the next row, had a nephew in Paris who had escaped from the Warsaw ghetto and followed a loved one to a camp where Jews were sent east to be killed within an hour of their arrival.

She had read about the six Jewish synagogues that had been blown up in Paris. *Les Temps Nouveaus* called it a spontaneous act of French people, which she hadn't believed at all. French people did not blow up other people's places of worship. It was Jacques who had shown her the magazine as well as the literary magazine, *Aujourdhui* which told of Nazi roundups of people and how great these roundups were to clean and purify France.

She thought, 'No one in my village is Jewish.'

From what she had heard, the Nazis were drunk with violence and power, superior because they were together, and could do whatever they liked without being subject to anyone. Not even their own courts.

They were clever and manipulative, these Nazis with their rallies and night parades. They were such masters at the psychology of manipulating people that they could put them into ecstatic states, as if Adolf Hitler had sprinkled sinister powder over every German and some residents of occupied countries, so they would pledge their obedience to his orders.

Could they take old Monsieur and Madame Gille away just because they looked like Jews depicted in *Aujourdhui*? Could they send someone whom they merely thought looked Jewish to one of those camps?

"Qui Messieurs? A votre service." She was the gracious hostess her father would have expected her to be when receiving official guests. Her arm pointed them into the entry hallway where their heavy black boots left a trail of dirt clumps on the newly polished floor.

As the door closed behind them, the officer in the middle, the tallest, stepped towards her, clicked the heels of his boots and said, "Mademoiselle, your father sends you a message."

Antoinette felt more surprised by the officer's fluent French than by the fact that he carried a message from her father, the mayor.

"He has offered quarters to us at this house. He says to tell you to ready all rooms on the first floor immediately. You are also to prepare food for us. Our first requirement will be the evening meal served precisely at . . ."

When he hesitated, another officer spoke, "Major Hurst, tonight, might I suggest the hour of nine so the young mademoiselle will have time to make preparations . . .

Antoinette's mind raced with what she heard—empty their own bedrooms *and* prepare a meal. What right did they have to occupy their home and make demands. However, she reasoned quickly enough, on the other hand what a wonderful opportunity to be so close to the enemy—to hear their secrets.

"Lutjemeir, your suggestion is out of place. You know I prefer the Abendbrot earlier," came the sour retort of their leader, the major, the one who carried so many medals on his chest and the death's skull on the peak of his hat.

The officer who had been first to speak, the youngest, the one who had such skill with their language that if he were not wearing the black uniform he could be mistaken for a Frenchman, put in, "Sir, Lieutenant Lutjemeir is well intended. If you would not mind, Sir, that extra time today would let us get on with our business . . ."

In a tone of finality, the major roughly gestured the discussion closed and the officers' comments ceased. *"On this first day, it will Abendbrot at seven, as is our custom,"* he said sternly.

"And, set all clocks ahead one hour. We are now on German time!" Roughness of his order made Antoinette cringe.

Then the major's tone changed. His voice took a softness as he addressed Antoinette. "We return soon. Be ready for us to occupy our rooms. There are four of us. I am to have a room to myself."

He stepped out from the group of officers and pointed from the hallway up the steps. "That one up there with the balcony." He stepped back even further for a better view of the upstairs, causing the other officers to separate from him.

"Yes," he continued. "That room. That one at the top there. That will do. Yes, it will be quite right."

They turned on their heels and marched down the steps into the narrow, cobbled street towards the Place de la Madeline.

The footsteps of Major Hurst danced across the cobblestone rocks in the street as he and his officers returned to the town square by foot, the row too narrow for their sleek Mercedes. A faint smile with a sensuous glint appeared on the major's face. For a fleeting instant, as Antoinette watched them depart, everything seemed to come alive, to be in a state of brilliance. That moment of supreme fullness vanished into the newness of the morning as she raced through the door and down the steps toward the house of her friend, Danielle.

The cat ran out the door after her as if chased by the devil.

Chapter Three

The grandfather clock in the dining room struck nine times as Antoinette and her friend, Danielle, finished emptying the last three of the first-floor bedrooms of family belongings.

They carried the last armload of clothing to the third-floor attic, a place which years ago had been converted into three tiny rooms for overflow of visitors and storage.

Danielle plunked down clothes she had in her arms. "How exciting for you. I wish I were you. There is nothing exciting happening to me. I can't even visit my grandmamere in Marseilles because we don't have enough money for the train. If I did find money to go, it would be hard to get out from under the embroidery hoop she hangs over me."

Antoinette stooped to pick up a sweater.

Danielle continued. "You'll be right in the thick of those handsome officers. What do you think they'll be like? Are they better looking than Jacques? What will it be like with them in the house?"

"Work. Hard work. See how discourteous they are? Bringing in so much dirt. What horrible guests they are going to be."

"But, did you think they are good looking?"

"Let's not talk about those Nazis. We have so little time. Instead of telling you what I think about them now, help me finish up. Help me hide the best silver, the porcelain, the heirloom rugs. I'll use second and third best of everything, even dishes."

Antoinette knew her friend well, knew she could easily be swayed by her emotions, become giddy over men with blond hair and blue eyes. There seemed a mighty pull for Danielle to such men. When they were little girls playing with dolls, Danielle would say, 'Someday, I will love someone just like this,' as she dressed her handmade, blue-eyed, blonde-haired boy doll she had begged her mother to make.

They changed the bedding, scrubbed the wooden floors in the first-floor bedrooms, and set the wide-polished dining room table for the guests' dinner. Then they finished hiding the last of the items in the attic rooms. The clock struck twelve.

"Oh, we forgot to put the clocks ahead," cried Antoinette, calling out all the rooms in which there were clocks to reset.

Thanking her friend, Antoinette opened the front door and whispered, "I'll tell you more about *them* tomorrow. Every detail. Maybe I'll even find a way for you to meet one."

Chapter Four

Major Reinhard Hurst's large body sprawled over Mayor Gautheir's desk. He shoved a slew of papers off the desk onto the feet of the mayor who was standing gravely in front of the him.

The chief leader of Villepente, mayor Henri Gauthier, watched the violent actions of the man before him. Arrows shot warning signals throughout his body. His wisdom about the ways of men, achieved through a long life of observing and participating at leadership levels, warned him that the village was in for trouble. The mayor's fist could be seen rubbing into the palm of the other hand. His dark eyes were alert but steady.

The Nazi pushed a few remaining sheets off with violence. "Anyone can be taken into protective custody for suspicion of activities inimical to the state. Do you follow me?"

"Perhaps it would be helpful if you clarified Nazi policies and all you intend us to do," cautiously replied Henri Gauthier, alert to every nuance of the man before him.

"Eric, bring up a chair and get him something to write on." Lieutenant Larsen brought forward a wooden chair and handed Henri a pad and pencil.

"Remove all crucifixes from homes and school classrooms. Replace them with pictures of Hitler. I see you have no such religious tripe in here. Good." A red Nazi flag with its crooked cross inside a white border, for racial purity, was tacked behind the desk. Henri breathed deeply and was glad he had stripped the crucifix off the wall before the Nazis entered town hall.

"Every Friday you are to prepare a detailed report on the preceding week's attitudes of local citizens. I want accounts of any joke about Nazis. I want names of anyone who opposes me or my men or our war aims. I also want the name of any Jew, Communist, gypsy, or member of a resistance group."

Henri vigorously shook his head, to indicate none such lived in Villepente.

"Every village has its Jews," he countered.

"No music of any Jewish composer is to be played, especially that Jew, Felix Mendelssohn! No dancing either.

"Appoint ten ward leaders. Each will have a block captain responsible for eight houses. The first thing they are to do is take a count at each house for every living person in the house and each and every pet. This includes servants.

"Any organization such as a church, club or school will also be part of this census.

"Employers are to give a complete account of their employees, tell their special skills, salary, and number of dependents.

"Especially emphasize to these ward leaders and block captains that they are to put down the name of anyone who neglects to give any of us the 'Heil Hitler' greeting. Those persons will lose their ration card for two weeks, to start, longer if there is a second offense.

"This is enough for your first bulletin for the villagers. I will have more regulations for you tomorrow. These I have just given you must be by posted tomorrow morning, no later.

"Oh, yes, most importantly, if ever a German soldier or civilian is killed, we will select thirty hostages to be shot at once. For any other act of terrorism, we will also shoot that number. That is all for now. You may go."

Henri stood up and gripped the top of the chair but his feet seemed locked to the floor. His eyes riveted upon the major's regulation SS officer's circular belt buckle with its death's head which he could see from his standing position. He read the German words, "Meine ehre heisst treue", meaning "Loyalty Is My Honor." He pounded the palm of one hand into the other as he so often did when deep in thought. Finally, he turned and as he was almost through the door, he heard Major Hurst say, "Oh, incidentally, I must give you my compliments."

"Yes?" replied Henri with a degree of apprehension, uneasy about what Major Hurst might be inclined to be flattering him.

"Your daughter is exquisite. I shall look forward to getting to know her better while we are here." The sinister smile left no doubt in Henri's mind as to the Nazi's intentions.

Chapter Five

Later that afternoon, Antoinette and her father whispered together in the Gautheir kitchen. Antoinette held a stenciled draft of her father's official notice.

"But, what do we do about Leon when the count is taken?" Her fingers clutched the paper. "Pierre's too young. He's only ten. No one's going to care about such a little one."

"I'm thinking of what to say," replied her father, veteran of the Great War, who at fifty-nine was too old to carry a gun in this war. The gassing he suffered in the trenches now caused frequent dizzy spells. He was tall but often said he would trade some of his height for more hair on his balding head. However, his height gave him respect from men and women, and, his wife often reassured him she liked men with less hair on their heads.

Henri had a way of getting people to work together, with a presence that put people so much at ease that they felt safe in speaking their ideas. He had a quality of goodness that even when he labored in a sweaty work shirt at the farm, or had an unmended hole in the heel of a sock, his demeanor appeared immaculate, which lent him an air of confidence.

His genes were evident in Antoinette's rich brown eyes. She had his quiet self-confident ways, although life had not yet worked out the rough edges through experience, especially the naive belief that all people were good. The trying days ahead would eliminate the deficiencies of her worldly wisdom, but not without exacting a price.

Her father assumed she could handle physical and mental challenges better than her brothers. He had seen that quality in her risk-taking and fearlessness ever since childhood. Now that her mother had taken over activities at the farm, he had to caution himself not to overly burden Antoinette with his problems.

They sat at the wood plank table. Antoinette had interrupted meal preparations to embrace him and was listening to him tell about the Nazi directives.

"I'll have to come up with some reason for Leon's absence." Henri spread the palm of his large right hand over the draft. He pounded the fist of his right hand into that of the left, the habit that so annoyed his wife.

"I've met many men in my life but this one I truly fear. I hate having him in this house with you. He's a man with Nazi training, Nazi ideals. He believes things to be true that are false. This kommandant, as he wants to be called, will expect all of us to bow to his will. I've been watching these Germans almost a lifetime and I know how he's been raised . . . like a prince. And now he's following the devil.

"Hurst, this Hurst, is someone who'll smile and tell you one thing, then do something different. Watch and see if your ol' papa isn't right. I would not have a man like that in my town or my house if I had a choice, but I can do nothing. They came in, demanded." Sadness and pain shown in Henri's eyes.

"Papa," replied Antoinette as cheerfully as possible, even though she felt the same gloom as that emanating from her father. "I know. They will be with you day as well as night. They picked our house and what could you do? Papa, come over here and stir this carrot soup so I can roll out these apple dumplings. Then, I'll dish you up some soup. But, I can tell them after they've eaten, that the carrots were infected by this terrible field worm, but I used them anyway." She tried to joke a little, to help lessen the tension.

"I saw Maman this afternoon. I took the bicycle . . ."

The mayor paused as he stirred the big pot on the yellow porcelain stove to study the daughter bending over the table rolling out pastry.

"They're all doing well." She lifted the rolling pin. "I had to get more vegetables for dinner. Leon was there so he killed a chicken for me. Oh, he's fine, just so thin. I told him about the Nazis at the house. What about you and dinner tonight? Will you eat with them?"

"They have not asked so I will not impose," he replied, angered that he was not asked to eat in his own dining room.

"Oh, Papa. I won't have time to go through the phonograph records to pull out the Mendelssohn. Maman so loves Mendelssohn. Can you do it?" Her hands fluttered through the air, specks of flour darting to the brick floor. "And, pull the drapes tight, too. Then, come, I'll fix you something else to eat."

With a glitter of tears in his eyes, Henri composed himself and said, "Come here to Papa."

She came to him as he stirred the pot on the stove. His frustration and anguish were plain when he put down the spoon. "I know what that Nazi wants. He wants you, Antoinette. He's said as much. If you resist, he could send you to one of their camps, could say you're Jewish, a gypsy, anything. I don't know what to tell you to do. I wish your mother were here. She'd know what to tell you."

"Papa. These days are so terrible. You here. Maman at the farm. Our family split apart, each going our way alone. Things we need to make it through a day so hard to get. Everything wearing out. Then, these Nazis come here to our very house." She paused and with great love continued. "You've given me seventeen years of your love. You must believe that I have listened to your wisdom and will do the best I can. I have faith that God will not desert me."

"Daughter, just get through this. Do whatever you can to endure. Brighter days will be here. I have lived long enough to know that life moves in cycles, up and down, always returning to a time when the sun shines."

"Don't be concerned about me, Papa. You have so many others to think about. I feel I am always in God's hands."

Under ordinary circumstances, the kitchen of the Gautheir house radiated a coziness. This afternoon there was tension, a feeling of apprehension. The blue and white tiles, with their little pictures, along the walls over the high, white wainscot boards usually beckoned Antoinette to visit with them. This afternoon in the heat of the kitchen, if Antoinette and her father were not so anxious, they would have seen the hat droop on the man who was riding in the cart, a tear drop on the cheek of the girl carrying the water buckets, a cloud form over the rainbow.

Chapter Six

It was late. The Nazis were sprawled about the massive dining table after the huge amounts of red wine they had consumed with dinner.

Music of Wagner encompassed the room with richness, blending often with the drone of an aircraft formation and the clacking of the railroad tracks in the distance, often becoming loud enough to blend with a crescendo of a musical phrase.

Antoinette placed a gold-bordered dessert plate with an apple dumpling and sauce in front of Major Hurst who sat at the head of the table.

"Mademoiselle, Gutes essen. The food has been more than satisfactory. He reached over and grasped her wrist.

"Thank you," she replied attempting to break away. "Someday I will study culinary arts in Paris and do even better." She backed up, her wrist still encircled by the major's firm grip. Then he released her and held out a crystal goblet with a long stem. She poured more wine and thought, 'How glad I am that I hid the silver goblets.'

"Jahowl. But, you must also study the German arts of cooking. Do you know how to prepare Rahmosschnitzel? . . . I will immediately send for recipes. Fortunately, you French keep the postal and phones functioning . . ."

"Rails and highways, too," put in Lutjemeir.

"Don't go," said the major to Antoinette as he gave Lutjemeir a stern look for interrupting. "Sit with us. We are all proper gentlemen and we will officially introduce ourselves to you."

Lutjemeir, eager to please his kommandant, jumped up and placed a chair next to the major. Antoinette found herself surrounded by Nazis.

"We have the most superior Nazi officers here . . . in this very room," continued the Major. His head nodded slightly left as he said, "You have already had the honor this morning of meeting Lieutenant Karl Walther, the one who speaks such good French we often look twice to see if a Frenchman has joined up.

"We call the officer next to him, 'The Professor' because he knows so much about art. He has just told me his mother would like that painting over there. And, by the way, we have heard there is a relative of one of those impressionist painters in your village. Do you know who that might be?

"Be that as it may. Hans, here," he continued, reaching over to pat Lieutenant Lutjemeier on the shoulder, which caused Lieutenant Lutjemeier's face to brighten considerably, "likes to be out in the country. He'd rather be farming than fighting, but tonight he seems to be in no condition to do either because he's had too much of your fine wine.

"And, then, you have the privilege of knowing me, Major Reinhard Hurst, number 1245 in the Waffen-SS, career officer, proud to have served the Führer in the Czech Sudentenland, Austria, Poland, and Greece.

"Ah, but now that we are guests in your home, you will become well acquainted with each of us.

"We will expect a meal like this every night . . . that is, unless we tell you otherwise, as we might take a meal at the cafe, or have other plans for the evening.

"Don't worry about our laundry. We can get recommendations for a laundress. I give you permission to find a friend who can help you with whatever you need. You'll clean our rooms on a daily basis, make the beds, and collect the laundry.

"Each week, beginning with tomorrow morning, before we leave around 7:30, you'll give Lieutenant Lutjemeier a list of provisions you will require for our meals and those things will be delivered to you. No longer will you need to go to the bakery, the grocer, or wonder if you have enough left on your ration cards. See how good we are."

Antoinette sought the eyes of her great-great-grandfather in the painting, seeking to find strength in the courageous legacy of her ancestor. The gall of this Nazi was almost too much to bear.

"Tomorrow night you and a female friend about your age are to come and join me and . . ." He paused and looked from officer to officer . . . "Karl . . . yes, that's right, Karl. After dinner, we'll have some nice plans. You and your friend will enjoy the evening we have in mind. Eric and Hans, you may join others at the cafe tomorrow night."

Antoinette thought immediately of Danielle. *'Now, you can be among these officers and see for yourself.'*

Major Hurst pulled himself unsteadily to his feet. "We're going to retire, except for Lieutenant Larsen, that quiet one, the one most sober. He can help you get these things to the kitchen."

Antoinette and Lieutenant Larsen watched the three officers leave the table and tramp up the stairs. Lieutenant Larsen held a goblet and swirled the wine around. She could see that Officer Larsen wasn't going to be much help, so she sent him off. Then she sat at the table and began making a menu plan for the week, listing the foodstuffs she would need.

Although some items were unobtainable, she still included them to see what would happen. Things like sugar, red meat, cinnamon. There were daily rations but not many foodstuffs available anymore.

She was registered with the butcher, who now was only open Wednesday, Thursday and Friday, and, with the baker. She had not worried about them being out of things when she finally got to the head of the line. But, lately, even they seemed to be running out of pastries and chicken for their important customers.

As she wrote out the list of items for the week's meals, she felt as if she had gone back to a time when she could get whatever foods she wanted. What a wonderful time that had been. She hated wasting time lining up in queues just in the hope that the meager food she needed would be available. Now, she'd no longer would have to stand in line. Suddenly she thought of *him*, the Waffen-SS officer, the prince, the king, the person who granted these gifts. What an unbearable, pretentious, despicable person he was.

The grandfather clock struck the half hour after midnight. She jolted like a kitten caught on a tabletop. 'I must get some sleep in order to be alert tomorrow.'

Antoinette quietly climbed the rickety steps past the floor where Nazis were asleep. She found her way in the dark the steps to the tiny room in the attic that now was hers. She fell into bed. The new day was there almost before her head hit the goose-down pillow.

The day of the arrival of the Nazis had been so filled with happenings that she had no energy to dream or picture in a nightmare the traumatic event which would take place the next evening.

Chapter Seven

The next day found Antoinette folding linen napkins on the large kitchen table. She was so absorbed in her thoughts, she didn't hear Lieutenant Lutjemeir when he strode into the kitchen.

When he said, "Mademoiselle," she startled.

In a thick German accent, in French words, he apologized if he had frightened her. It was all she could do to keep from giggling at his attempt to pronounce the French words he was looking up in a little German-French handbook for soldiers.

"Here is my list for the week," she told him, saying each word clearly and very slowly.

She felt comfortable in his presence, even though he wore the black uniform. He fumbled the large cap he held and the language dictionary fell to the floor. She gracefully bent down and found it under the table, then gestured that he take a seat. She noticed the hands into which she placed the book. They were so large, he might be able to hold more than a dozen eggs in them. Village men bragged about the number of eggs they could hold in one hand and she recalled that fact when she placed the thin little book into his hands.

He hesitated, unsure about whether he should continue to sit down or not, his strong jaw and square cheekbones indicating discomfort in the decision.

I like this one, thought Antoinette. He doesn't look as if he would harm anyone. I think he was the one who drank so much wine last night. I think the major said he once was a farmer. He does look like one, with his big hands and the big chest and shoulders.

"I am going to the farm," she continued, trying to find short, simple words he might grasp more easily. "So, I must go now." She pointed to the direction she would be bicycling. "I need carrots for the soup tonight." She laughed as she tried to depict a carrot with gestures. Her face brightened when she realized he might think she was describing something else.

His face muscles relaxed and his eyes brightened when he comprehended. He laughed, too.

"I am Antoinette, remember from last night?"

"I don't . . ." He fumbled looking for the word "to remember" in the dictionary. "I am Hans." He blushed.

"Yes, Hans. Thank you." She handed him the list she had made late the night before. "I hope you will like Villepente." There was genuine sincerity in her voice. Then she realized why. He acted like one of her mother's brothers, her uncle Jean Peju. Uncle Jean often showed similar frustration in the presence of females and unfamiliar situations.

"I like it here," he grinned. "I like this house—my bed. A good bed, good—" and he started thumbing through the book again, but the word sheets wasn't in the book. Soldiers had few occasions to use the word, except, perhaps when they were on leave.

Antoinette was chuckling when he started using hand motions to describe bed linens.

She was recalling their conversation as she bicycled back from the farm where she had collected carrots and apples. Now she now was heading for the Phantoms' secret hiding place near the bridge.

As the bridge came into view, she thought of the violent act she had witnessed that morning as she left the village. She had heard the loud roar of a truck coming, so she stopped the bicycle beside the stairwell of a building and waited for it to pass by.

A German truck roared up to the street lamp several buildings ahead to the lamp post where she had put up one of the signs. Two soldiers in brown uniforms jumped out and tore down the sign. They flung it off with a bayonet, then slashed it in two. Each soldier crumbled up a section and threw it into the back of the truck, along with the other ones they'd taken down.

The German words they spoke in anger were not in her German dictionary. She knew they were saying bad things about the person who left the signs. When the truck took off, she heard two windows slam shut on nearby buildings. So, she thought, others had seen what had happened. Again, she hoped that no one had seen her put up the signs.

Fortunately, as she drew near the timbered area on the hillside close to the bridge, she saw no vehicles or people, so she slipped the bicycle into the woods and pulled back a large bush which hid the passage opening.

Creeping between the narrow limestones, like a needle going through a hem, she hit her head and scratched her forehead on a sharp protrusion.

The thin light from her candle revealed two directions and a tiny arrow pointing the direction. She pawed her way the last few yards to the hideout and knew Jacques now was only a few feet away. She could sense his presence. She fell into the dome-shaped area. Jacques and Francois were huddled over a piece of paper laid out upon a large stone but didn't hear her enter.

She whistled softly several times like a bird calling in the forest.

Jacques and Francois turned around. "Oh, it's you," breathed Francois.

"They're angry. They're whacking down the signs."

Jacques etched out a large "V" with a knife he drew from his belt on a stone.

"If we let you come and we don't resist, we will die," declared Francois. "So, we resist, but we said it better, didn't we?"

The Resistors showed that when a nation is defeated and occupied by an enemy, words take on precious meaning of defiance. The signs they left were a declaration of independence, their bill of rights, a refusal to exist without protest. They dared risk words to present a challenge to the oppressor.

Antoinette, come here. We were just going over a diagram of the bridge. We've just got a radio. Left it at the farm. Now we're waiting for the British guy who'll show us how to use it . . . tell us what they want us to do."

Jacques put his arm about her shoulder. "Things are going fast," she breathed.

Then, Francois told more about his recent meeting in Paris with other Resistors fighting the Germans. "They aren't inclined to rally to de Gaulle, who has left for England. They say they resent the men who have fled France. The real fight is here in the internal Resistance, like us."

"It has become a serious dilemma." Jacques explained the politics of the situation. "To continue to accept London's arms and help is to place our cause under de Gaulle's command, but to refuse is to risk losing what little help we have."

"What if we disagree with what they tell us to do?" she asked.

"We can't. Not if we want their help." replied Jacques. "And, should you ever need help from the Resistance and you can't find any of us—Leon, Francois, or me, just get to Marseilles in the unoccupied zone south of the demarcation line. It's still free of German occupation. It's a big city, Antoinette, with many buildings, cellars, and warehouses with hiding places and safe houses.

"Go to the Cafe du Moulin Joli or the Cafe de la Poste. Ask for work, say you have been sent by Butterfly. And, there's also another shop, La Lingerie Pratique. That's owned by two women who are part of the group 'Combat.'"

"But it's huge!" Antoinette had never been further from Villepente than Cher. "Surely, you must know . . ."

"You disappear into a crowd easier in a big city than in a little village, especially if you know who to contact. Ask

Danielle. She's been to Marseilles. She'll explain how easy it is to find your way around. Just learn how to read the bus schedule so you can find your way to the right people."

Antoinette was disturbed. Jacques felt it wasn't about Marseilles but something else.

"What's up?"

"They want me . . . and Danielle . . . to be with them after dinner tonight."

Antoinette thought, *All our discussions and planning since we were defeated and formed this group are ending in a way I never anticipated. Will Jacques see my being with them tonight as a way to glean information or will he react like father, with fear and alarm?*

"They've taken over our house. Father and I have been sent to the attic." Antoinette flared. Her eyes flashed.

"I can't let them know how infuriated I am."

She realized a night with the Nazis might prove difficult but she knew she had courage to face whatever happened. Just like Joan. Wasn't Joan the same age when she led French troops into battle?

Jacques and Francois told her they thought the invitation was slightly dangerous and for her to be extremely cautious. "Report everything. Even small details. One might be a piece that fits into the bigger puzzle of why they've come."

"The wine will help, I'm sure."

Antoinette savored a few more minutes before she went back into the passage. As she going through the tunnel, she felt exhilarated by Jacques faith in her. Now she could play as important a role as the men.

Chapter Eight

The mayor's office was crowded the next morning with the ten block captains and ten ward men who had been chosen for the census. They were pressed together, sweating profusely in a combination of anxiety, heat of the day, and the crowd of bodies in the room.

Mayor Gautheir stood beside Major Hurst. The kommadant stood behind the desk poised like a giant predator. Lieutenants Lutjemeir and Walther flanked each side of the inner doorway. Armed German soldiers guarded the exterior of the building and hallway.

The last ward man arrived and squeezed into the herd of bodies.

Major Hurst roared, "You—you leaders of Villepente—I am holding you responsible for this!" He flashed one of the grim signs left by Antoinette, the message of the Phantoms. "Step forward anyone who knows anything about this!"

Tension was thick as the putrid air. No one spoke. The room filled with rapid breathing.

Henri Gautheir opened his mouth as if to speak and finally said, "As we are all here, perhaps, if Major Hurst would agree, this is a time to begin our new ways. I have his administrative directives to hand out."

Hurst fumed. His eyes darted about the men like bees.

"Major Hurst, may I present the operatives to these good men? I've put the papers in the top drawer . . . at your left there . . ."

"Touch nothing in this desk—!" Hurst yelled. "This is MY desk, now, mine, and don't anyone touch it *ever* !"

Lieutenant Lutjemeir squeezed through the crowd. With a nod of okay from his kommandant, he opened the desk drawer, removed a sheaf of light green papers, and placed them in front of Major Hurst.

"Is there anyone who does not read," barked the major. A rumble of no's were heard.

"As part of these directives . . ." the major held the papers in the air waving them about . . . "each one of you, as part of his report, will list persons you think may be responsible for this." He held the piece of cut-up sign above his head, and waved it as though it were on fire, then flung it to the floor behind him.

"Now, go ahead, pass those things out," he said to Lieutenant Lutjemeier.

Lieutenant Lutejemeir went through the crowd handing out the papers with the kommandant's directives, the ones the mayor had taken down the day before and run off on stencil.

Peering into the crowd of sweating men, Major Hurst thought, 'Everyone here has something to hide . . . an undeclared radio set, a Resistance pamphlet, a forged ration card, even a letter unflattering to us. Especially, it may be a matter of not being able to explain the absence of someone.'

"Are there questions?" he barked. "Now is the time to ask them, you leaders of Villepente. Now is the time to get thoughts, misconceptions clarified. Ignorance is not an excuse. There are no excuses, only performances.

"The mayor here will assist you captains with your wards. Any questions? You consult with him. He will be in the office next to me. No excuses. Only answers. Do you understand?"

A timid voice was heard. "Will the Ministry of Food continue to issue ration cards?"

"Still the same seven cards?" another asked.

"Good questions. Ration cards will be distributed locally as before through your mayor's office. However, if there are discrepancies with the information in your reports, there will be noticeable reductions."

"Yes, another question?" asked Major Hurst acknowledging someone in the back.

"Pictures of Hitler. Where are we to obtain those?"

"Good. Good. Right here. You pay ten francs for each."

"Can anything be substituted?"

"Yes, if there is already a picture of the Führer, we have flags for sale—same price, through your mayor's office. Do inform everyone."

Major Hurst thought. *These idiots. They think of nothing but trivia. His stomach took a cartwheel and his head felt ready to explode. Too much wine. These people, why are they packed in here? This can not go on.*

"Get out—all of you—out," he demanded, pounding his hand on the desk.

Henri Gautheir edged to the door, and eased his way into the doorway. It was a signal for the villagers to follow. He strode into the hallway and stood under a doorway where a hinged nameplate read Tax Collector. The poor tax collector had been bumped out of his office to a tiny closet.

As the leaders of Villepente trudged bleakly into Henri's new office to measure further the changes in their lives, they felt frightened, suspicious, alarmed, and each felt alone. No one knew where anyone stood and everyone was afraid to speak out or to take a stand. There were so many sides to be on. Pro-Ally. Pro-Vichy. Pro-Nazi. Gaullist. Communist. Black Market. Collaborator. Informer. Resistor.

Each man in his own way thought, *If kommandant in there ever questions me, what will I say about my friends, my brother? What about my brother? Is he immune to their temptations? Would someone send an anonymous letter about me? What should I do if I see something to report?*

It all happened so quickly. By the second day after the arrival of the Nazis, the leaders of Villepente were already regarding their neighbors, some even their families, as the enemy.

Lieutenant Lutjemeier closed the heavy wood door as the last villager left. Major Hurst bellowed, "Do not close that door! Can't I have some air in here? Get this place aired out!"

Major Hurst got up and strode out the door, out the town hall, and into his waiting Mercedes. Lieutenant Walther, who was in the driver's seat, started the engine and without directions, knowing his kommandant as well as he did, pointed the vehicle towards a spot by the River Sienne.

After a stormy confrontation, the major liked to relieve his frustrations with a good swim. Hot as it was, the swim would do them both good. Within a few minutes, the village was left behind and the green countryside began to work its calming magic. Germans could appreciate the beauty of the rolling French countryside. Major Hurst said, "Karl, we'll fix those bastards. We'll adopt their charming 'V.' We'll paint our own 'V's on their town hall. We'll let them know the 'V' stands not for their Victoire but for our Vergelting, *Vengenance.*"

As the weeks went by in Villepente, a sign painter in the village turned out posters and handbills, red-bordered handbills with white interiors and the letters "VH" and the words "Vive Hitler" underneath. And "V —Deutschland Sieght an Allen Fronten—Germany Victorious on All Fronts." The Germans adopted the French counter-charm to the German swastika and made it their own.

Chapter Nine

August continued insufferably hot. Antoinette, for the second dinner, decided to make Chou Rouge Landois. She began by putting layers of cabbage, onions and apples into a deep red clay casserole dish. Then she added seasonings of salt, pepper, sugar and herbs and a little orange peel, moistening it all with a bottle of red wine. Before serving the casserole, she stuffed little sausages into the cabbage layers and baked it a little while longer.

The rich fragrance from the dish, which had been baking for hours, filled the house with an appetizing aroma even now after the officers had devoured it and were finishing the light meal with dishes of fresh raspberries and clotted cream.

Danielle put the serving tray by the sink as Antoinette washed up the clay dish. "The major has eyes only for you. He's terribly handsome. His blue eyes are so powerful. His skin looks so soft, I just want to stroke it. But, I think Lieutenant Walther is even better to look at. When I saw them earlier today out driving in their big black car, I couldn't wait until tonight."

As she scrubbed the sticky dish, Antoinette was going over in her mind the dilemma of how to conduct herself. She disliked Major Hurst. How would she act if he touched her? Her father warned her not to upset the major. She wasn't certain what might happen tonight. She had been frequently asked, directly or indirectly by female friends, and especially, Danielle, if she had ever made love with Jacques.

She never said what she and Jacques did when they were together. She knew her friends talked about them. They were obviously in love, yet, there was something that led others know she was a virgin. She exuded a naivete. Perhaps when they were together, they maintained a quality of being separate. There was a bit of standoffishness between them, the way he hesitated before he touched her, and never too familiarly.

Sex was not a topic for discussion when Antoinette was around. Antoinette only hinted about the topic with her mother. She remembered what Mama had said several months ago before she left to run the farm.

"You're a good girl, Antoinette. You have a fine friendship with Jacques. If you ever decide to be the kind of girl who can't resist temptation, tell me. I can show you what to do to protect yourself." Those were Mama's parting words.

Antoinette could not imagine making love until the night of her wedding.

Her body tensed with hatred when she thought about Major Hurst. *His flashy uniform and earthy cologne mean nothing to me.*

For many months Antoinette wanted to share her feelings about how it might be to make love with Jacques. But with whom? Certainly not the priest or her papa. Or, Jacques. Maybe, if times were different. But with the war, there were always things of greater importance than what she should do about her longing to be joined to Jacques in body as well as spirit.

She longed to be held. To have someone whisper things in her ear. Have strong arms about her, to make her feel protected from the horrors of war.

Lately, this illusive feeling of wanting to show Jacques how truly much she loved him kept surfacing. If times were different, Jacques might have asked her to marry him by now. His invitation would come as naturally as the changing of the season, the rustling of the wind through the leaves as they walked on the bluffs above the river. Now asking Jacques about making love with him was impossible. There wasn't even time to be alone.

Danielle chattered on, shattering Antoinette's reverie. "I wonder what it's like to have someone make love to you. Especially if they are exciting. The boys from here are just boys and now they are all scattered. We could be killed by a bomb. Or, we might freeze to death next winter as we almost did last year. So, I say, why not enjoy the only thing we have left to enjoy—making love."

Danielle's eyes shone with anticipation. "We're only going to be young and beautiful once. I don't think these Nazis are so bad. They are just here to do what they have been told. Their politics should have nothing to do with you and me.

"When I peeked out from behind the curtains this afternoon and saw Karl going into your house, I lost my heart. He is the man I've dreamed of. He is so nice. Of all of them, I find him . . . irresistible. Best of all, I think he likes me."

Antoinette barely heard Danielle. Her thoughts kept returning to how much she loathed Germans, who only twenty years before caused her father to suffer so much in the trenches. Now, here France was, again, occupied by Germans.

If she went along with their plans this evening, she might ask the major why they had come to Villepente. Uncover the real reason.

Antoinette emptied water from the dish pan into the sink. "Before we go back in there . . . listen to me. I want you to promise me . . . something."

"Oh, I'd never say anything about hiding . . ."

"Yes. Don't do that. But more important, we must not tell anyone what happens here tonight. Can you imagine what people would say if they knew we were alone in the house with them."

Danielle nodded in agreement but her face revealed wistfulness.

The girls returned to the dining room, Danielle glowing with anticipation, Antoinette more than ever determined that she would get the best of this German, this Major Hurst.

Eric and Hans soon clicked their heels and said good night. Antoinette and Danielle were alone with two Nazi officers.

Lieutenant Walther went upstairs and brought down a movie projector. He set it on the dining room table and began showing a Charlie Chaplin movie on the wall.

The fourth reel ended. Lieutenant Walther was attaching the last reel. Danielle and Antoinette were laughing together. Major Hurst watched them. "So you like the little man. Our Führer likes to watch Chaplin, too. He finds him splendid. I like the way the girl looks at Chaplin. Now that's the way we want you to look at us."

Antoinette's head came up. She stared at Major Hurst across the table and smiled.

Lieutenant Walther moved his chair closer to Danielle's and put his arm around her shoulder.

"Ah, that's much better. See, Antoinette, how your friend, is behaving like the little vixen in the movie. She is showing Karl she likes him. Women like Nazi officers. Everywhere we go, they fall all over us."

"For good reason." Lieutenant Walther grinned. "It's our patriotic SS duty to sire at least four or six children. Women need us. We must bring the population of the Reich up to the quality and quantity Hitler desires. We encourage racially pure unmarried women to have children with us."

Lieutenant Walther looked directly over at Antoinette. "You could have a child free of cost through the Fountain of Life Bureau. We've set up luxurious Lebensborn Centers throughout Germany for pregnant women. Stay there many months before and after the birth of a child."

Danielle appeared fascinated by their ideas for the fathering of children. She looked up at Karl. Antoinette stared at the painting of her great-great-grandfather.

"Come over and sit by me," the major beckoned to Antoinette.

The lieutenant and the major went on to describe more

of Himmler's "marriage" policies. They especially emphasized the fact that producing a child was a woman's sacred duty to the Führer.

Major Hurst kept beckoning to Antoinette. "My Aryan pedigree has been certified. Any child you would have with me would be legitimate. There is no shame to have a child out of wedlock to an SS officer. It can be your greatest happiness.

"And, if you want to take the parcel with you after the birth, you are entitled to be called 'Mrs.' But, if you do not want the parcel, the Lebensborn Center will place it with a suitable family. Or, I might adopt it and increase the size of my new family to be."

"We have a 'Fetching Home' operation, you know," continued Lieutenant Walther. He related how fair children of other countries were being taken to Germany to be raised. The program was also called Lebensborn.

Major Hurst motioned to Antoinette again. "Officers can't receive a promotion if they are childless."

"How many children do you have?" Danielle looked deeply into the eyes of Lieutenant Walther.

"None as fair as any we could have together," Lieutenant Walther said after a moment, considering her question. He laughed. "As for the Major, he has been a 'conception assistant' to SS friends so many times, there is no count available. Which brings me to say, Major, if you and the lovely lady will excuse us, we will begin work on the possibilities for my next promotion."

Danielle took the hand Karl held out to her and they disappeared up the steps.

The major pushed his goblet across the table for a refill. Again he encouraged Antoinette to come to sit beside him.

"Ah, my lovely one, Antoinette. Bismarck said it well—'Wenn sich der Deutsche seiner Kraft recht bewusst werden soll, dann musser erst eine halbe Flasche Wein im Leibe haben, oder hesser noch, eine gauze.'" He translated what he said. "If a German wants to be properly conscious of his strength, he must first have half a bottle of wine inside him—or better yet, a whole bottle."

"Did you know you have 'Schondecken' qualities?"

Antoinette became drawn in by his worldliness. She came over to take the chair he kept nudging out. He told her why she should feel honored to be so acknowledged. "Schondecken" meant she set a beautiful table. He was talking about the things she loved so much and she began listening with an intensity she didn't realize.

The major sought her eyes. She felt the intensity of his desire for her.

"A handsome table is the pride of every German woman. To use the special table coverings, the special dishwares, these are as much a part of the meal as food or drink. I see you know flowers bring a grace to the table, too. We Nazi officers appreciate these touches.

"We Germans favor the prolonging of pleasure." His words slowed, the timbre of his voice mellowed and became even more seductive.

"Our national sport is gut essen gehen—dining out well.

I remember one evening in particular after the theater in Berlin at the Hartke in the Meinekestrasse. The Berliner Riesenbrotwurst mit Kartoffelsalst dish I had was as lovely as your meal tonight."

"And what was that? She looked into his eyes. They were hypnotic. She found it difficult to look away.

"A crispy, giant fried sausage accompanied by savory potato salad." His sensuous voice continued.

"Being here reminds me of a garden restaurant I know near Frankfurt. It's an old, old place with a rustic dining room, something like this. A leafy terrace dining room, too. A garden. The place makes its own breads and wines. You would enjoy their wild boar and the whipped cream parfaits."

She was now completely caught up in the enchantment

of the what he was telling her, as well as the feelings she was having when she looked into his eyes.

"*Sich verwohnen lassen*—let yourself be pampered." It was the way the Germans felt about food. "We like to have wide, wide choices." He continued to intrigue her with stories of many fine foods and restaurants. He even mentioned the tavern at Althier where he had asked for the Dammerschappen. Those were the times when he had began drinking at twilight, singing and dancing and drinking beer from a glass boot until dawn.

"You have, what do I say, such a distinctive quality about what you cook. About you, too. Undoubtedly, you are to be successful, very successful. What I like best is not your creations for the table but the perfection you achieve of even the most simple of dishes. Your chicken last night and the soup were perfection. And, this one tonight was equally memorable. You create with such a light hand and intellect."

He reached over and picked up one of her hands and enfolded it within his. "Your touch is light, so gentle," he said, continuing to stroke her hand. "You are so beautiful. This long hair. The way you float as you move. Ah, you don't realize what an utterly charming creature you are.

"You are like a lovely summer flower, one of the sweet ones we see now, wild in the fields. I will unpeel you, petal by petal and you will enjoy every moment as you abandon yourself to the pleasures of this night. As you do, remember you are enjoying one of the richest emotional experiences you will ever know. You are with a master."

He lead her up the steps to the room which once was hers and seated her upon the high-backed upholstered chair by the bed. She watched him begin unfastening the collar of the gray uniform and felt captured by the gracefulness of his actions. He unfastened the pistol holster and waistband and he laid them at her feet as if they were a gift. His eyes never left her.

He hung the jacket, shimmering silver in the dimness of the warm room, over the back of her chair, and reached into the pants pocket.

With a silver lighter he drew from the pants pocket, he lit the candle in the holder on the bedside table. She could see his broad shoulders, his narrow hips, the bulge between his legs. His bare arms accentuated the fine muscular structure beneath.

Her heart pounded. She began to feel hot, so very hot. An excitement built within her body. She found herself unable to reason.

He reached for her. She knew she should look away but she could not. The closer he came, the more details she could make out in his face. Fine cheek and jaw line, soft skin, huge blue eyes with long lashes, perfect teeth.

She meant to take a deep breath to clear the tension but it turned into a sigh.

He took her hand and kissed it. She did not pull away as she meant to do. His other hand began to stroke her thigh, going ever higher up her leg. She wished he would stop, then she became confused and didn't know what she wanted.

His hands, oh, those hands of his were moving ever so slowly, stimulating, exciting parts of her that were thrilling and throbbing under his ministrations.

He kissed her neck. The kiss sent heat waves up her throat and into her ears. She began to perspire.

He was murmuring things to her in German. He took her hand, pulled her from the chair, swooped her into his arms, laid her upon the bed and knelt beside her. He gave her a huge, wet kiss which soon she began to give back. He breathed passion into every bone of her body as they kissed. He opened the button on her skirt and slid it down her hips.

He approved of what he saw. Her mound was round and fleshy. He nibbled on the short dark hairs, licked the insides of her thighs as he unbuttoned his pants and boxer shorts and stepped out of them. His male member sprang free, huge, eager to please.

One broad hand pulled the blouse off her shoulder. He began to coax each nipple into erection, murmuring in German, the sweetness of her. Then, he suckled each nipple in turn with a touch perfected by the many golden opportunities available to a magnificent SS officer.

His pleasure expanded as he watched her expression turn into lust. When he saw her eyes close as the intensity of passions within her body heightened, he knew she was almost ready for him to enter.

But, as in all things, he was patient. He would wait for his pleasure. He would bring her to peaks of ecstasy. She would learn to beg for him.

He began to stroke the mound he knew had never been touched before. This was like taming a wild animal. He had all the time in the world.

Later, much later, when he entered her, he whispered, "It is pain once only, then it is wonderful. You will see. I will teach you the wonders of love. It is my best talent. Tonight has been for my pleasure. Tomorrow night it shall be for yours as well as mine."

He knew exactly what he was doing, saying. He had done the act so many times before. But, the first time for the woman made sex even more exciting for him. His whole body had exploded, the orgasm lasting seconds more than usual.

Antoinette, a naive young girl, who had never traveled far beyond the limits of her small village, was swept away by the skills of the older man, lured by his sweaty masculinity, the lusty cologne fragrance of ginger and lemon. Her skin, bones, hair, her very insides tingled because of his expert slow hands, sensuous lips, powerful muscles.

Afterwards, when dawn neared and she lay in his arms, a sense of betrayal came over her. No matter what reasoning she had used to justify giving herself to him, no matter what the cause, what she had done made her different than she had been before. Virtues she once possessed had vanished, especially purity of body and mind. His expert lovemaking had transformed her into someone so passionate she couldn't wait until the next time.

She slid out from under his enfolding arms and went up the servant's stairs to her room in the attic.

She poured water from a pitcher into a bowl. She washed the stains from her loins. She looked at her flushed face in the mirror and gasped.

She realized what she had done. She had made love with a Nazi. She had made love for the first time. But, it was too late for regrets. She knew she no longer wanted to consider anything but to be with him again. She was infatuated, pulled by the attraction of the sensuous and powerful Nazi. The man with hypnotic eyes.

Chapter Ten

It was insufferably hot. In the third-floor attic rooms where Henri Gautheir and Antoinette were quartered, one small window opened from each of their tiny rooms to let in air.

The sky was beginning to lighten as Antoinette gently tried awakening her father. "Papa, wake up. I must talk to you."

"Ah, my little one. You look as if you have had no sleep at all." Her face appeared flushed, her eyes wide with anxiety.

"Papa, I'm so afraid. Monsieur Ricco comes today. What do I tell him? He might think Leon is in a . . ." Antoinette caught herself before she said Resistance group.

Henri got up and sat on the edge of the bed close to Antoinette.

"When Monsieur Ricco comes to take the census of this household today, tell him . . . ah, I've been thinking about how to explain Leon's absence, the situation not out of my mind a moment for months. Yes, I know Mr. Ricco to be a smart man. Of course, he'll know Leon is still around somewhere. How can we say he is in the woods with the Resistance? In times like these, you can trust only a handful.

"Then, yesterday, I heard someone coughing, and the solution came to me." He reached under the bed and pulled out a certificate.

Henri handed the paper to Antoinette.

"See, it says Leon has leukemia and is excused from any war effort."

"Oh, Papa, you are wonderful."

"Not I. Dr. Renet."

"Both of you are wonderful. It's good, Papa. If they ever see Leon, he looks so thin that they will think he has such cancer. If they ask me where he is, what do I say?"

"The farm—but, of course, for the sunshine and good air."

"Then, I will get this to Leon at once."

"Yes, go as soon as possible. And, take CiCi with you."

"But, I like having CiCi here. I would miss her too much."

"Daughter, I can't explain. Just take the cat out to the farm, please. Next week Monsieur Ricco will come again. The Nazis are asking membership dues to pay for their occupation costs. Each house and business must pay with things that have value. Of course, they have a list which will say approximate monetary worth of anything.

"Start by giving one of those ugly bronzes in the living room. I've never liked their looks and your mama has only been keeping them in case one of you children want them someday."

"I'll tell Mama about your sacrifice." She laughed at her little joke.

"My little girl. It is so good to hear you laugh. It's too long since I've heard laughter in this house or anywhere."

"But, the good silver," gasped Antoinette remembering she hadn't told her father about the silver.

"It's hidden here under the eves. The only thing of real value I couldn't hide was the painting in the dining room. It's been hanging on the wall so long, we'd have to paint the wall, and there's wasn't time or the materials for that."

Her tone of anxiety changed to gentle concern as she asked, "Papa, is there anything you want me to tell Mama?"

"Tell her to watch out for the village men who come to trade their services for food. She can be much too generous. Your Mama would feed the world if she could." Whenever he mentioned his gracious and capable wife, he always felt such pride.

"Dr. Renet and I will drive out one of these days. Don't tell her so it can be a surprise."

"Now, come give me a big embrace to last me through this ugly day." His arms encircled her and she hoped his closeness and love would insure the same for her.

Chapter Eleven

Antoinette grabbed a bicycle from the communal stand in front of Danielle's house down the street. She stuffed CiCi inside a big box, closed the lid, then tied it onto the rear luggage rack, and pedaled toward the Place de la Madeline on her way out of the village.

Nazi swastikas flew overhead on buildings. There were two tanks on the street. The black Mercedes was parked in front of the town hall, but there was no sign of Nazis. No villagers were about.

Turning the corner of the Place de la Madeline opposite town hall, two Germans emerged from the Poulet Cafe and yelled, "Halt. Mademoiselle, halt."

One of them stepped in front of the bicycle and held the handlebars. His huge hands and stocky body created an immobile wall. "Where do you think you are going?"

"I am preparing food for your officers tonight. If you don't allow me to pass, Major Hurst will not be happy," she challenged defiantly attempting to push his hands off the bars.

"Ah, you must be the daughter of the mayor about whom we are hearing so much. You must not be aware that no one is to leave their house today because of the count being taken."

"I am aware of it. But, I am certain the major would permit me to go to my parents' farm. I need herbs to make their omelettes tonight. I can be back before Monsieur Ricco comes. So, if you just get out of the way . . ." and managed to pull off, pedaling hard and disappearing around the corner.

She pedaled fast and did not look back. The sweetness of the summer air uplifted her spirits. Half mile north of the village, she could see the Villepente Railroad Bridge, an arched marvel of massive stones. She loved its classic design. The masterful bridge had been constructed by tradesmen generations before to resist strong winds in the gorge. She thought the bridge beautiful from a distance, but, close up its sheer size could be frightening. The amount of stones in its arches were beyond count. What if one of them came tumbling down to start the fall of others?

Once out of sight of the railroad bridge, she concentrated upon the sweet summer fragrances mingling in the slight breezes. Anticipating seeing her mother and sharing with her all that had happened brought tears to her eyes.

When Antoinette pedaled up the tree-lined lane to the farmhouse, she was crying hard, the tears streaming down her cheeks. Her mother who was in the vegetable garden saw the bicycle coming along the main road.

The bicycle had a noticeable wobble and erratic pattern to its course.

Helene had been pulling carrots and shaking off the dirt before placing them in the large basket at her feet. She stopped and stood with a bunch in her hand. Something was wrong.

It was unusual for her to feel anxious. Why did she feel this apprehension?

She raced across the garden to her daughter, thinking: *'What has happened? Is it Henri? Is he alright? What is troubling her?'* She worried about her husband and the fragileness of his health. Any time she felt trouble in the air, her thoughts flew to Henri.

The bicycle dropped. The box opened. The cat fled to the barn. Tears streamed down both their faces. They held each other a long while. Neither spoke until they were kneeling across from each other underneath the low branches of a gnarly, old apple tree.

Both started talking at the same time.

"Tell me, nutchkin, tell me." A mother's heart went out to her daughter.

Antoinette told what had taken place the night before with the major. *"Mama. Part of me was willing. I am so ashamed."*

"You are very beautiful, my Antoinette. Ready to love and be loved. You must realize that there are too many differences between you and this German for him to really love you."

"Mama—I am two weeks from the menses. Will I . . ."

"Don't worry until you know for sure. I can give you herbs, but you must take them every day to prevent future misfortune." Then she added, "If staying in Villepente is all too terrible, you must go to Marseilles and find work."

"I can't leave you, Mama. Or, Papa. He needs me. He doesn't say much, but he's not the same since these Nazis have come."

Pierre ran up. "Antoinette, Antoinette, can I ride your bike? Can I?"

"Come here, first, you little one. So your big sister can give you a big squeeze."

Pierre ran off and Helene asked if she were hungry. "I have some bread and cheese."

"I can't stay long, Mama. The man is coming for the census. It is only a miracle I got here as it is. Oh, but I have this important paper for Leon from Dr. Renet. He must have it immediately. And, yes, I am starving."

They strolled arm and arm to the house, Helene fraught by an inner turmoil. *Should I tell her? It might help her to see the situation more clearly. After all these years, I still feel shame. I've told no one, but . . . still, how would I feel if her father found out what I'm telling? How can I justify what I did so many years ago? Can what happened to me help her? If so, then I must do it.*

"Mama. You're not listening."

"No, nutchkin, I was thinking about something. Before

you leave, I must tell you something. Let's enjoy this brief time together," she said and smiled despite her volatile feelings.

"Oh, there's Leon." Antoinette ran off to greet her brother who was coming out of the barn.

There was a pleasant respite around the kitchen table before Antoinette said goodbye many times over to the people at the farm. A box was filled with produce and strapped to the back of the bicycle.

Antoinette walked the bicycle along the lane, her mother by her side. They stopped at the junction to the main road.

"I can't help but worry about you, my little one. You have become a woman in the flash of one night. A mother wants her daughter to think the most of her. But on the other hand, a mother wants to teach about life, to protect a child by her own experiences," she said gently.

"Perhaps I can make you feel better about what took place last night if I told you what happened to me . . . there are certain similarities . . . so you can see *it is possible to be happy again.*

"I was a few years older than you are now when the Germans brought a military agricultural expert to our farm during the first world war. He was with us several months.

"I remember the same feelings as you describe. Dread. Feeling terribly wound up. Being mixed up. Just being scared. And, of course the worry of being with child. I desired him. He made me feel good, transported me out of the terrors of all the fighting around us. The guilt has never left. I try to forget but it sits like a little bird on my heart.

"His name was Sigfried. Our lives were hard then, too. But, he saw to it we kept our animals, our food. I can see him yet, sleeping in my father's woolen night shirt. He would have long periods of silence when he would be thinking about going off to the front. He said he would be traveling to his death in one of those slow-moving trains we could hear in the distance in the night. I remember how much he appreciated the little things, the cold nights we sat around the kitchen table as he checked off another day on his German calendar.

"He would say lovely things. Once he told me, 'Today I saw you hang up the wash and I will always remember that lovely vision. I will press it to me like a dried flower in my book of memories.' He said war was not natural, that it seems to go on forever, but, at least we could try to kill the heart of war by our kindness to each other.

"You see, I did what I had to do for us to survive. In a few weeks, they went away. He had a family. He showed me their picture. My parents were away so they never knew. I never told your father. Every farm in our area had its German agricultural technician so it appeared natural. I told no one. I have kept my secret until now."

Antoinette threw down the bicycle, went to her mother, enfolded her in her arms and said, "All these years and you never said anything. Then, you risk everything to tell me."

Pulling away, the mother said, "Sometimes there are parts of us we try to deny. I tried to tell myself then it was not right to have someone like him love me. But, those were bad times and even though he was the enemy, he was a good man. Many years later, when I could see things more clearly, I still felt it was my only choice.

"I remember telling myself many times since then - it is only one chapter in my life."

"Oh, Mama, I've hardly begun to know you."

"And, of course you know the next chapter." Helene's warmth and love for Henri reflected in the eyes of Antoinette.

"Oh, yes. They needed women to cook for the wounded French soldiers and you went and that's how you met Papa."

Antoinette pedaled off, the tiny seed of hope given to her by her mother growing in her heart. She carried fresh tarragon and eggs in the box bouncing on the rear for the omelettes and what was hoped to be preventative herbs to protect her from conceiving a child.

She left behind a medical certificate for Leon, a few minutes of fun for Pierre, a fluffy orange cat, and one very worried mother.

Antoinette turned to wave goodbye one last time and saw her mother clutching the bottom of her apron to her chest.

Chapter Twelve

*H*enri Gautheir was trying to wade through a massive 600-page manual Lieutenant Lutjemeir had just dropped off, compliments of the major.

It was late in the day. Henri thought the organizational book of theirs was a salute to German thoroughness. He was pawing through the book looking for the page with information about the colors to use for pins to denote homes of the ward and block captains.

A huge map of the village made by the Danish-now-German engineer hung on the wall. Henri's instructions were to signify each home with the correct color pin on the map.

The manual, by Robert Ley, was crammed with complex charts and job descriptions. It codified every branch, rank, uniform and insignia of the Nazi Party. Lieutenant Lutjemeier had joked about it when he tossed the book to him. "Here you go, Mayor. Ley's Fairy Tales. Parts of this book will soon be studied soon by children twelve and over in your school."

Perhaps Henri was having difficulty finding that particular page because he was in a quandary over the first weekly reports. On two of them Jacques Deval was named the person responsible for putting up the "V" signs.

If he did nothing, the Nazis would post Jacques' picture and offer rewards for information leading to his arrest.

As if his search for the correct pin colors weren't frustrating enough, and the discovery that Jacques' life was soon in jeopardy, he had just been handed a notice by Lieutenant Lutjemeir which caused his heart to ache. He felt ugliness of the directive: "You are to declare IMMEDIATELY the following:

Possession of a pet is a criminal action.
Whoever gives a dog or cat a place which a child
    should have commits a crime.
All pets must be brought to the Place De La
    St. Madeline Sunday morning between the
    hours of 9 a.m. and noon.
To harbor a pet thereafter is a serious matter.

What would they do with the animals?

To give up the solace of a pet during hard times, especially for the elderly and children, was an inhumane requirement.

It was hard to imagine their reason behind the "no pet" requirement—winter perhaps, when foodstuffs were scarce, but, now in the middle of summer when things had eased up a bit, such a demand seemed mean, vicious and horrific.

I'll know more about that Sunday. I must worry about whether or not to erase Jacques' name from these reports. It's easy to see that people are afraid.

I suppose what they'll ask for next is names of Jews and gypsies. Ah, here's one person who says the Gilles are Jews. Monsieur Gill would not be repairing shoes if he were Jewish. Everyone knows Jews haven't worked in the trades for generations and that's why they're merchants, doctors, lawyers, accountants.

I must see Dr. Renet at once. There must be a way out of these horrors.

Chapter Thirteen

A few minutes later, Marie, the doctor's housekeeper, ushered Henri Gautheir into the home of his friend, Dr. Jean-Claude Renet.

"Coast clear?" asked Henri. "Patients gone? I feel like a walk. Hope you do, too. I need a walk. Twilight feels good, although I must watch the time. Must be home by eight P.M. You lucky doctor—no curfew for you."

They walked along the crooked, cobbled rows of Villepente and passed no one. Shutters and drapes were pulled across windows. Their footsteps made eerie sounds in the early evening.

"A little cooler now. Appreciate the little things don't we?" The doctor was a man in his early sixties, tall and lanky, with gray hair, moustache and beard, spectacles, and kindly eyes in a weary, wrinkled face. His was a face which bore all the concerns of his patients.

"I have a situation—need your help. My daughter's boyfriend, Jacques, is going to be wanted by these Nazis . . . and then, there is this thing about one ward leader's report about the Gilles being Jewish." Henri looked up when he heard the noise of a shutter closing.

The doctor stopped and thought for a moment, then replied, "I have to pick up some medical supplies over the border in the Vichy section—I could jump that trip up and go a couple of days from now—Jacques and the Gilles could ride along."

He was the only person in the village now allowed to keep and use a car, an old black Citroen.

Dr. Renet continued, his thoughts in order. "That would give us time to pull together their travel papers. I think it would be best if they joined up with me outside of Cher, don't you?"

Henri agreed. He said, "I know someone in the PTT (Post-Telegraph-Telephone Ministry) who could get Jacques official papers. Those employees of theirs seem to travel everywhere looking out for the lines."

Then they began to speak about Henri's concern for the Gilles.

"They won't believe we have no Jews."

Dr. Renet was more realistic. "No, they *would* expect a Jew or two. Therefore, I, too, would be concerned for the Gilles. I agree. Something must be done."

The doctor shook his head and pointed out that the Gilles fit the Nazi caricature of the Jew—Monsieur Gille with his long, bushy, white beard and hair, and his plump matronly wife.

Henri stopped and put his hand on the doctor's arm. He spit out the heaviest thing on his mind—the edict that all must turn in their pet. He offered shelter for the doctor's dog at the farm.

The doctor shook his head, no. "For Angie's sake I wish I could. She's getting along in years. Known only me. She'd be miserable out of her territory. I'm afraid she'll have to go, but, I will miss her. I've had her awhile. She's been one of my better companions."

The fox terrier accompanied him on trips when he went to see patients in the country. The doctor talked to the tiny dog in the passenger seat as if she were human. It wasn't what he said but the lost-soul way in which the doctor said the brief words about "missing her" that let Henri know the doctor's pain.

"I wonder where Jacques is?" wondered Henri.

"What say we drive out and see if we can scare him up," said the doctor enthusiastically, looking up into the sky. "Nice night for a little drive. Have all your papers with you?"

The mayor reached into his pocket and reassured the doctor he did. Then a smile spread over his handsome face. "If you could vouch for me and get me back to town hall before the roosters start, I could even spend the night with my wife."

They arrived back at the doctor's and were soon enroute in the Citroen, Angie curled up on the floor of the back seat upon her favorite blanket.

"Oh, oh. Looks like trouble ahead," the doctor said when he spotted a makeshift roadblock. Several German soldiers in brown shirts lounged near vehicles parked across the cobbled roadway at outskirts of the village.

The Citroen stopped. A soldier approached.

"What's all this about?" asked the doctor in precise German.

"There was an unauthorized departure this morning—Major Hurst wants to make a point. The curfew must be obeyed."

"I see. I see," muttered the doctor. "I'm on my way to see a very sick patient—have the father with me. It was the first he, an important person like our mayor, could get away." He nodded his head to indicate the mayor in the passenger seat.

"Let's have a look at your papers."

Each carried: identity card, work card, seven ration cards, all with authentic stamps and signatures.

The brown-shirted soldier looked through the window and his eyes traveled across them.

"Next trip out, you'll also need authorization papers signed by Major Hurst in order to leave Villepente." The soldier ordered the vehicles moved and the Citroen sped off. The doctor said, "None of this is easy, is it?"

The sixty-acre Gautheir farm, a home place for many generations, had started out as a storage shed for grapes. It had become a refuge for Henri, as it had been for many Gautheirs through the decades. It passed from father to eldest son and was a work of agricultural art.

As they rolled up the farm road, the farmhouse looked like a postcard photograph as it sat on the crest of a rolling hill that overlooked a field randomly broken by a creek. Ten acres of woods spread out on the creek's far side and were accessible across a tiny, wooden bridge. A lane led off a dusty main road. It was lined with old apple, pear and plum trees and led up to a clapboard house with wrap-around porch on two sides and maze of add-on rooms on the other.

The farmhouse served like a familiar, wrinkled old friend welcoming ailing parents, a new child, or an extra hand. It was an unusual farm by French standards and not contained within the walls of a village like most.

Generations ago, the first building put up had been for a grape crop. A free-thinking ancestor had gone against tradition to ready the building for occupancy.

Beyond the house a large gray, L-shaped barn with a central area for farm equipment, supported two lean-tos at each end: one for pigs, one for cows. A hen house, smoke house, open area for blacksmith, spring house, store shed, root cellar appeared like big ant hills along the side of the house.

The place was important. Henri felt sustained by the continuity of life it represented. The farm, more than a livelihood, was a scrapbook of memories. He thought back to the months of his recuperation after the war, the times he rambled by the creek; when it took as much effort for him then to walk to the creek as it would now to walk from town out to the farm.

He remembered the beautiful spring Helene came to prepare for their marriage—the seamstresses who came every day to make the wedding clothes for their June wedding—the month he estimated he would finally be able to walk without a cane.

Substance. Pride. Roots. Memories. Challenges. Like all farms, it had seasonal challenges. Would the farm be a good coverup for Leon, a son going about risky business for the Resistance?

Leaving a dusty cloud behind, the Citroen drove up to the back door.Pierre ran out and yelled, "Mama, it *is* Papa. I told Antoinette to tell him to come and he did. He *did*!"

The household gathered. Bread, cheese and wine were spread out on the kitchen table. It was good, always good to be together at the farm. After all the latest happenings had been shared, and the servants and Pierre were sent off to bed, Helene whispered, "They're in the loft. Jacques came in to see if there were any messages. I told him Antoinette had brought a work release certificate for Leon. I am so glad that he's here."

"Two sons are better than one, eh? But, my dear, the good doctor and I must go now to discuss some things with Jacques. I'll be back soon so we can talk more, so if you'll all excuse us."

"I'll walk out with you." She led them outside to the porch.

"If you wouldn't mind, Helene, I'd enjoy sleeping outside here." The doctor's eyes saw a large wicker sofa, filled with stuffed, print pillows, placed near an array of potted plants.

"It's been too hot in Villepente to sleep well lately. The air out here is so fresh." He breathed in the cool, fresh air.

"Sorry we won't be able to stay long. We must be up early. I've got to get Henri back before those SS in his house are aware he's been out for the night. Ah, but I forget, you're all probably up before the sun anyway. If, I'm still sleeping, please . . ."

"Of course Dr. Renet. I'll have Nanette bring you some coffee au lait and bread and a little something for the dog."

The doctor smiled. He hoped the coffee was better than the fake nut coffee he'd been swallowing the last few months.

A thin moon traced the path of Henri and Dr. Renet to the barn.

Chapter Fourteen

"A qui est? Venez ici."

Major Hurst's tall silhouette filled the door frame. Antoinette kneaded bread dough at the table.

"Il est vous." She used the less familiar pronoun.

"Shouldn't you say 'tu'? We *were* quite familiar last night."

"You see, if I used 'tu', everyone would know how familiar we were."

"Everyone will certainly know two days from now."

"Sunday?" She stopped and looked at him. His eyes drew her into the depths and she felt as if he were crushing her to him.

"Yes, Sunday afternoon. I am taking you . . . on a picnic. I found this lovely beach the other afternoon. If you like, we could go alone, or you might like to invite your pretty friend, Danielle, and Karl. He tells me he is asking her parents, in the proper manner, if he may court her. If you like, I would be inclined to ask your father the same."

She kneaded the dough forcefully, thinking what if he did ask her father. What would Papa say? What would Papa think? What would Jacques do?

"What do you think my father would say if you asked him for permission to court me?"

"He would be more pleased with you than he was this afternoon when we both found out you disobeyed the curfew and pedaled off somewhere, who knows where, on your bicycle. Because of your little trip, I have had to close the village and put men on guard, just to prove my point. No one is allowed to break a curfew."

"You said the things I needed on my list were to be delivered. They weren't so what could I do? Either way you are angry with me."

The day had been trying. She was near tears.

"I've made you cry. There, there now." He came to her, spun her about, kissed her fervently. Flour from her hands dusted the front of his black uniform.

He released her and pulled out a chair by the table, sat down and began watching her knead the bread. Her hair was rumpled, her face flushed, her eyes unsteady.

"Yes, let's go on a picnic. We could start with a loaf of the bread you're making . . ." Like the clever intelligence agent he had been trained to be at the RSHA—Hitler's Secret Service School in Hamburg—he tapped into her expertise, easing her into being amenable.

No woman should be unhappy because then she won't be a delicious playmate.

"Add sausage. Greyere cheese. Ah, black olives. Hard boiled eggs. And wine, of course, wine. Incidentally, mother would be charmed with you. You're much alike. She has *Schondecken* qualities, too.

"Remember the first night you served dinner. I told you about *Schondecken.* It means you serve a meal with perfect grace and finesse which makes the meal a work of art.

"I know you'd find her charming. When I was a little boy I loved the little *Kaffe* parties she gave for her friends. She'd have the gardener bring in flowers and she'd arrange them for the tea cart and table.

"There would be little sandwiches, the Obsttorten, the little fruit tarts. Later one of the servants would wheel in the tea cart and pour coffee from a huge, ornate silver pot. She'd spoon in great globs of whipped cream and let me put in as many lumps of sugar as I'd like.

"After all that, we'd have vanilla-flavored pretzels served on a silver tray. Later there would be more sandwiches with a decanter of Madeira. Even though she wouldn't let me have sandwiches with anchovies or olives, because she thought they were bad for children, she would let me have a tiny glass of wine.

"My mother, a great, elegant lady. Much charm. Men still think she is very beautiful. What is your mother like?"

"Mama. She is very beautiful, also."

"I understand she operates a farm you have. Commendable. Commendable. But, tell me more about your family. You see, I am rather impressed with your father. He could be a much, much more powerful person in a bigger place. You are a lot like him, I can see. Who else is there?"

Tears came to her eyes. He took out a white handkerchief and handed it across to her. Then, he took off his jacket and threw it onto another chair, his white, short-sleeve shirt better suited to the hot kitchen.

"My brother, Leon, is a year younger than I am. . . ."

"Leon?" he coaxed.

"He does not have long to live . . . Dr. Renet is doing all he can for the leukemia."

"Perhaps another doctor . . ."

"There are no others. Oh, I've told you enough about my family. Tell me about the beautiful lady in the picture, the one in the frame on your night stand, the one in the bathing suit. I've always thought it would be lovely to have long blonde hair like hers. What is her name?"

"My fiancée's name is Ellen—Ellen Laudier." He drew out the words slowly, as if he were picturing Ellen in his mind as he spoke. "She lives in Berlin where she is making plans for our Verlobung." He said their Verlobung engagement party would be announced by formal engraved card soon. Before Christmas, he was to return to Berlin on leave, and a formal reception would be hosted by their parents with many speeches, and special remarks about each of them by her father and he, himself, of course.

"She has only one flaw," he continued . . . pausing to let the information he was about to reveal sink in. "You see, she wants but one child and we SS officers have sworn to have many more than one child, four or six children are best. However, she is agreeable to my efforts to fraternize with potential mothers of good blood and breeding. She very much respects my judgment in all matters. She'd rather have children who are half mine than older children who might be sent by Lebensborn from another country. She also knows part of my pay each month is sent to support this program.

"The picture you saw of her—in the bathing suit—is not as good of her as the one I sent of her with our application for the license. You see Himmler himself must approve the marriage partners of his Waffen-SS officers. I wanted him to see her in the best way possible. I know he places a woman in one of three categories. The woman is in complete accordance with SS principles and meets the Nordic measures of shape of skull and forehead, distance between the eyes, curve of the nose, breadth of the hip . . ."

"Ellen will be in complete compliance, of course. . . You would be, too. Then, there is the average woman who is also acceptable, but, of course, women in the third category are those not suitable. It is my duty to increase the pure population of the New World for the Reich. I deem it an honor and it should be yours, too."

"Danielle and I discuss these so-called duties of you Waffen-SS officers."

"And . . ."

"She finds the idea exciting."

The conflicts Antoinette was suffering were almost too confusing to be sorted out. He was the enemy; on the other hand he was a man whose presence was mesmerizing, powerful, appealing. From time to time she struggled, like a drowning victim, to try to resurface to where she had been before, a time when her feelings for Jacques were pure and straightforward.

Jacques? How would he react when he found out she had been intimate with the enemy? Would he turn his back on her? Was what she had done—was doing—irreconcilable? Could things between her and Jacques be as before?

Confusion. Guilt. Fear. Conflicts over feeling passion for two men. Guilt for the tender, newly born feelings for a Nazi. Fear she might be pregnant. Guilt because she had not found out one thing of value yet for the resistance.

Shame. The terrible, hurtful longings of her body were shameful. The Nazi had introduced her to the passions she never knew existed. It seemed horrible in retrospect. He had the power of the devil.

Just to think of him brought a rush of desire. When he was near, to look at eyes created wellsprings of lust and the desire to feel his hands upon her body. She wanted to feel them caressing her with their slow, dreaming way of exploring, seeking, finding.

The future seemed to have vanished. She wanted only to exist in the moments of their togetherness.

Can he be the devil? Why is being with him electrifying?

Should I go to the farm and send Nanette here to cook for them? Should I go to Marseilles? What if I am pregnant? If I am, I can't stay in Villepente.

"It is my job to convince you, the future mother of an Aryan child, of the joys inherent in giving birth for the Führer. Are you worried about support for the child? Do not give that a concern. You either bring up the child and I send money, or Ellen and I adopt it, as I would hope.

"You are not to worry about not being accepted in society. You would be esteemed. You would be put upon a pedestal. You would be called Mrs. Hurst, nice sound, eh? Or Mrs. Gautheir. Your preference. Every woman in the world wants to have a child by an SS officer. It is a duty, your lifelong mission. Women would envy you. Waffen-SS officers would bow to you in your aid of the Führer's work. We Germans love, respect our children."

"But, if you love and respect small things, how can you make us give up our pets?" Antoinette asked.

She rolled the dough into tiny balls but avoided looking at him.

"If you saw my notice, which indeed you must have to bring up the subject, you would have read that I said - 'To give a pet a place which a child should have is not correct.' We must have children in the world to raise, to love, to protect, for our perfect World Order, the Third Reich. Pets do not have a war-time role. They are a hindrance. They eat food which might cause a child to do without. Incidentally, where is your cat, the one I saw earlier?"

"There's no cat here."

"But you said 'us' when you said *we were making you give up pets*."

"I was thinking of Dr. Renet's little dog, Angie . . . of Danielle's parrot, Lindy . . . of the sweet little kittens on the next row."

He noticed her obvious dishonesty. He had seen the orange cat run out the door the first day in the village, and, come to think of it, hadn't seen it since.

"Trivia. Put thoughts of pets out of your mind. Replace them with thoughts of our picnic soon."

She put the shaped dough into pans and coated them with beaten egg whites. "You must excuse me now, Major. I must reach the post office before it closes."

Untying the apron ribbon from around her neck, she turned her back on him, hung the white, cotton frock on a peg on the wall, and went out the door.

Her heart longed to stay with him as long as possible, but her mind told her to go from his presence as quickly as possible.

Chapter Fifteen

*T*he lobby of the PTT, the post-telegraph-telephone building, was crowded. There was an odor of stale sweat hanging about in the air. It came mainly from persons who had
only a tiny cube of soap to wash with each month. However,
there was not enough time for cleaning or ventilating public
buildings either so the odors of the unwashed persons who
came to the building lingered and progressively grew worse.

Antoinette entered the lobby. A small circle of villagers
near the door caught her attention. "There she is. She'll know,"
buzzed the butcher's wife, Anna.

Puzzled by their agitated expressions, Antoinette came up
to the group. Anna, cried out in a loud voice, "What do you
know about this turning in of our pets! They already ran over
and killed mine."

"No more than you do. I saw the same notice. It is a bad
thing. Why do you ask me?"

"Everyone knows the Kommodant stays at your house.
We thought you might have heard why he is asking for our
harmless pets." The voice was that of an elderly man whose
only son had been killed June 6 last year in the nine long days
when the French were fighting back.

"I won't give up my son's dog. No, I just won't, no matter
what they do. I promised him before he left I would take care
of JayJay."

"Excuse me, please. I must see if there is anything for us
today."

She left the little collection of villagers and heard the
butcher's wife say, "What must her mother think—Antoinette

alone with those swine."

Then Antoinette heard a barely audible shushing. "Someone might hear you. Turn you in for calling them that."

"What do I care," said the butcher's wife. "He is a swine and someday I'll tell him so. And, if anyone collaborates with them, I will show them what I think of them, too."

Chapter Sixteen

In 1749 stone masons built the town hall. It was a solid structure, with high vaulted ceilings.

Eric Larsen, the Danish civil engineer who had been captivated by Hitler's visions for a Third Reich, and who had been so excited by their promises for him to engineer marvels around the world with their elite group, had eagerly let himself be recruited for the Waffen-SS. He was at work in one of the rooms in the town hall.

Lieutenant Larsen had seen his world collapse in a matter of a few weeks. He felt the Germans meant the dawning of a new era, so he went into a German recruitment office in Copenhagen in 1940 and enlisted. He was sent to an SS training camp at Sennheim in Alsace where he and other volunteers from countries in Europe were taught arms and Hitler's ideology. He was the son of a prominent Danish banker and artist mother.

He was very blonde, hair laundered white by the sun. A university graduate in civil engineering, he dreamed of designing dams, bridges, roadways around the world. He was an officer of the 33rd Waffen Grenadier division de SS Charlemagne.

His talent for art, encouraged by his mother, a prominent sculptress, was evident. So, he had been assigned the job of cataloging the art treasures soon expected to come in each week from this and the surrounding villages.

He didn't anticipate many. As far as he could determine, they were such poor, little villages. He deliberated: Should I explain why I don't think we'll turn up much of value to the kommandant? Or, should I hope these villagers have more to offer than I'm able to see? And, where are these paintings by the impressionists some of the ward men had told the kommandant about? Could there be a VanGogh, a Renoir, a Matisse hidden behind a wall in one of those connecting row houses?

He had just supervised the clearing out a huge room which once housed the village water office. The room had two closets and many large, built-in cabinets. There were rows of shelving along one wall.

He worked at the only piece of furniture in the room, a large table where he was making labels for the shelving: JEWELRY, SCULPTURE, TAPESTRIES, PORCELAINS, RARE COINS, ORDINARY COINAGE, COSMETICS, METALS, PAINTINGS. Cosmetics, he thought, and wondered why they were needed. But, he was not to question the why behind an order.

"Herr Kommandant. Heil Hitler." He saluted the major who came into the room.

"Things going well?"

"Quite nicely, Herr Kommandant. We've readied this area and requisitioned the only carpenter to start making the crates."

"Fine. Excellent." Major Hurst put his hands on his hips and looked about the room.

"Someday, we will be there in the front row when the Führer's art museum is dedicated. With our help, he will have a collection that surpasses the New York Metropolitan."

"Jahwol." Lieutenant Larsen's eyes shown. "I want to see the Führer's birth place—Linz, Austria. His art museum there will be filled with superb pieces. By the way, Kommandant, are you aware of the painting in the dining room of the house where we stay?"

"You think it has value? Major appeared surprised.

"I believe it has all the makings of a Watteau. If you will notice, for example, the outline is most minute, touched in by brush point, thick and light. It is very expressive and fanciful."

"Now that you mention it," said Major Hurst, "I have admired the old man. Somehow he appears so alive, so sensuous."

"It's the golden atmosphere Watteau could achieve. It's like a symphony of joy in his paintings. However, if it is not a Watteau, it may be a later artist who took inspiration from Watteau. I can't be certain but it definitely has historical presence. Imagine, finding such a gem."

"The Führer will be delighted. I must find out what Antoinette knows about the artist."

Lieutenant Larsen wasn't so sure getting the painting would be easy."These French are very proud of their relatives. The gentleman looks like Herr Gautheir so it may not be easy to extract the portrait of a great-great-grandfather from them."

"Nevertheless, keep looking for that type of rarity. Accompany the ward captains on their rounds next week. Have a look for yourself in these homes and businesses. Your thorough eye will find what these villagers are hiding. Our Führer's source should not have been mistaken about the paintings the Führer knows are in this village. Especially those works by the Impressionist painter. I leave it up to you."

"Should I put off surveying the rural area?"

"No, Lieutenant Larsen, do that, too. As you are well aware, we have several missions here. Visit the homes when you find time. See what you can turn up. These peasants may not be unaware of the worth of a historical item, or they may not be giving us their best items.

"The rare items—those you keep out for the Führer. Do not talk about them. Keep them very quiet. Store anything of great value out of sight. Mark it delicately, so as not to collect attention of the War Ministry to whom we are sending all the others. The rare items are for the Führer himself. Wrap each one separately. Put my name on the parcel. I will personally see that they get to the Führer in December when I'm in Berlin."

"Excellent, Lieutenant. I'm putting in a commendation for you."

"Thank you, Herr Kommandant. Heil Hitler."

Chapter Seventeen

Dr. Renet and Henri wrestled the barn door open. Once inside Henri was assaulted by a pencil-thin shadow. Leon grabbed him and whispered, "Papa, we heard the car and almost ran off thinking it was *them*."

"Yes, they'll be here. We'd better tell Jacques they'll be looking for him." The doctor looked about for Jacques, then told Leon about others who'd be on their wanted list.

"We fear for others in Villepente, too," and spoke about the possible Nazi roundup of Jews. "Without a doubt, Monsieur and Madame Gille who came to Villepente . . . "

"After the Great War," reminded Henri. "One day we had no shoemaker and the next day there he was."

Jacques joined them. "Am I missing something? Does this has conversation have anything to do with me?"

"You're wanted." Henri said two villagers reported Jacques as the one responsible for the inflammatory signs speaking out against the German occupation of the village.

Leon started moving toward the door. "Father, we're leaving to meet the Englishman, the munitions expert. We've got to get going. Jacques are you coming or not?"

"Do I run to save my life or stay to fight for my country?"

"No. You go, help save the lives of two innocent people, the Gilles. If they'll go." The doctor put his hand on Jacques shoulder.

Jacques argued that if the Gilles left the village, the Nazis still might have a quota to fill of Jews. Henri said the two most questionable would be gone. Finally, Jacques agreed to listen to the doctor's plan.

The doctor outlined his thinking: "Both the Gilles have a condition which might be judged a light case of tuberculosis, so you and I say we're taking them to a TB clinic in the south. But, they're old and will help once we get past the border. If we send someone like you with them, they will be less reluctant to go."

"What about their nephew, Gerald? Is he going?"

Henri said they wanted the lad to stay for a lot of reasons.

Henri explained why they couldn't ask either Leon or Francois to go with the Gilles.

"If Leon left here now, it will cast suspicion upon too many. And, we want to ask Francois if he'll go across the border to alert the physician friend of the doctor's in Bourbon L'Archambault that Jacques is on his way with the Gilles."

Jacques gave a nod to the anxious Leon and Francois that they should be off to meet the Englishman. Then he requested some time alone to think over this new turn of events.

"Take your time son," said Henri. "I know we're asking a lot, but we're confident that you can bring this off. Dr. Renet can come back in a few minutes for your answer."

The doctor and Henri left the barn and Jacques went up into the loft. He stood looking into the night through the large opening. Moonlight fell softly upon the countryside and he tried putting down the gut feeling that if he left with the doctor the next morning he regret it.

Chapter Eighteen

Henri and Helene carried a heavy quilt to a place on the hillside overlooking the creek so they could talk privately away from the others at the farm. The air, fragrant and cool, wrapped itself about their shoulders. They sat close together, their hands entwined.

He told her of the many problems he was facing. "I feel as if I've been fighting these Germans my whole life. I've asked Jacques to leave with Dr. Renet in the morning. Two persons are turning him in. He might have been safe enough in the woods . . . but I know these Nazis have devious ways of finding out the information they need. They also know how close Antoinette is to him and might torture her to find his whereabouts. Jacques must go tomorrow."

Helene sighed. "There's really no other choice, is there? He's so capable. If anyone can do the impossible, he can. Remember all the times through the years we've watched them playing together and all we ever hoped was that they someday give us grandchildren. His mother has said the same. My, these neighbor Duvals have been such a comfort."

"We've made beautiful memories, Helene. My life began the moment I met you. I remember the first time I saw you. A nurse bundled me up like a package and wheeled me out under the trees. Then, I saw you, the prettiest girl in the world, filling plates, smiling and flirting with all the walking wounded. I wanted so badly to run up with my plate but I couldn't walk. Suddenly, you were there, dragging up a chair next to me and saying, "Hello, soldier, my name is Helene. I'm the best cook in the world so why aren't you eating my stew?"

"Henri, dearest, God was watching over me, too, that day. The moment your eyes met mine, I felt I'd known you forever, that you would be someone very special. You have been a devoted husband, a caring father, a source of inspiration to the village. Other women complain about their husbands. I can only compliment mine. I feel very fortunate to have all that I do. In spite of the war, I know things will work out and our family will be back together."

He took his arm about her shoulder when Antoinette's name was mentioned. "I would not have them in our house but there was no choice." His voice steeled with anger. He took his arm from about her shoulder and pounded one fist into the palm of the other hand.

"I thought about the possible ramifications of them being in the house so I took some measures."

Helene gripped his hand. "What did you do!"

"Last night when the house was quiet, I took the painting by Watteau out of the frame and rolled up the canvas. I'm sending it with the good doctor tomorrow. Should anyone stop them, Dr. Renet will be the only to know the painting is hidden in the car.

"Dr. Renet won't tell Jacques about the valuable cargo they have on board until they've crossed the border. Then, he'll tell Jacques to take it to the art dealer in London and sell it. It should bring a tremendous sum. The money can be there until one of us claims it."

"Indeed, indeed." The wonder then in Helene's voice turned seductive. "But, Henri, I've noticed that something is missing."

"What's that, my dear?"

"The night is slipping away . . ."

"Oh," Henri chuckled. "You can't mean you've missed me."

A thin moon smiled upon Helene and Henri as they again expressed their love for one another.

Chapter Nineteen

Dr. Renet and Henri left the farm early. Their knock at the front door of the shoe shop was soon opened by Monsieur Gille.

Recognizing his important visitors, Monsieur Gille's face was resplendent with joy. "To what do I owe such an honor?" he asked. "You have shoes needing work?" His soft, indigo-leather eyes fell to their shoes.

"We'd need to talk with you and your wife," replied the doctor matter-of-factly.

"So it's not shoes today," replied the old man, "and, some other reason for your visit, then, please come up the stairs to our humble place."

The two town leaders followed the shoemaker up a narrow flight of steps to a door which led into their living quarters.

"My dear. We have visitors. Is Gerald about?"

Madame Gille came into the room which served as a combined living-dining and kitchen from a bedroom. She was closing the ties of a dark blue apron behind her as she came into the room. A dark dress with a cranberry pattern lay under the apron over her ample form.

"Good day to you," she said. "If you wish to see Gerald, he is already gone to deliver shoes."

"No, it is the two of you we're here to see." Henri radiated a warmth in his voice as he tried to put them at ease.

The madame motioned them to take a seat at the table."Let us sit down," she encouraged. "May I prepare something?"

"Oh, please nothing, but thank you, madame." The doctor sat down at the small wood table. Henri took a seat across from him and then the Gilles sat down. For long moments no one said a word. A grandmother clock chimed the half hour. Henri could sense they were afraid.

"It is not easy for us to come," Henri began.

"It isn't something about Gerald?" Monsieur Gille asked the question cautiously.

"No, no," responded Dr. Renet. "He is a fine lad, we hear. What we've come about is that we must tell you immediately that you aren't safe in Villepente. As we came into the village this morning they were putting up signs, 'No Jews Here. That, among other incidents leads us to believe, even more strongly, that we must help you leave.

"At the latest—tomorrow morning," Henri added solemnly.

The old gentleman and his wife looked at each other with sadness in their eyes, acknowledging their predicament.

"So, these Germans consider us Jews," sighed the Madame.

Henri said packing up so quickly and going away would not be easy. But, he explained that Jacques Duval would be accompanying them and stay until they were settled in a new location.

"But, what about Gerald? We have him to think about. What will come of Gerald?" Monsieur Gille shrugged his shoulders.

"The main concern," replied Henri, "Is to get you two out of here—now. We'll find a place for Gerald after a little time has passed. If he stays at the shop and carries on business for awhile, it will make your absence not so apparent."

The doctor was impatient now. "Border crossing are still lax. The sooner we go—"

Madame Gille got up and began looking about the room. "How much can we take?"

"Two, three suitcases," Dr. Renet was saying, "and tools for starting up again. With no shoes being manufactured, you'll be welcome in any community."

Henri tried relieving their fear about Gerald. "Jacques will have ways of keeping in touch. You'll always know how things are for him. Dr. Renet and I will do all that we can to protect Gerald and your business."

Dr. Renet stood. "We must go. Leave everything to us. We'll round up some money, take care of getting new identification and travel papers."

Henri wrote down information from their current identification papers and concluded the visit. "Send Gerald to the doctor's office later today to pick up your packet of new papers and train tickets. You'll be leaving on the early train for Cher."

As the doctor began climbing down the stairs, he looked back. "We're doing our best to throw them off. That's why the train to Cher. We'll take my car from Cher across the border.

Goodbye until tomorrow when I meet you at the train station there."

Chapter Twenty

*I*n sending aid to the French, the British parachute-dropped very fragile radio sets, each weighing thirty-five pounds. Many broke. When the Phantoms found theirs a few days before, it was intact. Now they waited for a British radio operator to show them how to use it.

The British also supplied the Free French underground with munitions and sent a munitions expert to France. He was Chester Bailey, a British Special Organization agent, and since boyhood had been rather a genius with munitions. While other youths played soccer in the street, he had been tucked away in the basement of his family's London flat happy as a lark with experiments, chemicals, wires, and physics books.

As a roving instructor for British Special Organization, he followed a secret trail through the French countryside teaching resistors the art of the 'planned accident.' His talents also included radio instructions.

When he met up with Leon and Francois, he said he would teach them the use of explosives and time detonators. "In case there is need."

Leon responded immediately. "We've got the perfect candidate—that bridge right below. Hitler may want to send troops to Russia across it."

Chester was cautious. "Bridges present reprisal problems. Must weigh the blowing up of a bridge against the return measures. Many innocent lives would be lost . . ."

"I'll study the bridge closely when morning comes. Meanwhile, here are some things about sabotage.

"Achieve the objective without killing of wounding civilians or bringing reprisals. Seize their ammunition, medical supplies. Search out the shipments of gasoline, oil, wood, cloth. Then, help them catch fire accidentally. Who can be blamed?

"Grease rails on sharp curves. Why not? Put sand in axle lubricants of cars. Loosen train couplings. Tamper with brakes. Unbolt rails. Jam switches. Partially cut or loosen cables anchoring armored vehicles to flat cars so the loads rip loose on a curve. Trains go through Villepente. I've heard 'em. You'll find plenty of opportunities."

Francois and Leon followed along best as they could trying to understand his limited French. Learning became easier when Chester removed a cluster of explosive devices from a duffle bag.

"I'll find you tomorrow and show you how to use these— we'll practice in daylight."

Chapter Twenty-One

*R*iver sand washed up between a stand of scrub trees to make a beach that was a local favorite. When the Mercedes roared up, villagers, who were at the little spot, quickly gathered their belongings and left.

The beach's new inhabitants got ready for an afternoon in the sun.

Antoinette reclined on a German army blanket. She studied a swastika patch on one of the corners, then looked over to the large wicker basket under the low tree branches. She peered up and saw the Mercedes and thought it looked like a giant lizard crawling along the side of the road.

As soon as they arrived, Karl and his kommandant stripped out of their uniforms down to their white boxer shorts and rushed out into the river to begin racing to the middle and back. They were in a tight finish to the shore.

"Mon Dieu," shrieked Danielle, standing knee-deep in the water.

"Karl! Karl! Karl! Bravo! Karl! Bravo!"

She yelled to Antoinette. "He's strong, that Karl."

Karl, cheered on by the clapping Danielle, rushed up and caught the laughing girl, clad in yellow shorts and little print blouse, into his arms. He marched with her into waist-deep water, then submerged her. When they surfaced, Danielle had on no top. After another dunking, she had no shorts. After a third, Karl's short's floated off and made their way in a zig-zag pattern to the current running by the opposite side of the river.

"Come. Let's join them." Reinhard Hurst stood before Antoinette. His shorts dripped water upon the blanket. His hair fell over his eyes. He pulled her up to him.

"Now, see, I have gotten you all wet. So, you must either take everything off, or come for a swim."

She looked into his light blue eyes which vibrated the energy which created the sensuous warmth within her. She followed him into the river.

Danielle and Karl rushed out, hand in hand. Karl yanked up a blanket and they disappeared behind a clump of bushes.

"Karl," Danielle squealed. "Teach me more."

Danielle sat with her back to the river upon the blanket. Karl came behind her, nuzzled the back of her neck as she sat with her feet tucked under her bottom.

"You smell like sunshine," he said. His right hand wandered into her lap. He had a light touch—not too hard or too rough. His wet fingers opened the pink skin of the lips and he felt thick creamy moisture.

"Ah, you are sweet." He purred, like a golden tomcat.

Since they had last been together, Danielle had thought a lot about the new things he might do to her today.

She breathed deeply of the warm summer air and closed her eyes. He played with her, toyed with his fingers. "Come to me, my sweet." His fingers and his words brought her to ecstasy.

She murmured. "Yummmmm." Hesitating to come back to reality, she finally turned and faced him. "Oooo-la-la." She picked up the thickened, hard staff which rose up before her.

"I make him do tricks." She moved her hands up and down, admiring the long stiff member, the moist tip.

"This is what happens when I am with you, or when I think about you," Karl said.

"Then you must be very careful not to think of me when you are on duty." She laughed.

She kissed his eyes, his cheeks, nibbled on each ear. She placed her hands once again upon the hard shaft. "Handsome, so handsome, so warm," she murmured.

"There is something I would like you to do." He smiled and looked into her hazy eyes. "Bend over and place your sweet mouth, yes, that's perfect," he said, guiding her, instructing her with new lessons. "Not too rough. Better. Too many teeth. Better.

"Now come over here to me." He laid back upon the blanket and pulled her onto him, penetrating her slowly, fitting his hardness into the waiting space, bending into her inner curves. She finally sat down all the way upon it and he reached up to fondle her breasts.

She began to move up and down, bent over to kiss him, shouting gleefully, "Ummmmm. Ummmmm. You're doing it. You're doing it."

Karl and Danielle took a break from making love. They spread their wet clothes out to dry. They returned to their blanket and Danielle pleaded, "Tell me everything about yourself all over again. I love hearing about your family and how you became a Nazi."

"As I have told you, our last name is Walther. I am twenty-one and my father has a factory which used to make tin cans. We live in Nuremberg. My Father was recently glad to hear his factory could be converted into making bullets. If a company does not do over 400,000 marks a year in sales, they can no longer stay in business. My brother has decided to help him instead of joining the military.

"I decided to become a Nazi when I was thirteen. My parents took my brother and me to hear the Führer speak. I remember the date exactly. It was the night of Sept. 5, 1934. There were over 100 searchlights sending beams thousands of feet into the air. I heard the roars of 'Seig Heil, Seig Heil' filling the night. It was like being in a glorious outdoor cathedral.

"The red-and-black banners with swastikas and the red, white and black swastika arm bands on the soldiers fascinated me. I thought I heard the huge eagle, perched high upon a wreath on top a gigantic swastika, call me to join these elite SS men.

"I heard Hitler say that he and the Nazi party would save Germany from Jews and Communists. I knew I could help Hitler right the wrongs of the world. I vowed to join the Nazis as soon as I was through school and do my part to help Germany become a strong economic force again. Then, you see, my father would not worry so much about the ups and downs for his business.

"As for my French, which you think is wonderful. That is because I had a French nanny, Marcella, who taught me so well for ten years."

"Karl, my sweet Karl. Are you happy? I am so glad you are here." They kissed and after another long kiss, she said, "Let's do what we did before, again. Then, show me something else. I like being your student."

After another lesson, they ventured out of their hiding spot to rummage through the picnic basket.

"Antoinette, where are you?" teased Danielle. "We are having wine. Come here and join us."

They looked about. No Kommandant. No Antoinette. They looked up to the roadside and saw the long automobile still stretched out.

Karl opened the bottle of red vin ordinaire and was just pouring a glass of wine for Danielle when they heard rustling.

They froze, rushed to put on their wrinkled clothing.

"We heard you," said Antoinette.

"She is like a wild tigress," grinned Karl, saluting Danielle with his glass.

"Antoinette is more like a little kitten I stroke." The kommandant strutted about the group clustered upon the blanket.

The afternoon wound down into early evening. The Mercedes returned to the village like a satiated animal to its lair. Then, it halted at the improvised road block.

"Heil Hitler."

Karl, who was driving, acknowledged the soldier's greeting with a cool nod of his head.

The soldier whispered to him.

Karl turned to the backseat. "Herr Kommandant, there has been an incident."

A soldier opened each of the car doors for the two officers who bruskly stepped out of the car.

Danielle and Antoinette remained in the car. They gave each other worried looks. Danielle whispered, "Can you hear anything?"

"Shush. Let me listen. " Antoinette said, "It seems there are bad words on something."

"What! Where?" shrieked Danielle.

"On the steps of my house," replied Antoinette.

"What words?" asked Danielle.

"Swine. Traitor!"

Chapter Twenty-Two

A little after ten o'clock Sunday morning, Henri Gautheir sat on one of the little wrought iron benches in the Place de la Madeline.

Nearby were two enclosed, old, farm trucks with signs on them labeled, Chats et Autres, and, Chien.

Only a few persons had come so far with pets.

Marie, the doctor's housekeeper, could be seen slowly making her way up the Rue de Lille with Angie on a leash.

The mayor's eyes were watery. He had accepted the first few pets from their owners. He had expected a lot of noise from the animals but instead there was an eerie silence. The dogs cowered, the cats fled to the darkest corners of the truck so noiselessly it made the task even more devastating.

"Monsieur le Mayor, so you are the welcoming committee?" she asked.

"Madame Marie. Not so welcome, I'm afraid. This is an unwelcome task for me. But, unfortunately, yes, I am the one who must collect the pets today," he said sadly. "I wish the doctor had left Angie at the farm but he felt she was too old to make such a big adjustment."

She unfastened the leash. Henri picked up the dog and carried Angie to the truck, agonizing over every step.

He returned to the bench. He and the housekeeper sat in silence, the hot sun spilling its penetrating rays upon them as well as the caged animals.

She arose, and put a gnarled hand upon his arm.

A little boy about Pierre's age, after leaving a bird in a cage, volunteered to help him. "I am so sad for Monsieur le

Mayor. I am sad, too. I would like to help. I am good with animals."

"With a brave fellow like you by my side, maybe we can make it a little easier for our friends and family who must bring their pets. What's your name young fellow?"

"Gerald. My friends call me Ger. You may call me Ger."

"I know all about you, Ger. Had hoped to talk with you before your uncle and aunt, make sure you knew they had to leave."

"Don't worry, Sir. I've been around a lot . . . for someone my age," he added quite proudly. "I get along wherever I am."

"Tell me more about yourself," encouraged the mayor, taking in the confident manner of the skinny kid, the huge, wool tweed cap shading his eyes, the woolen baggy pants and shirt too hot for the sweltering summer day.

"My parents sent me to live here so I could help Onklen. Onklen told me I could trust you. I think I can tell you some things.

"I am a mutt, a half and half, half-Jew, half-Gentile. I used to live in Warsaw where there were a lot of Jews. And, a lot more rules, even more than here. But, different rules. If I wanted to go to the toy or candy store, I could only go after hours, through backdoors. Usually I do things right, but one day . . ." He stopped for a moment as he thought about the incident.

"Mother took in sewing. It all started that day. A big lady came for a fitting. I asked the lady where she got so much food to eat. The fat lady got mad. She threw off the dress my mother was putting on her. She screamed at me, 'I will make sure your mother doesn't work much longer.'

"Mother called Father to come up from his shop. I was very sorry at what I had asked. They were very upset, but not at me. They didn't know what to do. They decided we should go immediately to a cousin's for a few nights. The holy days were coming up. When we were coming back to the flat, we saw the Gestapo padlocking our door. We went back to our cousins again. The Gestapo came later when just my mother and I were there and they yelled, 'Where is he?'

"'Two men like you came and took him away, I said.' It was a lie, but, they didn't know.

"One day not long after that, my mother put on her best clothes and told me to stay in the flat, but I followed to see where she was going dressed up so much. Father had already gone to a different hiding place. So, I followed her and saw that she and a lot of other ladies were scrubbing slogans off the street. The Germans were there with big clubs and they kept yelling at them, 'Sarah, do this, get that place there,' and if they weren't fast enough, they'd hit them. People were coming from everywhere to watch and one of them yelled and pointed to my mother, 'Get her, get her.'

"When Mother came home, she wouldn't talk. She just sat and stared at the wall. I tried to tell her everything would be all right, but she would not even eat. She wouldn't.

"Finally, in the middle of night, Father came back and I heard them talking together. I thought, well, finally, she is talking. That's good. She will be all right now. But, she was telling him that one of the women in the street had whispered to her, 'I want to warn you. They will find you. Don't hesitate. Flee at once if you can.'

"Then Father burned some papers and came and told me that we were leaving the ghetto. I am always proud to go with him. I didn't know where we were going, but we ended at the train depot "Father said, 'I'm sorry I can't be with you any longer. He told me that I should remember as much as he had told me about the family, about life, and how sorry he was he couldn't be with me for awhile. He gave me a ticket.

"Then, the train came in. He took this out of his pocket and gave it to me." Gerald's small hands cradled a gold watch. He opened the cover with respectful fingers, looked at the insides, then handed the watch to the mayor.

Henri knew the watch was the last link for the lad to his parents. "I know someone just like you who has lost his family. I think you'd be good for each other. I think you know Dr. Renet. After this is over at noon, I wonder if you would go with me over to discuss whether you might want to live with him. You'd be a big comfort to him."

Ger and the mayor sat on the bench, looking like relatives waiting for the results of surgery to be announced. Gerald saw the stocky, rotund priest, Father Molterine, struggling with a large, yellow tomcat, wiggling under his arm. Ger ran to him. The seventy-nine-year-old servant of God, who had served the parishioners of St. Mary's for over twenty years, whispered cautiously to the mayor as Gerald took the cat and raced off to the truck. "We must meet soon. The weight of this action could prove devastating."

Henri said, "Come to my office this afternoon—it's now at the tax collector's old place, and we can talk."

"Freely?" asked the priest.

"Only God will know," replied Henri, grimly, adding, "I will say if asked, it is your custom to often go over the topic of a sermon with me."

"I have begun now to think about St. Francis and how he might counsel all who will mourn the loss of our dear departed ones."

The mayor placed an arm about the priest, then went to help another villager with a pet.

Henri watched the priest depart. *That man has courage. God, why have you deserted me? Given me these impossible tasks. Father has the guts to speak before the whole village. My wife has moral strength. Antoinette, Leon, Jacques—with the resistance. That lad, Ger, so cheerful in spite of his great losses.*

His thoughts turned again to Antoinette, the daughter he cherished, in the special way of a father. *I've left her alone to that Hurst. I'm a forgery. I don't have the strength to watch her have to give up a cat. I knew what was going to happen but*

I spared her pet but not those of others. Have I done anything right?

The noon deadline approached. An avalanche of villagers suddenly poured into the square. Many were weeping. Several uttered curses, but beneath their breath. Some thrust a pet into the hands of the little boy and left after the mayor wrote down the name their name and that of the pet. Others seemed more reluctant and spent much time uttering words of endearment before handing over their animal.

As terrible and difficult a time as it was, most owners held their pet, calmed it, expressed a final, loving farewell, these last moments together as acts of mercy. The animals could sense the owner's intense feelings of doom and did not seem upset.

Although Henri attempted to put reassurance into his voice, when an owner asked, "Just why, why do they want my pet?" His words seemed as empty as the promise made Major Hurst when Henri had asked him the same question.

"The kommandant said they were being taken to a breeding kennel. He said you are to be proud that this village has been chosen."

Gerald looked at his watch. It was past noon. It was over.

"Is it time to meet your doctor friend?"

The lad's courage displaced Henri's inner feelings of inadequacy.

That afternoon, the priest and Henri discussed the situation, and the priest pondered how to help the villagers deal with the catastrophe. "So many are already emotionally injured and suffering from major stresses. I fear the death of a pet could set some off into shock, so much that they may lash out and vent their rage, double the tragedy."

"Indeed, Father. We cannot even offer sympathy to each other. My first reaction is naturally to strike back . . . self-destructive as it might be.

"The sermon you're preparing is difficult but God's words will come and will sooth the villagers. Now I fear that many may be so weighed down by their loss that they will be too miserable to venture out to church."

"Tell the Nazis my sermon is meant to pacify the villagers." Father Molterine's jowly face, framed by scraggly white hair, looked most angelic. Issue another edicts so that everyone from the village must be at the service."

"But, if the Nazis take offense to what you say . . as, well they could, Father . . ."

"Explain to the Kommandant about my role—helping parishioners understand and prepare for death, even the demise of pets. I'm certain his Germanic logic will accept such reasoning. He will see that my message can possibly diffuse any anger a villager might hold. God will help me choose words which may prevent any act of retaliation."

A few days later German soldiers drove the butcher into the country where the animals had been penned up with no food or water. Many had already perished. The stench was repulsive.

One by one, a German soldier chose an animal with good patches of fur, then shot it and passed the creature to the butcher to be skinned. The butcher later treated all the pelts which were shipped to a factory to be turned into gloves and coat linings for officers enroute to the Russian front.

Forbidden to tell of his role, once back home, the butcher could not eat or sleep, thinking of the tiny bodies he had mutilated. Completely worn out by the ordeal, depressed, unable to function properly, he was constantly at the sink washing his hands. He was pumping water from the little red pump at the kitchen sink when his wife encountered him.

"Tell me. I know you have done a horrible thing. I have this feeling. I have known you twenty-five years and you have never been like this."

"No. No. I know what they'd do to me."

"You don't trust me—your wife!"

He turned to her and saw her hands upon her hips, anger in her eyes.

His face fell.

"I am not angry with you," said Anna. "It is them. All of the Nazis, especially the tall one, the kommandant. I will kill him."

"Please," he said. "You must not insist. I cannot. I wish I could cleanse my soul."

"Then, you must tell the priest what you have done. Father Molterine will be finished eating." Her voice softened. "We have time to go before curfew."

A week later, Henri's count and the original count taken by the block captains of all the inhabitants of the village, showed two households which had not turned in their pets.

An elderly woman and the elderly man who would not turn in his son's pet were marched before Major Hurst. The shutters of the town closed cautiously as they passed.

In the Place de la Madeline, after several hours, their frail, beaten bodies were placed at the end of a high, suspended beam, much like a teeter-totter, toes not quite touching the ground, a noose around their necks. They lay on their backs with their heads tied to the center. When the man managed to get his feet on a cobblestone, the woman strangled, and struggling, pulled the man back up into the air where he in turn strangled. This went on for a long time until they were both dead.

The pets they could not bear to part with were tied to a miniature beam and died in the same manner. The big joke for Reinhard Hurst was that he had not killed them—they had killed each other.

Chapter Twenty-Three

*A*ntoinette genuflected and squeezed into a back pew next to Danielle who was sitting with her mother and Lieutenant Walther. She glanced about quickly in the dim interior of the church and saw Major Hurst and several other German soldiers standing by a side door. Her heart leapt. Whenever she saw him, the pull and attraction for him felt as intense.

Henri finished reading the lesson, from Genesis . . . about God making all creatures of the earth, telling man to care for them. All eyes were riveted upon him. She thought how much they each relied upon him.

I wish I could be as kind, thoughtful, and generous. Who's the new altar boy? Is it Gerald? Light shone about his face, an old face for one so young, the depth of his soul radiating through his eyes, steady, fearless. Although the black cassock fell loosely from his thin shape, there was steady firmness in his stance, and directness in his actions when he easily placed the heavy cross in the standard.

He appeared supercharged with a vibration, a bundle of dynamic energy. Antoinette felt her spirits were lifted just by looking at him. Father Molterine would have said, if asked, that the lad was in harmony with vibrations of the universe, especially from God.

Father Molterine climbed into the centuries-old wooden lectern. His chubby hands took hold of the rails. His eyes swept the pews and landed upon the cluster of Germans. He sent a silent prayer heavenward and began . . . "In the Name of the Father, Son and Holy Ghost . . ."

His voice was steady as he began one of his most challenging sermons, a message that would be memorialized in later years, repeated as much as many could remember when the memorial statue to the pets was dedicated in the village after the war.

He began: "If death is the ultimate destination of every life, why can we so easily accept birth but not death? Birth is life's beginning, death, its ending. We have made death an unknown because we find it disturbing, and try to deny it is around the corner of every life, which leaves us frightened and unready when it comes.

"Birth—death—marking points of a life. All our powers, all civilization cannot revoke death. No one can control God or be God. We are but human and frail.

"Do not hide your feelings about death from the children or try to shield them from death. Death is learning. In times of war, death is not an unknown. If a child asks questions, don't try to explain fully, it is too complex. Children can assume it was their fault and blame themselves for death, think that they have caused death because they have been naughty or think God might be punishing them.

"Explain death is a normal ending to life, as birth is the beginning, not bad or to be feared. If they ask, 'Will I see the loved one again?'—emphasize as *long as we remember and love that dear departed, they will always be with us.* Be especially loving to children for blessed are they who mourn for He shall comfort them.

"Your grief may be aggravated by an earlier difficulty. We must let go of what we have held so dear. It doesn't mean to forget or end memories, just let go of painful thoughts and go on living. *We must go on living.*

"Time will heal all wounds if we can learn to live with the pain. We must let go of the pain, but not the loving memories. You owe their memory to continue on with your life.

"St. Francis of Assisi felt that we are all part of nature, each a segment of God's plan. Perhaps, it is not a coincidence Christ was born in a manger.

"It is natural to grieve. Grieve we must. Again and again scripture tells us how God grieved, and still grieves for that which is created when it no longer lives.

"It is not important to search for answers which only God knows. It is God who punishes, God who forgives.

"Trust that what God has created is always in His care."

Father Molterine, having lived a lifetime carefully concealing his feelings, turned to leave the lectern, knowing that the pain in his own heart was magnified in the hearts of so many.

His moment of sheer courage came a few minutes later when, as was the custom in church, he encouraged prayers of the people and announced the name of his departed pet, which led Henri to take out a list of the pets and recite each name in a loud, deliberate manner.

Henri slowly recited the name of each pet. Villagers reached for handkerchiefs or tried not to crumble by steadying themselves with hands pressed to church pews.

Chapter Twenty-Four

"We think you're a member of the Resistance."

Anna Perrin had been delivered to the kommandant's office directly from the butcher shop. The white uniform and apron she wore were spattered with flecks of dried blood. She swelled her massive chest with a big breath and turned angry brown eyes directly into those of the kommadant and with such force that he shifted his vision. It wasn't often someone challenged his authority.

She laughed, a lusty guffaw, which noticeably annoyed the German confronting her. "I wouldn't have the hours in the day after what you've done to my husband."

"And that was . . ."

"You know what you made him do. But you don't realize what those acts have done. I have to do all his work as well as mine. Father Molterine tried talking to him, but it didn't help. You've made him useless."

"Hah," retorted the major. *"He is the one who chose his line of business, but,* we're getting away from our purpose here. What do you know about the slogans on Mayor Gauthier's house. Who painted them? Did you?"

"If I'd had the guts to put them there, I'd have the guts to tell you." She twisted her hands together behind her back.

Hurst smiled, a smug little smile. "You wish you were younger, don't you, so you'd have a chance with one of us?"

"Monsieur Kommandant, I am a proper married lady. If I were young and not married, and, if I did have a chance with one of the likes of you, I would not take it."

"Yes, do continue. What you say might interest me." The spunk of the big woman pleased Hurst because rarely did anyone fence with him like she was doing. A person who could do that in a pleasing manner was a challenge. He liked dueling with a competitor, not shadows in the wind.

"My soul—I do have one—would be doomed if I did fraternize with one of you. You—and your soldiers—should stay away from the village girls or that's what will happen to them."

"My, my, you do have opinions. Ah, you might know something about someone we're looking for."

Anna became quiet. It wasn't often that she had the opportunity to match wits with other than village women.

"Jacques Duval. Where is he?" Hurst commanded.

"Ask Antoinette—you see her every day. She'd know."

Major Hurst sat quietly a moment, then asked, "Who's the relative of the impressionist painter in this village and where are his paintings?"

"Under some shoes, maybe. The Gilles, of course. Should be easy to find anything you'd be looking for now that they've gone."

"Why, thank you, Anna, you have been most helpful. In the future, we must talk again."

As soon as she left the room, Major Hurst strode down the hall to tell Lieutenant Larsen to search the Gilles' shop and residence.

Anna hummed through dinner preparations. She behaved so gaily, her stricken husband finally had to comment. In a rare little speech he said, "I was worried when they came for you. What happened to make you so playful."

"I may not be a part of the Resistance, but, I certainly have my own tricks. You should have seen the way I completely threw him off. He'll send his troops looking for some old paintings in a vacant house with nothing but trash."

She saw a question on his face, then said, doing a few cumbersome dance steps, "Faira jacqua. Faira jacqua. Dorme vu. Dorme Vu . . ."

The butcher thought, *And, Father Molterine told me I was crazy. He should see her.*

Chapter Twenty-Five

Lieutenant Lutjemeier told Antoinette that the officers would be busy several evenings and she could do what she liked with her evenings and would not have to prepare meals.

Her eighteenth birthday was in a few days, so Henri suggested that he take her to dinner at the Poulet Cafe.

On that day, Antoinette and Henri were in good spirits when they arrived. The cafe was on two floors. It also had private rooms for dining upstairs, the floor also housing the water closets.

They were being led to a first-floor table by Madame Zonek when Antoinette excused herself. "Papa, I'll join you in a moment."

She went up the stairs and as she neared the area of the water closets, looked into one of the dining rooms and noticed a Nazi officer sitting at one of the corner tables, his back to her, his head tilted in a particular way. He had his hand protectively over the hand of a woman.

Something in that romantic gesture reminded her of Major Hurst. She looked again. It was the major. She felt betrayed and burned with rage. On her way downstairs, she looked again into the room filled with partying Nazis and village women.

The woman with Hurst was older. Antoinette felt acute rejection, the loss of self-esteem, and double-crossed. She slunk down the steps.

She rejoined her father and a massive wave of white hot rage shot through her.

I must talk to someone. I must.

She could never be with him again, and, yet, she felt she could not live without him. She recalled that at dinner the past several nights he had been aloof and had not issued invitation for her spend the rest of the evening with him.

The following night, she told her father that she was going out for awhile, but would return before curfew.

"Want me to come along," he asked, pleased when she indicated no because he had directives to write out for the village.

Antoinette stepped into the twilight, the night beginning to wrap itself in black. No airplanes were flying overhead which made the quiet eerie. Dusk, that murky in-between shadow of day, cast a mood of foreboding. She crept along the rows, hugging the edges of the buildings, until she came to the edge of town, looking for the an out-of-sight entrance in the back alleyway.

There it was, the small white sign she was seeking. The words were painted on a wooden board with cheap paint which was fading, the hand-painted black letters—Madame Mana—Past and Future Revealed barely visible.

Antoinette hesitated, then rapped a few times on the wood door.

Seconds raced by. She heard sounds inside. The door opened. A stout middle-aged woman in a long velvet red dress stared vacantly at her.

"Yes?"

The woman's dark brown hair was held back from the unlined face by a patterned, dark kerchief. The plain simple dress highlighted her enormous dark eyes.

"I need help," Antoinette stammered.

The woman told her to enter. She saw a room that almost bare. A curtain was closed about one corner.

The woman led her to the curtained area. She threw back the plain brown fabric attached to a half-circular ceiling tract. There were two wood chairs and a low circular table. The table was covered with a dark cloth on which many candles were clustered.

Madame Mana went behind the chair nearest the wall. She motioned Antoinette to take the other chair. She bent over to pick up a match stick, struck it and began lighting the candles.

She got up, pulled the curtains closed, then eased into the chair, asking, "Palm, horoscope, or . . .?"

"Palm." Antoinette watched as the coins she took from her pocket and laid on the table simply vanished.

"Give your right hand to me, please."

Antoinette placed her hand in the cool, upright waiting hands of the fortune teller who placed one of her hands on the top, the other on the bottom of Antoinette's. As she did, Madame Mama said in such a loud voice it startled Antoinette, "Make two wishes!"

Antoinette stared at the linoleum floor as if it had wishes in its pattern.

Time hung by a thread in the cubicle; it seemed to float like a bubble in a thermometer.

Madame Mana leaned closer and in a deep voice entreated, "Then, tell me one."

Antoinette looked up. Madame Mana's body shifted toward her.

"One wish," she encouraged.

"To be happy again."

Madame Mana bent over Antoinette's hand. She studied it as if it had the key to happiness imprinted upon it. "You are very disturbed. Who could be happy with such clashes? They are tearing you up. You cannot go like this."

"Oh," sighed Antoinette.

"I see a married man. I see you have strong feelings for him—very strong, runaway feelings. Am I right?"

Antoinette nodded.

"I do not judge whether they are right or wrong, they are your feelings. I see someone strong—another man—your husband, perhaps?" She looked at Antoinette but Antoinette was staring into her hands.

"I see another woman—the married man's wife?—no, another woman. So many women for one man. No wonder you are so torn." Then, she gasped and, clasped both Antoinette's hands within hers.

"I know now why you came. You had to bring me this burden. I pray every day. I pray for many people and now I will pray for you. I help those in big trouble—like you—but, only if you believe I can."

Madame Mana's soothing words continued. "Then, I do what I can. If you want happiness, it will take another visit so I can work out this evil from your soul."

Shaken, Antoinette groaned. "Can't you do anything for me tonight?"

Candles flickered as if a terrible wind swept into the little cubicle.

"See," Madame Mana exclaimed, "the spirits know you have been weak. But, you are too strong a person for evil to defeat. You are a very strong. Very." Then, Madame Mana became very still and was silent.

"Please . . . go on . . .," begged Antoinette.

"You do not know how much you ask. You came to me because you need someone to hear you. You have no one to talk with, then finally you come here." She sighed, then took Antoinette's hands and placed them firmly upon her breast. "I can feel your heart break."

Madame Mana braced herself back in her chair and released Antoinette's hands.

"I can't go on. The spirits are too strong. You must come another time. Before I say more, you must tell me if I am right."

"Yes . . . I . . ."

"Do not say more," cautioned the clairvoyant. "We must work this evil out. Do you believe I can do this?"

"Oh, I believe you can," immediately replied Antoinette.

"Then, this is what you do. Go out and come back again tomorrow at this same hour. Bring three things. I need time to pull all my power together."

Flames of the candles moved up and down, became tall, then almost diminished, then tall again.

"Bring these things tomorrow night—a used handkerchief belonging to *the* man, a large red tomato, biggest you can find, a small jar of dirt. Go now. I see you tomorrow night."

Antoinette ducked through the curtain. Madame Mana called after her as she opened the door to go out, "I will use the time to meditate."

The next evening when Antoinette arrived again at Madame Mana's, the door was slightly ajar. Instead of knocking, anticipating that she was expected, she entered and called, "I'm back."

Fear crept in behind her.

"Go in. Be seated," commanded Madame Mana from some unseen place.

Antoinette trembled as she sat down and put money on the table. She heard Madame Mana approach the cubicle.

"We begin at once." Madame Mana briskly relit the candles. "We both prepare by remaining silent."

The atmosphere thickened. Antoinette found it hard to get her breath.

"Now we can begin. Please place the things I asked you to bring upon the table."

Newspapers rustled as Antoinette unwrapped and took out of the sack she had placed on the floor, a tomato, *his* handkerchief, and the jar of dirt.

"Your left hand, please. Ah. You are unhappy because you have looked for happiness in the wrong place. You will soon realize what brings happiness."

Madame Mana appeared grave. "I know things. My mother did before me and her mother before her. Many come to me with different problems.

"To have answers for you, we must go back to your people—those who came before you. Your mother—a saint—but, she has had a cursed life, too, yes? Yes. Your father, most respected, feels inadequate. Ah, here is something . . . I am trying to see . . ."

The candles flicked wildly, the air turned murky.

"No, it is not your mother or your father—they are not the ones. *It is the tall man in black, the one with the force of evil.*

"Do as I tell you. Take this jar from the table and go to that room. Behind the door there is a bucket. Empty the dirt into the bucket. Fill the jar with water you'll find in a bowl. Then, bring it back quickly."

Antoinette fumbled with the jar of dirt, emptying it and filling it with water as she had been told.

She came back to the curtained cubicle wondering why she was here. However, something was compelling her to continue. She reached for the curtain, pulled it back and sat once again on the chair across from Madame Mana.

She was never certain what happened next.

"We will be quiet again." Madame Mana, as if she were summoning the spirits, became oblivious to everything and appeared as if in a trance.

Suddenly she commanded."Give the jar to me. Undo the top button of your dress—push it from your shoulders . . ."

Madame Mana became still. Her eyes closed. Her body quivered, then shook. She opened her eyes, took the handkerchief from the table, bent over and dipped part of the handkerchief into the water in the jar.

"With this water, I will take his evil from you."

The handkerchief felt cold as Madame Mana rubbed the wet linen cloth roughly across Antoinette's shoulders and breasts. She picked up the tomato, held it in her hands above Antoinette's head—then, crushed it upon the middle of Antoinette's chest, saying loudly, "Be gone from her you spirit of this evil man—go—I tell, you—go. I demand you leave."

Madame Mana sagged back, her hands in her lap. "I did what I could—now it is up to you."

Antoinette rebuttoned her dress. She looked at the table and saw no items—no mess. Had she imagined the wet handkerchief, the squish of the tomato, the cool hands upon her shoulders and breasts?

Very shaken, she stood, turned and went out the cubicle, out of the house, her thoughts wild, chaotic.

Chapter Twenty-Six

When they reached Bourbon L'Archambault, the town nearest the line of demarcation, the Gilles said they were staying and would go no further. Dr. Renet understood their reluctance to go to Marseilles, as they were accustomed to Villepente, a small village.

"We've lost everything, except our will to live," said Monsieur Gille. "Someday we'll return to Villepente, in hopes Gerald's parents return for him. If they don't, God forbid, we will be his only family. From this place, it won't be as far to go back to Villepente."

Then Monsieur Gille told the doctor how a Jew had learned the trade of a shoemaker. "My mother apprenticed me when I was seven to a shoemaker. I used my eyes and hands well and when the Great War was over and the men returned, I went back to my academic studies and became an accountant. I found it good to have the skills and tools of a shoemaker to fall upon when I want to start life anew."

And, Jacques. His mission with the Gilles was done. Now before him lay the challenge of getting the painting to London. Through the Resistance network, he knew contacts in Marseilles. He and Dr. Renet discussed the few limited countries through which he could get to England: Spain, Ecuador, Brazil, North Africa.

Francois reminded him before he left the Villepente area that one of the passwords to try was: "Can you give me English lessons?" Or, "What is the level of the Seine, today?"

Jacques decided to walk instead of taking a train to Marseilles. He had led an out-of-doors life so he felt going by foot was less risky, even though the route was entirely unknown. Once away from towns and railways, with knowledge of nature and the heavens, he felt he could hardly fail to make it safely if he went by night. When the stars were out, he planned to walk by their aid; he would carry a compass for times when the sky was dark.

With him were cut-up sections of a map which would lead him through the wine country. He would always willingly trade the most direct route for a longer one which offered a better supply of water or safety.

After much difficulty, he finally reached the outskirts of Marseilles. Marseilles, the port, the wide-open town where everything was for sale and where he could purchase the things he needed.

Marseilles, the second city of France, after Paris, with a population of some 600,000, founded centuries before as a trading post by the Phoenicians, was gateway to Africa, the place Jacques was headed.

The port teemed with Czechs, Poles, and French from other occupied cities of the North, and Belgians, Dutch, and Jews of many nations fleeing Nazi persecution. Little-known to the Jews, however, were sweeps by the Vichy government. The rounded-up Jews were sent to the French concentration camps filling up outside the city limits.

Jacques wandered about the warren of streets near the Gare Saint- Charles until he spied a likely hotel off one of the main boulevards, the Blvd. Charles Nedelec. Somehow, he felt a strange secureness amongst this throng of people who all looked different and seemed to be speaking many languages.

Jacques changed his coat and hat often, sometimes wore glasses, sometimes not, so there would be no recognizable pattern to his appearance. It was no trouble to buy second-hand clothes. He removed the painting from the raincoat and was relieved to see it was not damaged from the abuse of his travels.

Needing a new identity, he decided to be a wine merchant. That afternoon when he was in the vicinity of the merchant docks, he overheard a man talking with a sailor about a wine shipment. By luck, the man resembled him.

"Monsieur," he said, stopping the person, implying he was the police, and demanding to see the man's identity cards, he memorized the details. Now, all he had to do was find a forger and get a ticket to Algiers. He had heard through the Resistance that getting passage on a ship would be almost impossible because bookings had to be made so many months in advance and there were so few, if any, vacancies.

But, that was a problem he'd face later. First, he'd find a forger.

He had heard of a possible contact at a religious book and article store on Rue Bonnefoy near the Basilica of Notre-Dame de la Garde so he began the arduous uphill climb along the winding streets, the gilded, monumental statue of the Blessed Virgin on top the hill guiding his footsteps upward.

The little store appeared, lodged between two tall buildings near a little parkway of trees.

He walked into the quiet interior and was looking at St. Anthony medals in a tall case, when a low, sensuous voice asked, "Might I help you, monsieur?"

"Can you give me English lessons?"

"Monsieur, but, of course. Perhaps you might wish to take a cup of tea with me." It was the voice of small woman, a widow, who had a role with a network of people whose occupations gave them reason to travel throughout France, moving from occupied to unoccupied zone. They held occupations for which they could obtain official passes: lawyers, movie makers, book publishers. They used code names of animals: Wolf, Eagle, Hedgehog.

"I am pleased you have come," she said as she made tea in the back of the shop, first turning the sign on the front door to Closed and locking the door.

She moved quickly, with assurance, the skirt of her dress swishing sensuously.

"They call me Fox." She smiled when she heard the name of his fifth-class hotel near the train station where he had paused to admire the elaborate marble and format of wedding-cake steps leading up it. The bronze statues and the lamps, too, were strikingly appealing even to a fugitive. He liked the area of busy, twisting streets near the station and the tangle of different races parading the boulevards.

She took his photo and he gave her the information he had taken from the wine merchant for new passport and identity cards.

Casually, she asked, "What if I asked you to go to bed with me?"

There was no mistake. He had been admiring her. Was she also a mind-reader in addition to being a forger? Astonished, he coughed, "I'm sorry, but I couldn't."

Fox drew up a chair close to him. "Am I not attractive to you?"

"Yes," he admitted. She looked younger than she was, wide dark eyes, thick brown hair, a bold mouth, a lean figure showing through the shirtwaist dress.

"And, if I asked whether you might consider me a friend." She looked boldly into his surprised eyes.

"Give me your hands," she said softly.

He felt the warmth of her hands. "Does that offend you? Then, I must ask a favor. Please kiss me. That's all I ask," she said as he withdrew his hands.

He abruptly stood up and so did she; he gave her a peck on the lips.

"No, a real kiss," she insisted, and wound her arms around him; "like this."

Jacques felt sensations stir in his loins as Fox's tongue flitted around the corners of his mouth. He could not resist the excitement and ran his hands over her hips.

"Are you surprised?" she asked as he caressed her all over, thinking what difference would it make? He felt her breasts harden.

"You don't like this?" she murmured, her voice a caress almost causing him to explode.

He felt resistance going out of him as his pleasure spread. "You're beautiful," he whispered. Her fragrance enveloped him, an aroma of orange blossoms, cloves and sandlewood, which triggered his pent-up need.

"Over here," she whispered, and pulled him towards a cot where she tugged him on top her.

She laughed as she began unpeeling the many layers of his clothing and saw the canvas of the painting plastered on his chest.

She pushed her dress away as she glided her body back and forth under him. He thrust deeply and she moaned in pleasure, their lips crushed together as his loins exploded.

As they lay with their bodies hanging over the tiny cot, she cradled his head, and whispered gently, "You've been through a lot, haven't you? Wasn't what we just did a pleasant way to replenish the energy you've lost coming here? I promise you I won't encourage you again. Today, I felt you needed a lift. It was the least I could do. And, I've been thinking, if you want to join up with us here in Marseilles, we could use a resourceful guy like you."

He left the store mystified, puzzling over the renewal of energy he felt. And the lack of guilt! In times of war, he rationalized, a person's vulnerability to temptation is going to be tested again and again just as their cool-headedness and courage.

The next day he returned to pick up the identification papers.

"Now, comes the hard part. Take these to police headquarters and get them stamped. Ah, but you were clever enough to choose a person who will have information that can be verified."

He was uneasy. "Fox, getting these stamped at police headquarters should be easy work. It's getting the ticket to Algiers that may be difficult."

"Ah, but, I've fashioned you travel papers: reason for visit: negotiating sale of wine crop. It won't be easy with the police, but, you'll do alright."

Her smile felt to him like the sun. He thought, when he drew her to him and kissed her on each cheek that he might just come back.

His steps were lively and purposeful enroute to the station but police headquarters was not without moments of sheer terror. The big gray, stone building was ominous looking. Inside, he agonized when the police checked his paperwork. He tried to think about other things as the long minutes passed while he waited for the papers to be returned.

Finally, they were handed to him and he was on his way back to the African Consulate to pick up his visa. On the sidewalk outside the consulate he ran into a person he met the day before when they were both applying for visas to Africa.

Jacques asked the man, "Do you know a way to get over to Algiers?"

"You're in luck," said the man. "I've booked passage for my family on the *SS Horatio* sailing tomorrow but can't use all these tickets because my wife needs an emergency operation. I was on my way to the ship agent to return hers."

The next day Jacques stood in a drizzling rain waiting in line to board the ship. The official searching the luggage of the passengers was doing it so slowly Jacques was afraid the ship would leave without him.

Jacques grew alarmed when he saw men beginning to untie the ropes of the ship. He had to take a chance. He left his place in line and went up to the official leisurely going through the contents of a trunk.

"Look here," he informed the official. "I don't have any luggage. Let me by. If I miss that boat, it will be your responsibility." His remarks were so emphatic, and in the tone and language the official must have valued, that the man waved him by. Jacques ran down the pier.

At the end of the dock, two police officers confronted him. "Your passport," one demanded.

He handed it over. One of the officers stared at it a long while and showed it to the other policeman. They asked for his travel permit, then studied it. Just as the ship began to move and the gangplank was starting to be hauled up, Jacques heard one of them say, "Heil Hitler." He hastily returned their salutes, raced up the plank, and dared not to breathe regularly until the ship was out of port.

Luck held hands with Jacques again.

He stood by the ship's rail, a steady rain coming down as he watched the city and coastline recede.

No one from Villepente would recognize him. His face was covered by a heavy beard. The heavy wool suit and vest, covered by the raincoat, and the canvas of the painting wrapped around his body, he appeared thirty pounds heavier and years older.

He hardly knew himself. A strange warmth and contentment grew within him and suddenly he realized why—the buildings on the hillsides he saw in the distance were the same ones as the ones on the postcard he sent to Antoinette. He was on his way to Algiers and from there to London.

Chapter Twenty-Seven

Kommandant Hurst sweltered in the warmth of the late afternoon. He paused a moment, ignoring the sweat dripping from his armpits. Strands of blonde hair curled above his ears and beads of perspiration sprinkled upon his forehead as he concentrated.

The pen in his hand kept forming two words over and over as he tried writing a long-overdue letter to his fiancée, Ellen Laudier, daughter of a Berlin banker. He promised he would write every day. How many days had passed since he had written?

"Darling Ellen," he penned in a variety of handwriting styles. Then, he drew from the drawer another sheet of water-marked SS stationary and began to write in earnest:

"I've told you over and over again that once we are married, we MUST HAVE a respectable-sized family, two children at the least. First, you say you'll have one, but now you tell me NONE. Why don't you like children? You were a child once. Ach, such a woman—you draw people to you like bees to roses, yet you put off children. No time now you say, with the engagement party and wedding affairs to even be thinking about children."

He pulled out her recent letter and smelled the faintly scented, gray monogrammed stationery. The script was carefully placed upon the page, just so, her handwriting beautifully crafted.

"Darling Henrich, Your letter of the 20th was so welcome. The news of your picturesque village assignment so well described, I could almost see you at town hall. You know my heart aches for you. I kiss your picture every morning when I awaken and your face is the last I see before closing my eyes.

"Father has started the invitation list for the reception which announces our engagement. Please arrive a few days early for the galas friends and relatives are hosting.

"So glad to hear that Himler liked the photo. About the child—do remember our early discussions. A child by me is not a possibility. And, I don't have time now to even consider such a thought with all the preparations going on. Don't you remember our agreement? I'll leave all this in your good hands.

"Hurry back, sweetheart. Berlin is not the same without you. I do the best I can. Friends try to help me pass the lonely hours.

"Until December. Yours, Ellen."

He thought, *I must prepare her for motherhood. She will soften once I lay a beautiful parcel in her soft hands. She will see for herself the wisdom of being part of the new Master Race.*

I must convince her that any time she'll spend with a child would be minimal. A greeting in the morning and evening, a little planning for their development, but, even that can be taken care of by servants. How do I convince her that I won't change my mind and demand a child by her? Who cares where the parcels come from as long as we present two perfect children at public appearance and in formal family portraits.

Surely, she can understand how important it is for a Waffen-SS officer to have a proper family. She wants to be a perfect bride. So, it should be easy to show her how little effort it will be to play the role of perfect mother.

Perhaps, I should just take things as they come, let things transpire naturally. Once she sees a beautiful parcel, she'll succumb. Working things out in person might be more effective than trying to put it into a letter. I certainly don't want to upset her.

He crumpled up the page and reached for a clean sheet of stationery.

Relieved by his decision to avoid the question of motherhood in this letter, his pen began to fly across the official Nazi stationery. He raved about her beauty, asked questions about her activities, requested details of the reception, and cautiously and carefully phrased a question about who was keeping her from being lonely.

He also asked for a guest list—surely, he thought, the Führer's name would be included. If the Führer is there, he could explain his new ideas for the Führer's art museum. What ecstasy it would be to see the Führer's face when he heard about the impressionist canvases.

The thought of opening day at the Museum, the crowd yelling, 'Sig Heil', 'Sig Heil' returned. It felt as if the crowd were yelling for him. A feeling of power, of pride, of appreciation for his virtues, swelled his chest. The kommandant glowed with delight over his vision of things to come. His future would be magnificent.

Chapter Twenty-Eight

"Lieutenant Lutjemeir," snapped Major Hurst.

"Heil Hitler." Lieutenant Lutjemeir came to attention before the major.

"Find Henri. He should be in his office. Bring him to me immediately."

Henri Gautheir also wanted time with the major. He marched up the hallway with the Lieutenant prepared to seek answers to *his* own questions.

"Heil Hitler." Henri saluted the kommandant.

"Take a chair."

Henri Gautheir pulled up an ornate wooden chair he'd never seen before, gripped its carved arms, slid it up to the desk, then said, "I am *very* angry this morning. To be called a swine and a traitor by my own people was unjust. It was humiliating . . . hurtful. And, then, you make me responsible for collecting pets."

"You're angry. *It was I who was called names,*" spit out the major.

Lieutenant Lutjemeir, who was standing just inside the door, interrupted, "They may not have meant it for either of you."

Distracted now by the interruption, Major Hurst's eyes flew up to lieutenant with distaste.

"Go on. Go on, now that you've started." The major pounded his fist upon the desk.

Unshaken Lieutenant Lutjemeir continued. "I heard a lady talking on the street. She was speaking about 'the naughty girls of the village.'"

"Go on. Go on," pushed the major.

"Perhaps there are some people who have strong opinions about you and Karl being out with . . ."

The major stopped him. "We'll have none of that. When you see the woman who spoke, bring her to me."

"Jahwol, Kommandant."

"Herr Kommandant," said Henri. "It is my daughter, my only daughter, we discuss here. Someone I cherish more than life itself. I cannot bear to see her hurt."

"My intentions are the highest," reassured the major.

Then, he thought of the perfect solution. *Hah, I have a way to keep track of all her actions!*

"I will see that from henceforth she is escorted wherever she goes. Lieutenant Lutjemeir, make it your responsibility. Go to the house. Accompany her everywhere. See that nothing happens to further embarrass us."

"Heil Hitler." The Lieutenant saluted and was gone.

Henri Gautheir pressed on. "These pets . . ."

"Ah, I already told you—for a breeding farm, but you don't believe that. You wish to really know what we want of them, don't you?" The major put his hands together on the desk, studied them, and, said, "All you need to know is they will benefit everyone. Now, that should take care of that. Meanwhile, you had other things on your mind?"

"Indeed. I have been thinking about your request for names of Jews. We have never had any of Jewish faith reside in our village," continued Henri in a stiff voice.

"I see you are an intelligent man. You seek reasons. So, I being a reasonable man of intelligence, respect that in you, and will explain why we ask for Jews."

The Kommandant said the Germans looked at France, or any other nation they conquered for the Third Reich, as a farm overgrown with weeds and they wanted to cultivate the worthwhile elements and allow the substandard to wither. They planned to increase the mixture of good German blood with the good blood of those elsewhere.

"But, you see, Jews are weeds. You and I, we men of good race, must hold our own against such weeds. Sending a Jew away from your village is an emergency defense measure. In fact, we have some books ordered for your school children—*The Poison Pill*—which should help answer the Jewish question."

In his training, in talks with people at home, or among his men, he said he heard many opinions about how to do this weeding.

"Some want a *Volkesch*—restrict their influence in politics, culture, but allow them unlimited freedom in the business world. Others, the extreme racial theorists, want to dismiss any Jewish official or doctor or lawyer or business person from our public places, our concert halls, swimming pools, restaurants."

He said the German Nuremberg Laws passed in l935 stated any business between a Jew and a non-Jew was a crime before the state.

"Personally, I would like to ship all of them off to Palestine. Palestine says it wants to have all of its sons backwho have been lost for over a thousand years. You know, we have even set up retraining camps for Jews so they can learn to do the farm work on the Palestine Kibbutzims."

Major Hurst said there were too many top people in Germany now felt that if Palestine became a strong Jewish state, someday they'd demand representation in the German government.

"It all gets very complicated. Britain may or may not permit them to have a state. The Arab Nationalists closed the frontiers. And, now so few countries are taking Jewish immigrants.

"The Police. The Party. The State. We have decided to put all the responsibility for the Jewish immigrants into the hands of one office. Into the hands of someone very organized. It's director is Eichmann, maybe you've heard of him?"

The mayor said he had not heard of Eichmann.

"As I have explained to you before, I wish to maintain good relations during my short time here—we could get orders to leave anytime—but, while I am here, I wish us to do business in a mannerly way. Incidentally, I am curious about something. The painting in your dining room. What happened to it?"

Henri replied sourly, "Since you started taking your evening meal there, I have not set foot in the room. I would not know. Are you telling me something has happened to it? That painting has been in our family for generations. The painter spent many weeks with my great-great-grandparents in exchange for his lodging and food.

"Grandfather Georges has been an inspiration to the family for years. His painting reminds us of his noble character and the will to be the best. Has it been damaged! I certainly hope it has not!"

"Damaged! Only the thief knows. We came one night and the canvas was gone. Officer Larsen was incensed."

Henri stood. "I am shocked. Such a crime in my own house!" He saluted, then said with anger apparent in his voice, "Heil Hitler."

He stomped out of the room. He felt the same fierce fury as the storm, which had rolled in during their session. He hoped the rain, now pelting the windows of the town hall with its fury, would fade the words "SWINE . . . TRAITOR" on the steps of his house.

Chapter Twenty-Nine

*D*inner was late for Dr. Renet and Gerald.

The doctor had just come from the bedside of a dying patient. As he approached his home-office, he murmured a prayer of blessing for the arrival of the sunny lad. If Gerald had not come to live with him, coming home now would not have the anticipation or feeling of being needed. Although Angie's presence lingered, and he occasionally would mention her to Gerald or Marie, he did not miss her as much as he might have because of Gerald.

Other pet owners were not so fortunate. Most feared sharing their grief or hatred with other villagers, which made their personal pain more intense.

For those who worked outside the home, they had their activities to occupy them while their inner reserves rebuilt. But those whose pets gave structure to their daily activities in the home were going through the most abrupt separation anxieties. They suffered grievously and either began to think about suicide or wonder about their sanity. There was no longer anyone to open the door for, to feed, or to caress.

Many former pet owners couldn't grasp what had happened. They blocked out the memory of handing over their pet or even that they had ever owned one.

The doctor, absorbed by the dying of someone who had no physical need to die, could not put out of his mind the many dishes of food his patient had put out for the dog throughout all the rooms of his house.

Gerald noticed immediately the doctor's quiet mood of deep introspection.

Dr. Renet burst out, "Oh, how he wants to believe his dog will come back. I could hardly find a place to put my shoes, there were so many dishes. I wish I knew how to help those who are suffering so much."

Gerald's sad eyes imaged the feelings of the helpless doctor. He, too, was aware of tormented villagers.

"Maybe we could help Father Molterine. He's having terrible headaches keeping him awake at night. I said you might have something to help him. But, Father said there were too many others with greater needs."

"Of course. Yes, of course. Take something to him. In fact, stop in and see Madame Sabrine. She hasn't gone out or let anyone into her place since—"

Gerald's eyes brightened. "I remember her house, Dr. Renet. I've taken shoes to her. She's the one who cried so hard even Mayor Gauthier couldn't get her to stop. Her little dog looked the worst, was the saddest of them all, when I picked him up. He was trembling and shivering. Maybe she'll talk to me, a little kid, about her dog."

"You're absolutely right, Gerald. Listening is what she needs, not explanations. She's overcome by her reasons why innocent, trusting, good animals had to die. They were pure love, so full of trust."

"Father Molterine says they are waiting for us in heaven and we should be the good persons the pets saw in us." Gerald was glad to have before him missions of good cheer. He was a child born with a shining spirit, someone who could bring hope to those in despair just by his presence.

"Gerald, you have great promise. If you want to be a doctor, I would feel it an honor to fiance your education."

"I like you a lot, Dr. Renet, and it's been awfully good here with you and Marie. However, I have to wait to see what my parents think, as well as my Uncle and Aunt, the Gilles. As for being a doctor—if I could be like you, I'd want to do it."

"Keep it in mind, Gerald. My offer is good for a long, long time. Meanwhile, how about seeing if Marie has scraped up any dessert."

"Oh, but she did. It's your favorite." Gerald's eyes sparkled. As he left the room, an old Chinese proverb came to mind to the Doctor:

When the winter is severe
The pine tree in this ancient land
Stays green throughout the year.
Is it because the earth is warm?
No, it is because the pine
Tree has within itself
A life-restoring power.

Chapter Thirty

Midmorning the next day Gerald tapped lightly upon the black door at Madame Sabrine's. He listened for sounds of someone coming to answer his knock, but, upon hearing no movement within, he rapped harder.

He waited and as he did so his glance took in a large black bow fastened upon the door above the brass knocker. His eyes went to the windows. Black bows were there, too.

He thought about Madame Sabrine. Dr. Renet was sending her liquid to bring her back to reality. He wondered what the doctor meant, however, he had not asked for an explanation as he knew he would soon find out. He remembered the tiny, stooped widow from the day of the pet turn-in. She was one of the worst, clutching her tiny Pomeranian dog, cooing, "Peppy, my little Peppy," over and over. "What will I do without you? What will you do without me?"

She was so bent over that he was almost as tall as she was. He remembered how he had tried pulling off her gnarled fingers to take the animal. His feelings of remorse and pity for her had been so full he felt his stomach ache and his hands tremble.

He went around to the back door. It felt awkward going into a house where he was not expected, but, he had to overcome his feelings of guilt with the fact that he was coming to help.

"Madame Sabrine? Hello." He called in a mellow child's voice as he entered the small entry hall. Again, he called out, "Madame Sabrine? It's me, Gerald. Doctor sent me," he announced as he entered the kitchen.

Then, in the big room, he saw a small form hunched in a rocking chair. The room was dark, the lace curtains over pulled shades at the windows.

"Madame Sabrine, are you there?" He approached the form in the chair. Is she all right? Is she alive?

"Oh, madame," he cried. He knelt by the chair and sought her balled-up, gnarled hands and placed his own about them. "My heart breaks for you and for your little Peppy."

Madame Sabrine's heart awakened from the depths of her grieving and flew up to her lips. "My little Peppy. Did you know my Peppy?" She began to cry, little jerky sobs.

"Tell me about your Peppy," encouraged Gerald. His heart was pure and full of love for someone in this mortal pain. "I'd like to hear all about Peppy." He stroked her hands.

Within a few minutes, she gathered a strength from him, and began to rise up from the chair with his help and move in mincing steps toward a large buffet.

"Is there a light? So we can see."

Madame Sabrine stood in front of the buffet. She pointed to an ornate lamp with a massive fringed lampshade. He found the knob and the room became softly lit.

For several hours the little boy listened with his whole being while the old woman recounted the story behind each toy and black-draped picture on the hutch.

"I can't go out, not with them around." She told him that Anna, the butcher's wife, came every night to bring a meal. The terror in her voice as she spoke left little doubt in Gerald's mind that she meant the Germans, especially Kommandant Hurst. Gerald wondered if he might feel the same if he were ninety-three years old and lost every living thing he loved. Would he take the medicine? Could being more optimistic about life improve her circumstances? The sincerity of his feelings for the old woman shone through.

When the lad left the house, the madame trudged to the kitchen, poured some water into a glass and took the medicine.

Chapter Thirty-One

Antoinette was placing silverware on the table when Major Hurst strode into the dining room.

"You're early."

"I want a few moments with you before dinner." He pulled out the tallest-backed chair at the head of the table.

He smiled and loosened his tie. Then, he became quite serious. "I am going to talk with you about practical matters." His left hand repositioned two pieces of the silverware.

Stricken by the tone of his voice, she tried to stand tall, to not look down into his eyes. She feared where he might be leading.

"How are things going? Are you still getting adequate food and wine?

"Yes, but I do more substituting lately," she confirmed. "In fact, I've been meaning to ask if I get a permit to go to the farm at once a week now that it's harvest."

"First tell me . . ."

What was he going to ask?

"This friend of yours, Jacques Duval? Where is he? You've seen the posters. You know he's wanted."

"Kommandant, I do not know. No one does."

"You were quite the friends, I understand." He looked stern.

"We grew up together."

What did he want?

"How is he different than me?"

"He's just a village boy . . . while, you are . . ." She took a deep breath to consider how to respond. "Educated. Have seen

126

things. Been places. Know things he doesn't."

"So I know things he doesn't. Then I must be the better lover."

At that moment, they heard the front door open, the other officers coming in.

"I must excuse myself." She rushed into the kitchen thinking, he probably censors our mail. I hope Jacques never writes. Oh, Jacques. Where are you? I'm sorry I called you just a village boy.

The next day, as if the kommandant's conversation had been an omen, she put her hand into the white box at the PTT and pulled out a postcard with a night scene of Marseilles. She dared not breathe. Her heart trembled. Could this be— finally, something from Jacques. Smoothing the front of the card, she shivered, looked about the lobby to see if anyone was watching, then hastily slid the card into a skirt pocket and left, slowly willing her footsteps to be deliberate.

She made her way down the familiar row, through the back alley and into the kitchen, through the hall, up the main steps and then up the rickety steps to the attic to her little cloister. Now it was safe. No one would see her.

She gently slid the shiny card out of her pocket. She looked once again at the lights of the hillsides, the night lights of a scene taken before the war. The suspense of waiting so long to hear from him was unbearable. It was a tumultuous thrill just to hold the card in her hands. She turned it over. Sight of the familiar bold handwriting made her gasp out loud. "You are alive."

His words were puzzling and would echo in her mind. She read over and over these words: "Dare to be who you are. The day will come for your happiness."

Chapter Thirty-Two

Antoinette watched for red blood stains to appear. Days passed without the beginning of the menses. Many times a day she went to peek. She hoped and prayed the menus would begin.

The only sure way to be certain would be to ask Dr. Renet. She considered going to see him after the first month went by, but she knew her father and the doctor were good friends so put the idea out of her mind. *I'll go in another month. Perhaps the herbs . . .'*

Days passed. Then weeks. She watched, waited. Nothing. No sign of blood.

'I must know,' she agonized. *'If nothing has happened by the 16th of October, I will make myself go.*

On the morning of the 16th, Lieutenant Lutjemeir sought her out. She was making one of the officer's beds.

"Bonjour, mademoiselle. What are we up to today?"

"We will be going out, Hans."

"Looks like another beautiful fall day. If it is anything like yesterday . . . but, you seem not your cheerful self, like yesterday."

"We did have such good news then, Hans. A postcard came from a friend."

"So, why are you gloomy?" The German officer had grown fond of Antoinette.

Lieutenant Lutjemeir was one of the last officers to join Hurst's group. His field gray uniform bore his Arm of Service color black, or Waffenbarken, on the piping of collar and shoulder strap. He was the son of a farmer who felt such pride in the Nazi cause, the uniform and their mission to conquer the world, he had encouraged his son to join.

"It's something I want to see Dr. Renet about. I shall be occupied with my daily work, say for another hour." She plumped pillows back onto the freshly made bed.

"I'll wait for you in the dining room." The lieutenant had become fascinated with the production of grapes and the art of wine making. He like to look at the Gautheir books on the subject as he hoped to grow grapes at his father's farm someday. He had become quite excited about the venture in September when he and Antoinette spent several days helping with the grape harvest and the beginning of the wine making, the time called the Vandage.

Following the Vandage, Antoinette came to him. "Hans, if you are truly interested in making wine, here are some books for you to read."

He was in the middle of a chapter about soil types when she called to him, "I'm ready, Hans."

They set off into the golden fall day. "To the PTT?"

"Not today, Hans."

Anna was coming towards them. "Bonjour, Anna." Antoinette called out as they met the stout woman. The butcher's wife turned her head and walked across the street.

"We can't make them like us," Hans said dismally, "it's times like this I miss Germany."

"Oh, Hans. I forget how hard this is for you, too."

"Waffen-SS do not complain. Ever. Overlook that. He spoke with military-precision, his ability to converse in French much improved due to the time he was spending with Antoinette."

They came to the gate by the doctor's large combination house and office.

"Do you want to wait inside?"

"No, I'll stroll about for awhile, then wait outside." He meant the sidewalk in front of a low wrought-iron fence which enclosed the house and grounds.

Marie greeted her as she entered the waiting area. "Doctor is with a patient. He shouldn't be long." She led Antoinette to the doctor's study after Antoinette explained that she really wasn't sick, but just had a few questions to ask the doctor.

'Waiting. Waiting for the mensus is more painful than having a disease.' Her mind could not be distracted from the question: Am I with child? The harder she tried not to think about the question, the more it seared, consuming and filling her with turmoil.

"Antoinette. How good to see you." Dr. Renet strode into the study. "To what do I owe this unexpected pleasure?"

"I think I am . . . I think I am going to have a baby, but I don't know for certain."

"Well, well, well. Have you missed the menses?"

"Twice. And, I never have before missed one."

"Um, I do detect a 'Mask of Pregnancy.'" He stood beside her and ran his hand across the bridge of her nose and cheek bones. "In a woman who is with child, we often see a darkened area here, caused by an increase in something called melanin.

"These hormones of pregnancy," he continued, "Also stimulate the area around the nipples—would you mind opening your blouse—yes, I see the area there is darker as I suspected . . . but, if you want to be absolutely sure, I could do the Ascheim Zondek tests . . . the Germans have come up with our only tests available to find out with a frog or a rabbit."

"But, you believe . . ."

"You *have* missed two menses and have the other signs. My dear, I do believe you are to become a mother . . . sometime mid-April is my guess. How do you feel? Any nausea? Upset stomach? Tiredness?"

"I can barely stay awake afternoons, so I run up to take a little nap, but I feel better than ever." She could sense he wanted to know more—know who the father was.

"I had to know," she stammered. "It was something I had to know. You won't mention my coming—"

"If I can help in any way, let me know. Come see me once a month. I'd like to be sure things are coming along as they should."

"I trust you, Dr. Renet. You have been so good to all my family." She stood.

"Stop in next month, or anytime. If you need someone to listen, I'm usually around. You might even like to come along with us—Gerald's with me now you know—on one of our trips to the country. Incidentally, any word from Jacques?"

"Oh, yes. I've waited so long to hear from him. Then, yesterday I received this postcard. It's such a relief to know he is alive." Her hand touched the postcard with respect as she showed the scene of Marseilles to the doctor.

He gave her some medicine for possible nausea. She took the sack, crammed it into a pocket, then said as she was leaving, "Of all the people in the world, you are one of my favorites."

Lieutenant Lutjemeir waited by the fence. "Home?" he asked.

"No. I must see the major. Do you think he's at town hall?"

"Let's see." He noticed she had a determined air.

At the town hall, several wooden chairs were in the hallway but none were occupied. "Take a seat here," he motioned. "I'll see if he is in."

She paced up and down the hallway, and hoped her father would not appear.

Hans returned looking jubilant. "Fortunately, I found him alone. He says he can see you."

The major leapt to his feet. "Please wait outside, Lieutenant."

"Heil Hitler."

"Why have you come?" he asked. She shuddered.

The door closed.

"Now, what has brought about this visit?"

"I'm—I'm here because . . . because." The words would not come.

"Come sit here." He pulled up a chair beside the one in front of the desk. "Why you are so anxious?"

She gripped the carved arms of the chair, trying to remember something her father had told her about the major.

"Now, what is this all about?"

"I've just been to the doctor," she blurted out.

"About your brother?"

"No. Not at all."

"You are having some problems?"

"Yes. No. I don't know what to do?"

"Now, tell me why you have come today." He was impatient.

"You see I have missed two menses and the doctor has told me I am surely with child." She could not look at him.

"When is the event?"

"Mid-April," she said, eyes downcast.

"Under the present conditions, you cannot remain here. Already there have been incidences, relatively few, but still, your condition would surely incite more. I won't be subject to such further gossip about the mayor's daughter."

"What will I do?" She felt forlorn, like a dog left outside on a rainy night.

"Leave, of course."

"But where? I have no money. No place to go. I cannot tell my parents."

"And, who is the father?

"But, you, of course. You know I have been with no one else," alarmed he would even think such a thing.

"Obviously you cannot remain in Villepente. I will make inquiries immediately with the Fountain of Life Ministry. We shall both hope they have a vacancy." The major went on to again explain the Lebensborn facilities scattered about Germany, one perhaps even in Paris.

Suddenly she felt queasy. She put her head into her hands. He arose in a gesture of dismissal and said as she went out, "The Führer will be proud."

Chapter Thirty-Three

*D*anielle tried feeling happy. It was the night of her eighteenth birthday and she was on the way to Cher to celebrate with Waffen-SS officer Walther, one of the privileged few to have petrol.

The car flew through the cool night, its headlamps making light on the road thin as pencils.

She shivered. Celebrating in Cher with Karl might prove unpleasant. Cher was slightly larger than Villepente and, although not occupied by German troops, its residents were being assessed their valuables each week, too. However, there had not been the nasty business of a pet turn-in; yet, Villepente news reverberated fast after the loss of the village pets and the deaths of two old people who had not given up their theirs.

Danielle was having a hard time deciding what really was making her feel uneasy. She wasn't afraid to be seen with Karl at the cafe or driving in the car making its way along the narrow road. It was something else. Maybe something to do with her recent conversation with Antoinette.

A long stretch of time had gone by without seeing Antoinette. She had almost disappeared. Or, if Antoinette were out, she was always accompanied by Lieutenant Lutjemeir. Danielle spent her time waiting for any moment Karl might be free, so she hadn't noticed the absence of Antoinette until recently.

Late one afternoon a few days before, Danielle looked out her front window and saw Antoinette leave her house alone and start down the row. Danielle rolled up the front window and called out, "Antoinette. Stop. I want to see you. Right now."

Danielle slammed down the window and rushed out. "I haven't seen you for so long, Antoinette. Where are you going? You're never alone anymore. Talk to me a little while. I have good news," Danielle continued excitedly.

So, they sat on the steps of the Ramaine house, Antoinette curled on the bottom and Danielle on the step above. Danielle gushed, "Karl is taking me out for my big birthday tomorrow night. Mother put two of last year's dresses together. But, you're not listening. What's wrong?"

"I *really am* pleased for you," responded Antoinette in a weary tone of voice. "You're happy—still?"

"I am happy, but I am not happy about not seeing you. You must be hiding from me. But, why? Have I said something to offend you? Or, is it something to do with the major? You can tell me."

Antoinette turned and looked at Danielle. "It is not you or anything you have said or done. There have been other things."

"Tell me. You don't look like yourself. I want to know why. I know there is something. And, what's happened with the major? You seemed to be good friends at the beach. And, I've seen you out with him in the car several times. Maybe it was those bad words someone wrote on your steps."

"Perhaps so. I know he thought someone put them there for him, but I knew they were painted for me. I think after that he grew afraid to be seen with a French woman."

"No. No. That's not so. I've seen Angelique and Monique, both of them, with him. Imagine, and both of their husbands gone."

Danielle saw the pained look in Antoinette's eyes before she looked away. "Mon Dieu! I am thick in the head. You really liked the major but he doesn't like you anymore."

Antoinette nodded. "As you say, there are *others* he'd rather be with. I should have known. Don't worry about anything you've just said. Danielle, *I am* glad to see you. Being with you never fails to cheer me up. I wish you were coming with me."

"Where? When? Maybe I can go, too?"

"I don't think so." Antoinette looked away and adjusted her skirt. "Things didn't turn out as well for me as they did for you."

She stood up and bid adieu to Danielle. Then, she looked back and called out to her over her shoulder, "Happy birthday tomorrow," as she began walking towards the intersection which led to the church.

Danielle puzzled over her friend's cryptic words and unshared plans. War makes things hard to figure out, she decided uneasily.

Karl noticed Danielle was too quiet and asked, "What is happening with you, Danny, my sweet. You are too solemn. Something wrong?"

"I've been thinking and thinking and that's hard work. I've been trying to figure out, why on the most special night of my entire life, I am sad beyond belief," she answered. She turned her body towards Karl, admired his profile, and smiled a sad smile.

Karl said she should tell him what she had been thinking about so seriously. Then she told him of her recent conversation with Antoinette.

"Perhaps I am sad because Antoinette is going away and I'm not. She wouldn't say where, just that she was going somewhere." Danielle sighed.

"And, where would you like to go?" the lieutenant inquired.

"Anywhere that's fun." Danielle considered the possibilities. "Yes, I think even a visit to my grandmamere in Marseilles, even with the old embroidery hoop she throws around me to keep me inside with her, would be the most glorious thing. Marseilles must be more active than Villepente and fewer sad things happening. Remember how I told you I like to go places by train. If I could go anywhere, I would like to go by train to see my grandmamere. Things would be happier where she is. The war would not seem as real there, at least I don't think so."

"Then, my darling, as your birthday present, you shall go on the train Saturday to Marseilles. I have been thinking about an appropriate present to give you. So that shall be it. I'll prepare your travel papers and buy the ticket."

"Oh, Karl, you are wonderful. I am . . . I started to say happy . . . and, yes, I am happy to have this present of a trip, but I won't be happy to leave you behind. I'll be sad." Danielle looked at the dark road and fought back tears.

"You have always been honest with me. You have reminded me time and time again that you may have to leave at any moment, so really that's not why I felt so bad after Antoinette and I talked."

Karl focused on the road and the shadows cast by the stone walls. He said solemnly, "If you want to know where Antoinette is going—she is going away to have a baby at a special place. The kommandant does not believe it is his, but he is providing a place for her at a Lebensborn."

"But," stammered Danielle, "I can't believe the baby is not his. Antoinette would not go to bed with Jacques until they were married, which wasn't possible until after the war, and she hasn't seen Jacques since you came. Poor Antoinette. She is so brave. I wouldn't be if I were in her place. Oh, Karl, I think I realize what has been bothering me so much. But, I'm afraid to tell you."

Karl slowed the car by a lane and parked. He pressed Danielle to him and said tenderly, "Men are as different as people and officers as the wars they fight. A woman must have a tough time knowing the man behind the words he says. I hope you know in your heart the love I express for you is true and that someday we will be together forever."

"Karl," she said gleefully, clasping him tightly, "what you just said is the best birthday present I've ever had—but the train trip to Marseilles Saturday is second best."

Chapter Thirty-Four

*M*ajor Hurst stroked the thick linen paper with its rich creamy color. The glow of his good fortune brought a wide smile to his handsome face.

He had just pulled an invitation from a black leather dispatch pouch, a top-secret SS document container with twin silver lightening streaks in the right-hand corner.

He was to attend a top secret SS conference. For a moment, the electric blue in his eyes softened and became the softness of the Mediterranean. Its cryptic message read:

Your immediate presence is desired.

A driver is waiting. I am waiting.

The scrawled initials were enough to put fear into the heart of any in the Order. Eleven other Black Knights of Heinrich Himmler, who ranked high within his black-uniformed society, were also being summoned. Hurst would be attending a gathering of one of the Waffen SS innermost circles.

Few knew the location of the former monastery which Himmler had refurbished into a castle at tremendous expense. The spot and what took place within was a source of mystery. Blood-chilling commitments were made before any attendee left.

Rumors within the SS whispered that these retreats were held in Wevelsburg, Westphaia. For hadn't Himmler searched in that area for months. He'd begun looking when he learned from his personal astrologer that in the next confrontation with the east a Westphalian castle would be the only stronghold to survive.

The road was narrow and moved through undisturbed shade with such subtlety that when it widened it gave the feeling of arrival to a great place. Travelers along the road felt that a great joy would be in store for them at the end. The quiet atmosphere erupted into a forest of flags, on both sides of the road, and before the road turned, a castle came into view, but just for a moment. Then, the road moved narrowly again through a silent tangle of thick brush, crossed a moat, and stopped in front of a massive carved wooden door.

Inside Himmler nervously paced flagstones in the cavernous stone entry hall floor. He was dressed as King Heinrich I might have been on such a ceremonious occasion in the eighteen hundreds. The King's spirit came to him in the night with invaluable counsel and told him what to wear and what people to watch out for.

He had on light blue pumpkin hose, his legs stuffed to make them appear more muscular. They joined soft skin shoes with pointed toes. The deep blue tunic was embedded with glittering bits of silver holding diamonds which formed twin lightening streaks.

He was of medium build, moved and spoke quickly and in so doing often said things that seemed to be without much thought or came out as slips of the tongue.

The cheeks in his usually pallid completion this late afternoon were bright red from anticipation. His eyelids were always reddish over the mouse-gray pupils behind the little round glass spectacles. The whites were so small they could hardly be seen if an onlooker were bold enough.

Dark and bushy brows almost covered the eyeglasses. His chin receded so sharply it looked like the mouth of a shark and did not help hide the fact that he was a cruel and evil-spirited man. This strange look gave him much power and ability to intimidate.

Enroute to the castle, Hurst perspiring. Would he be the one singled out for the concluding event? Was his not finding the treasure of Villepente the reason for his invitation?

A spiritual sensitive, an artist of pendulum practitioning, a dowser who used a pendulum instead of dousing rod, vehemently had insisted that the pendulum consistently time after time stopped cold over the little French village of Villepente.

The Grail is there . . . somewhere in that village . . . I'll find it. I will convince Himmler it has got to be among the things we've collected. It would be inaccessible to any ordinary mortal but I will know it when I touch it. I will understand what it is.

It is not gold or silver. It is a simple pottery goblet, because, of course, the guest then was given the best and the household probably only drank from bowls, but they gave him a goblet. Perhaps painted, the paint peeling. Maybe gray.

How victorious it will be in the eyes of the world when our Führer possesses it. He alone then will appear as the Messiah, the Führer of the entire globe. He will most certainly be head of the New World with Germany as the center. Mein Führer—the white race will be reunited to its eternal beginning and our Reich will be glorious for a thousand years.

Is that why I am here. Because I haven't given it over?

He turned the thoughts over and over and considered how to respond to Himmler's anticipated question: 'In your special assignment, what news have you? Would you be pleased to tell me?'

Yes, he knew Henrich Himmler was quite capable of saying please in private conversation. Hurst hoped if the question came it would be in private not in front of the group. If he were found delinquent in this assignment in Villepente, would it mean the end of him? Even though activities during the secret retreats were keep secret, a mention of the finale of one of these events couldn't help but leak out.

Even now as he put his arms into a deep burgundy velvet waistcoat with hand-worked gold embroidered collar and cuffs, a garment created by the Imperial German Opera Company, his fears grew. That's why he didn't appreciate, as he might have, the tall-ceiling of his castle room. The bed so high it had three wood steps up to it. The tall windows. The white bear fur skin before the fireplace.

Oh, he knew why he was here. He was the one to be sacrificed. His head would be cut off as a way of communicating with the Secret Masters in the Caucasus.

However, he would act like the well-trained Waffen SS officer he had been turned into. Hadn't he glided past Himmler's initial welcome without giving away the fact that he was anything but glad to be here. There had been no hint from Himmler either, he had just seemed like a host acknowledging a guest before he handed him over with directions to his quarters.

He must join the others. He glanced at his watch, squashed out a cigarette in a silver ashtray, then made haste down a wide hallway, trotted down the wide wood steps leading to the entry hall and burst into the dining hall.

A huge oval-shaped table was surrounded by high-backed soft-skinned chairs, a silver plate engraved with each Teutonic name hanging from the back on a golden chain. There were two vacant chairs, his and the highest backed one, Himmlers'. All conversation stopped when he had entered, and, because each Knight had anticipated it was Himmler and would have risen, however, when they saw it was one of their own, they resumed their quiet conversations, and continued to buzz.

Stiffly he slipped into the chair being held out for him by a costumed male servant.

Appreciative as he always had been for beautifully appointed tables, he saw with a glance, as his eyes swept over the sight before him that this was one of the loveliest presentations he'd even seen.

A heavy cloth of snowy white linen fell off the top with precision stiffness. Huge white napkins made a showy performance encased by the massive death's head rings of silver. Elaborate silver pieces lined up beside each plate like miniature soldiers ready for the duty of helping each knight feast upon carp, roast goose and wild boar—drawn from sphere of water, air and earth. Etched glassware above each place setting told of the many wines to be served, the finest, of course from France, ending with a champagne which would breathe tiny bubbles.

Silver candelabra held white candles and were placed so they would not obstruct the view of any knight to their chief lord. Open white rose buds floated upon a raised silver pedestal in the center as tiny white buds cascaded down the sides. A single, long stemmed white rose presided upon a delicate glass presentation plate. The plate had been especially etched with the knight's ancestral pattern.

As soon as Hurst was seated, a voice to his right said, "Baron Hurst, isn't it? I've been looking forward to meeting you."

Hurst took in the handsome man and wondered how they were connected and then realized, of course, his name was getting around and his reputation within the organization was growing.

"Duke Landruth, Peter," smiled the man whose broad, warm smile melted any suspicious thoughts Hurst might have had. "I'm one of the mercenary knights, you see, who give our loyalty to the highest bidder." He wore a slashed sleeve red jacket with yellow gold shirt showing beneath.

"Ah, I see you do not know the name. I am only one of your finance, Ellen's, great admirers. You've got quite a handful, there, haven't you? You're a lucky man none the less."

Before Hurst could respond, sounds of chairs scraping commenced and all rose as Himmler entered.

Himmler raised a hand and motioned them to sit. He went to stand beside his chair and announced, "This is a great night. I am honored you are here. So, let us begin.

Course after course was served to the accompaniment of his favorite Wagnerian series of six operas, Cycles of the Rings. It was favorite of course for the story it told—of the Norse mythology of rings which give immortal power.

The Knights followed the example of their leader and ate without conversation other than mummers of approval as the food was served.

The evening felt orchestrated, pre-arranged, and ominous. An expert observer, he watched the other knights carefully.

Himmler rose. All eyes fastened upon the chief knight who wore a waist coat and breeches of silver. The silver shoes with buckles and heels that made him seem taller. All items, of course, created by the most talented slave labor available.

"Men. Let us reach for the skies to grasp whatever men desire."

The knights, most of them new to the occasion, seemed uncertain about how to respond. Peter who was a regular assumed the leadership and raised his champagne glass. The others did the same.

"Thank you, Duke Landruth. An announcement now of interest. I decided due to your superior past record that you will be reassigned. Yes. We'll sending your great talents to Berlin. You'll have a thing or two to get them excited about at the Institute of Scientific Research. Your illusion work is quite superior from what I've hear.

"It is customary to exchange ideas about the success of our steadily deepening research into family genealogies. We spring from the greatest of men, our forbearers the great Germans of the Middle Ages. This places each of you under great obligation. Hurst cringed. Himmler picked up a knife and struck several empty glasses before him. The bell tones resounded through the hall.

"Hah. You should know what your obligation is. It demands you be liberated from any old world ideas and proclaim our own laws of the new community.

"As heirs to old German nobility, it matters with whom you mate and beget children. The future of the German people depends upon it."

Hurst squirmed. Did his French girl meet Himmler's criteria? Is that why he was here? Had he made a mistake by sending her paperwork in and requesting a Lebensborn assignment?

Himmler continued more loudly. "I single out Baron Hurst who has taken our racial program one step further—"

The eyes of the knights swiveled to Hurst.

"He has mated with a French woman. Yes, a racially pure woman of excellent linage. I've just seen the paperwork, Baron Hurst. Well done. Thus, take notice all you others. In this way we bring about a new world order. As links in the clan's endless chain, Hurst has been careful to be sure that she would pass the rigorous tests for entry to a Lebensborn.

"Ah, you are not ordinary mortals—you are Super Men. We gather tomorrow at dawn on the lawn to witness such an example."

Himmler yawned, then abruptly left. Peter leapt up and began beguiling the knights with magic tricks which ended the evening in laughter.

His illusions were impressive. Through words and actions he could make they believe a seated knight simply disappeared. Of course, it was only Landruth's ability to play on the unconscious characteristic of their eyes to react as if someone were gone even though they weren't. His illusions were believable.

"We SS men are eagles, souring mightily above mere mortals below. You two, go over to stand behind those statues. Yes, the ones with the eagles," he said directing to two he had in mind because there were so many other statues of eagles, too, in the soaring room. The officers went behind the statues. "Place a hand upon each wing," Landruth commanded. "Let's have a demonstration of our SS abilities." His deep baritone voice held the officers. What was going to happen? Wings of the eagles began to move, and then the birds appeared to be flying off.

"SS are eagles. We are majestic, magnificent specimens of men." The applause of the officers was deafening. Several men had tears in their eyes.

The next morning Hurst was awakened by sounds of a dog snarling. He pushed the tall windows apart and saw several men clustered together. A Viking pavilion with long oars and red and god sails stretched down blocked some of the view.

A man was striped to his waist and was trying to fight off a guard dog. A few of the men moved and Hurst saw Himmler standing nearby with hands on his hips. Two uniformed men stood beside trees with rifles readied.

The dog/man contest wasn't new. SS candidates often were required to go through this exercise at one of the schools of instruction. It was all part of their gruesome preparation. Through any barbarity, no matter what, one could thus show indifference for pity or sorrow. He had torn the eyes out of kittens with his bare hands and had told a lesser-ranking candidate to balance a grenade upon his head, stand at attention, then pull out the pin. Too bad it had been his cousin, but that was the way it was.

Himmler held up four fingers. It was a timed test. Hurst tried to see the man's face. He rushed to dress but when he went again to the window, no one was in sight.

Where were they? When Himmler greeted him upon his arrival, he had mentioned the library. Was this the library where all known literature relating to the cult of race was housed? He must see it. Would the breeding catalogs of Race and Settlement be there? He'd have to look to be sure his ancestors were properly mentioned.

It did matter who the heirs of the new German nobility would be. The future of the German people depended upon it. The little French girl's genes would polish and enhance the

Jo Ann Bender

qualities of his ancestors. He sped down the stairs to find the library.

The beauty of the sunlit library struck Hurst in the same manner as when he caught sight of a beautiful woman: first, he felt a sense of appreciation, then the need for further assessment, as no thing of beauty was completely flawless, and he did like to look for flaws in anyone or anything.

He went to a shelf and pulled out a new looking book, attracted by its red spine among the old gray volumes. 'Ah,' he sighed, 'Rosenburg's Myth of the Twentieth Century.'

He felt the presence of someone in the room and turned to see Himmler.

"When you read his new book, you will understand, as did I, that it is even a more powerful work than that of H.S. Chamberlain. Perhaps Baumler's book should also be of interest, Baron Hurst." Himmler turned to another shelf to seek a book. When he pulled one down, he leafed through its gold-edged pages. "Here it is. Concerning the Grail—he writes, but no, I'll let you discover the beauties of this work," and thrust the book on top of the other book in Hurst's hands.

"There is another you'd like, too. Did you know Baumler advocates that conception take place in a Nordic cemetery." When he saw the vague stare in Hurst's eyes, he added, "The baby inherits the spirits of all the dead heroes who lie therein. Lists of such cemeteries are published regularly in our *Das Schwarze Korps.*

"I also like the custom which can almost guarantee a male child. Baumler says the woman should do nothing but eat wholesome food and sleep for a week while the man abstains from alcohol, goes for seven-mile walks each day, and then comes to her to mate."

Hurst found his voice and said, "Without the ability to multiply our blood, we shall not be able to maintain the Great Germanic Empire. It is a noble duty which Ellen and I will strive to maintain."

145

"Excellent. Excellent. I have things to attend to but, oh, do regard my collection over there, too, on that lower shelf. It should give you some new insights about the finer aspects of the sexual arts, especially note what the Hindus have to say about the tantras. Ah, but I have things which need my attention. I do hope that all is satisfactory and that you are enjoying your stay."

Days at the castle passed quickly with tournaments. Hurst proved best at ones on horseback. He could slash a melon in two by riding by the fastest and because of the sharpness he could bring to his sword. He wasn't as good with foot fighting with the ax, but held his own in the drawn sword fighting. The other competitions did not hold his attention at all, especially the calligraphy contest. Or, the watermelon throwing contest.

The competitions all led up to the final night when at midnight the knights were to proceed to the lower depths of the castle to a funeral room.

Three foot stones climbed one upon the other, dovetailed without mortar, and stretched high into a vaulted turret that narrowed at the peak. On several of the stones were large metal engraved plates with a knight's teutonic name, birth and death dates.

A well was sunk into the middle of the room. There were stone pillars with raised stonework around the sides. When a top-ranking knight died, his ashes were placed in a cremation urn on the one of the pedestals and smoke would rise into the turret due to a clever ventilation system.

Upon coming into the room, the knights' eyes had to adjust to the hazy blue-gray lighting as they arranged themselves around the well, holding sputtering torches.

When all were situated, a rich male voice floated in the air above them and said:"The last days are at hand. The Jews - satan in disguise - must be prevented from taking over the world. Super Men - you fearless elite - are the Reich's modern warriors."

"You have been taught to think with your blood. One of you is to be honored. From the fruits of his bloodline will rise up the spirit of his ancestors to guide our great mission.

"Answer again, each of you, why do you obey so gladly, when given an order?"

The men responded together as if a rehearsed chorus, their voices firm, emphatic, definite.

"I obey from inner conviction, from belief in Germany, in the Führer, the movement, in the SS and from loyalty to all."

The voice continued: "If you fail to respond willingly, remember you betray the party and its Führer. Your wife and children will be destroyed. The one who does so with courage honors himself, the party, the Führer, his ancestors and those who come after him."

The voice stopped. It was silent.

Tension swelled within the chests of the knights within their coats of wire. Muffled irregular breathing could be heard behind the masks.

Hurst sweat profusely. Was he the one?

The voice began again. "OberguppenFührer Von Drexler. This will be your last and best command."

Hurst felt so full of relief he almost shouted, 'I knew my mission in Villepente was too important.'

Von Drexler, the lieutenant general so commanded, moved from within the ranks of his fellow knights. He made his way slowly to the hollowed out stone, removed the heavy metal mask from his head and let it clank to the floor. He unfastened the suit of armor and let it fall to a puddle.

He stood naked and said in a voice of triumph, "I am honored to serve."

He put his head to the stone.

A knife concealed within the fretwork, flew from the side to slit his throat. Blood flew out and spattered several knights. Hurst felt nauseated when he saw flecks on his armor. He hated the sight on blood when it was on him.

The knights went outside to view the rising of the spirits of the fine Aryan specimen who had been sacrificed.

When Himmler joined them, he made a spectacular sight. He had thrown over his armor a velvet robe of dark blue velvet. A wind came up and bellowed the cape so it spread out and he appeared a giant.

The wind brought the perfect finale to the occasion. Himmler could hardly wait to send out the next invitations.

Was the beheading of Drexler another Landruth illusion?

Chapter Thirty-Five

A long line of penitents waited to make their confessions at the rear of St. Anthony's. Two sets of chambers had three doors each and were made of carved, varnished wood. They opened and closed with a peculiar noise, followed by then eerie silence.

While waiting her turn, Antoinette strained to determine if the persons inside could be heard by those in line. In the past she had never thought about being overheard, as she had never confessed worse than eating meat on a Friday, disobeying her parents, or French kissing with Jacques.

'*How can I tell someone so pure about the sins I have committed? I have no words to describe what I've done, especially to someone I've known all my life and respect so much.*'

Once inside the closet-like enclosure, she knelt on the little kneeler and folded her hands upon the little shelf by the tiny sliding window. She studied the wooden grill with the curtain which hid the penitent from the priest.

Again, she used excessive effort to see if the person on the other side of the confessional could be heard. She heard whispers but could not make out what was being said.

The little grill slid open.

"Bless me, Father, for I have sinned. It was in August . . . two months ago that I made my last confession."

Father Molterine was old and often slept through parts of a confession. Antoinette felt his portly presence. She listened intently for the familiar sniffs and snorts which meant he was dozing.

"This thing . . . these things I have done . . ." She began to cry, a few tears at first, then big sobs.

"The Lord is gracious and has mercy for those who call upon him. Which commandment have you broken?"

"I have been . . . impure . . ." She began to dry her tears.

"In thought, word or deed?" he requested.

"In all, Father."

"Was it done alone or with a man or woman?"

"A man."

"How often?" the priest asked.

"Often."

"Were you forced?" he inquired.

"In the beginning when the Nazis came to my house, I had to make a decision . . . to either go willingly or . . "

"But, then?"

She began to sob.

"There are martyrs who have chosen death before submitting," he insisted.

"I am to bear a child—I cannot stay in Villepente. I would dishonor my parents. I am leaving and want forgiveness."

"You go and sin no more."

"I will try," she said.

"You must do more than try. *You must succeed!*" The old voice was firm, full of resolve.

"Also . . . something else . . . I went to Madame Mana, terribly wrong, but really I . . ."

"No more," he said gruffly.

"Of course not." she admitted contritely.

She heard the familiar Latin words of absolution.

"For your penance say six rosaries. For strength of spirit, read Psalm 86. Now go and pray for strength to resist further temptations."

The slide closed.

On her way to the high altar, she clutched a wet handkerchief. She knelt and began to pray. She held the cross of the rosary. "I believe in one God, the Father Almighty, Creator of Heaven and earth." She felt her heart twist with pangs of rejection, loneliness of having no one to share what she was going through, and, fear of the Lebensborn.

Chapter Thirty-Six

*A*ntoinette might have been a tiny, yellow rose on the linen wall covering in the dining room, once admired, yet forgotten once viewed, familiar but now overlooked. They forgot she was in and out of the room so she heard snatches of the officers' conversation as the meal commenced.

Eric Larsen mentioned "enough provisions when they come through." Karl Walther was trying to reassure the major he could control, let's see, what was it? terror . . . terrorist . . . terrorists under control . . . *enough soldiers to protect the troops and equipment on the cars coming through.* When?

It was two weeks since the day she had gone to Major Hurst's office to tell him she was having his child. The major had avoided her and since then had taken his evening meals at the Poulet Cafe. Tonight was an exception. He was here tonight to take dinner. He had been aloof and distant when she came within view. No longer did he seek her out for any reason. He had not spoken to her since the visit in his office.

This morning, when Lieutenant Lutjemeier received the provisions list from her, he said, "You must be ready to leave very early tomorrow morning. Put your things in one suitcase."

'Tomorrow, she thought. *'So soon. I must tell Papa tonight. What shall I say. Everything?'*

She put the kitchen to order, then began dragging herself up the narrow steps to her room when she heard the officers coming in.

She waited. She pressed her ear to the wall.

Over the jumble of their conversations, she heard the kommandant's loud voice, "Where did this order come from—who is doing this to me? Our job is only half finished. If we put the things we've collected from the villages on the late train tomorrow afternoon, Hitler won't be pleased. It can't be Hitler's idea to send us to the front, not at all, his art museum project is too important. We are too close to finding the paintings and other things he wants."

Then Karl Walther said something she couldn't hear.

Lieutenants Lutjemeir and Larsen were excited. Lutjemeir said, "We're going to the front—finally some action."

"The Russians should have caved in by now—summer is over—we're into autumn. They need more Waffen-SS at the front. We're the ones who really know how to fight," emphasized Lieutenant Larsen.

"It won't go on that long." Lt. Walther was emphatic. "Not when all of us Waffen-SS get there. The day after tomorrow can't come soon enough for me!"

Lieutenant Larsen said, "The furs we collected can go, too. They'll be needed."

"No," replied Lieutenant Walther. "The Russian campaign will be over before winter. But, just in case."

"I'm sorry, Sir, it looks like you'll miss your engagement party, " consoled Lieutenant Lutjemeir.

"Ellen will be furious," cursed the kommandant. "It's these damn Jews. It's their fault for taking up all our trains. I'll get to the bottom of this order. I'll find who's out to get me." He slammed the door to his room.

Other doors slammed.

Antoinette continued up the steps. She found her way into the darkened room where her father slept, feeling about for the bed.

"Papa, are you awake? It's me. I've come to say—goodbye."

Her right hand felt the cold, hard chill of the iron headboard. Her left hand traced the outline of the pillowslip on the heavy goosedown pillow. She collapsed on the opposite side of the double bed on which her father was snoring.

Assuming he was asleep, she poured out, "Papa, everyone I love seems lost to me. I may never see you or Mama again. Or, Jacques. Or, this village. I've heard people call me a collaborator. But what else is there to think when they have seen me with him so many times.

"He is horrible. You said he would say one thing and do another. You were right. I should have run away. Instead I did horrible things—with him. Tomorrow he sends me away—to Germany where they will hate me and think I'm a spy.

"He's *terrible.* I hate him. Hate him. I wish he were dead. If I were here just one more day, I'd poison him." Her anger gushed forth.

Henri suddenly was sitting and beside her. "Mama and I love you so much. We love you. Forgive me, I've been so busy with things I thought were important that I . . . I'll tell you something which might help you now. When I was wounded many years ago and alone in a distant place . . ." his voice trailed off. "I felt no one . . . no one was left who cared."

He put his arm around her shoulder. After a few long minutes, he said, "I'd get angry and say to myself, 'I won't let this stop my life. When a sad image would come, I would write down memories of good things to replace them. I would also say words from Psalm 86 over and over, especially these lines: 'Teach me thy way, O Lord, and I will walk in thy truth: O knit my heart unto thee. For great is thy mercy toward me; and thou hast delivered my soul from the Nethermost Hell.'"

Then he told her that he had taken the canvas and rolled it up and sent it with Dr. Renet who asked Jacques to smuggle it to London. "Remember—that art dealer? He offered to buy it when he was here for a sum which seemed phenomenal. I'm certain its value has risen. If you ever need money, go to him. And, he may also know where Jacques is. Here, I've written his name and address. Memorize it and burn up the paper in the kitchen stove."

"Oh, Papa. I must tell you what I overheard Lieutenant

Jo Ann Bender

Larsen say he was going to do tomorrow. That he is going to search every house—but, now that they're leaving so soon, he won't have time. I hid many of our good things under the eves and . . . perhaps re-hide them in the cellar next door."

"They're leaving, Villepente . . . after they've taken over my house . . . the village . . . our possessions . . . violated our loved ones, including the pets." Henri pounded his fist into the palm of the other hand.

"Something will happen to them, Papa. The kommandant is terrible and bad things will surely happen to him." Then, she told her father why she was leaving the village and remembered she had an urgent message to deliver.

The Nazis were leaving. She had to get to Dr. Renet's. The curfew be damned.

She creaked down the attic steps to the floor below, paused at the landing to hear if anyone were roaming about downstairs. Drone of planes covered sounds of her footsteps through the hallway, the kitchen and out the back door.

Night shadows began chasing her as she fled along the cobblestone rows. She stopped to listen for the familiar patterns of the German patrols, crunch, crunch, crunch.

Her beloved village, which used to be like a blessed mother protecting a child, had turned into a monster with eyes, ears and claws. The streets she knew so well by day were strange by night; identifying landmarks seemed only partially visible or missing altogether.

Near the town square and the street leading to the doctor's, the towering fountain loomed like a gigantic iron monster hiding Nazis in the skirts of its shadows. Crunch, crunch, crunch - a patrol was coming. Scarcely daring to breathe, she pressed against the side of a stairway; two soldiers marched by, not as she had often noticed them in the past having a conversation, or laughing; but, with resigned, heavy footsteps. The back door at Dr. Renet's was unlocked so she went in and called, "Dr. Renet—Gerald—Marie. Come quick."

Dr. Renet, always ready to be called to a patient, came into the main hallway dressed in loose pants and a shirt, tugging on socks. Gerald raced down the staircase followed by Marie.

"The Germans are leaving day after tomorrow." Her eyes were wild. "The late train tomorrow afternoon will have troops and equipment and our village possessions. Then, they all leave day after tomorrow for the front. Finally! The Nazis are leaving Villepente."

Gerald, who copied every action of the doctor, watched for the doctor's reaction to Antoinette's news.

It was Marie who said what they all felt, in plain words, "Good. That's good." She clutched the front of her blue-patterned robe together, for in her haste, she had fastened several buttons into the wrong holes and a few gaps were obvious.

"This calls for a celebration." The doctor started for his almost empty wine cellar.

"But, someone has to tell Leon." Antoinette's statement stopped the doctor. "And, quickly."

"Me. Let me." Gerald's eyes sparkled, his small figure brightly illuminated by eagerness.

"Gerald, it's too dangerous," cautioned Dr. Renet. "There's enough petrol for the car. I'll go."

"They might need you tonight, Doctor," reminded Marie.

"You're right," remembered Dr. Renet, "And, you, my dear, Antoinette, should spend the rest of the night here where you'll be safe. Next week after the Nazis have gone, we'll have ample opportunity to celebrate, won't we?"

"Without me." Antoinette told the solemn little group that she was leaving Villepente early the next morning. She rushed Gerald off. "Kommandant said there are two trains tomorrow. The first, the village local, then the freight late tomorrow afternoon following it. That second train will pick up the valuables they've taken from the villages.

"Then, there's a one coming for all of them the next morning. They're angry because they have orders to go to the

Russian Front. They are complaining that there are so few trains left . . . for them, such important, high-ranking German officers. Their car, goes, too, on the freight car tomorrow afternoon, as well as all their trucks and other equipment."

There were few hours left in the night. Antoinette lay on the bed made up in the doctor's study and alternately worried about the place she was going, the Lebensborn, where women waited to have babies for the Führer and about Gerald. Would he get to Leon in time? What about the babies? What happened to them?

There would be little space in the suitcase for other than a little food and few garments of loose clothing, the postcard from Jacques, a few photos of family, her prayer book, of course. But, what about the delicate perfume container the kommandant gave her? At the thought of the gift, she recoiled in distaste. Why hadn't she already disposed of it.

Chapter Thirty-Seven

Gerald ran to the Gauthier farm humming a refrain: The Nazis are leaving, the Nazis are leaving. It guided his feet. He loved the night. It was his best friend. It was in the depths of night he found hiding places along the dark streets of Warsaw when he left the ghetto foraging for food.

The outcome of the Phantoms' plans depended upon him. Dr. Renet and Antoinette trusted him to find Leon without alerting the Germans.

He skirted village patrols and ran along the roadside. He knew he was on course from the outline of the Villepente bridge on his left. The bridge was the large and tall. At night, it loomed to monstrous proportions, the holes in the arches making it look like the eyes of a sea urchin. But it didn't scare him. He had a mission: to find Leon and tell him how and when they were leaving Villepente.

It seemed easy, almost more simple than in daylight. He had a special gift. He could see and hear better at night. He reached the barn and found the opening between two boards to slide between, and the ladder by the mid-beam just where the doctor said it would be.

His hands held the rough boards of the ladder as he climbed. He was halfway up when he heard a low voice say, "KVA."

He wondered what that meant. When he neared the top, Leon was there to give him a hand up and ask, "What's going on?"

Leon led Gerald to the opening of the loft.

They studied shapes in the countryside. Gerald began his message: "Antoinette says the Nazis are leaving. A freight is coming for all the valuables from the villages, and their tanks and trucks. That's tomorrow afternoon after the local. Day after, another will come for them. Please make something happen to them. They've done so many bad things," pleaded the lad.

"Wish I had a choice. If it were me, I'd blow up the train with the Nazis on it, but, I don't." Leon was angry.

"Who says?" asked Gerald.

"The Brits. They want the second train tomorrow taken out because there's a double agent on it."

"A double agent?"

"Someone who works for both the British and Germans."

"How can one person be more important than getting all the Nazis?" continued Gerald.

"If we want the Brits to continue sending weapons and technical help, then we have to do what they tell us even if we're not in the military. I'd like to see the Nazis go down with the train just like you. That was the Brits just now on the radio. They said things were on the move."

"It'll be okay, Leon. We'll be rid of them, won't we? Someone else will get their chance to get them in Russia."

"Say, can you give me a hand getting a few things to the bridge?"

"Sure. Let's get going. It will be light soon."

Chapter Thirty-Eight

*I*f Leon came back alive from his mission, he would feel such a rush of adrenaline, a lifting of himself, an indescribable joy, that throughout his lifetime he would seek ways to recapture the intensity of those feelings.

He had just awakened from a fitful sleep in the cave near the bridge. Francois was nearby. Through his sleepy eyes he saw him sitting cross-legged and staring at him.

"It's almost time." Francois had a thin smile.

Leon wanted to talk about what he was going to do, but for curious reasons, he couldn't tell Francois how terrified he was about blowing the bridge. Instead he said, "I've just had a dream. My father told me to spread out and be less of a target, like they told him when he was fighting in the war. But, I only wanted to stay as close to you as possible. It was a terrible feeling. I was on the tracks above the bridge but you weren't below."

Francois clenched his fists. "I'll do my part—won't let you down." Agitation rolled through Francois. "You can take risks, Leon. I know you. You've bet on hands that were so marginal. You've got guts."

"This can't be as scary as the piano duet I played with Antoinette."

"I could never give a speech."

"Yeah. Dr. Renet, calm as he is, said he had to give a paper to a group of physicians in Paris. He said his heart was beat so fast that he took his pulse. It was 154 beats and normally is 67."

The two were sharing the danger indirectly, but their mission was forging the closest of human ties known. Their perceptions of risk varied with their circumstances. Yesterday's risk for a boy of nine years now felt the same as the serious task facing the lad of eighteen.

Mentally, they tried to shortcut their risky actions by a process of mental rehearsing, creating movies in their minds.

The act this afternoon was more risky due to the lateness of the day. The body has a clock of vulnerability, when blood levels of steroids, the Circadian rhythms, have an effect on alertness and courage. Leon would have been braver in the morning, less brave in the afternoon, and most afraid at night.

Within a few minutes, Leon and Francois left the cave for the bridge. A cold damp mist hung in the air. They made their way along the edge of the wheat field, up the hillside to the towering deck upon the bridge.

Leon snuck out to the center of the bridge and tied a rope to the edge of the top railing, secured it at the corner of one of the center columns where edge stones had been cut away.

The stone bridge, they had been informed by British Special Organization Agent Chester Bailey, could not be destroyed by dynamite due to its massive dimensions. But, they could derail it by blowing up the tracks at just the right moment, when the engine reached the detonation point halfway across.

Leon's morning task was easy compared to what was before him now. Germans routinely patrolled at one end of the decking. The Phantoms knew the Germans could see if a person were on the deck or under the bridge.

The second and third parts of blowing the tracks were more tedious, and, consequently, more hazardous. Not only would they hope not to be seen but they had to work against an element of time.

All they had between trains was thirty minutes!

The 3:10 train rolled by. Leon and Francois embraced. Francois scrambled to his position below and Leon started to crawl between the rails upon the ballast like a worm.

He felt surprisingly sharp. He sensed motion along the rails as he crawled along the decking. His body ached with fear but he shook it off. He saw everything bold and clear, was aware of every bite of the wind in the air, the green blur of trees in the distance, could almost smell heavy cologne of Germans on patrol.

His movements were forever being etched into memory: he would forever see the missing button on his gray pants, sense the tight feeling of the woolen shirt over his chest, see the anxious look in Francois' eyes as they parted.

The buildup of tension produced a huge erection. His countrymen used the term "aloler" interchangeably with "to cause anxiety" and "to excite sexually," the phrase "tu m'affolles" meaning both "you make me anxious" and "you arouse me to point of orgasm."

He felt the erection and thought, *'I should be scared more often. There is sex in fear.'* but that awareness was swept aside when a profound feeling of calm seriousness overcame him. Within him grew an enormous mental intensity. He gave undivided attention to the tasks before him now and disregarded any irrelevant information or feelings.

His heart pounded as he moved slowly between the rails, the coil of wire in a burlap sack attached to his belt shifting on his back. He knew he held his life in his hands; blowing the bridge made more sense than sitting by waiting for Germans to send him to a labor camp.

Again, he felt a fleeting moment of terror when he reached the hole he had dug earlier that morning under the rail. Was a German watching? He couldn't take time to look. He pawed out a few pieces of rock, unwrapped the waxed paper from the brick-shaped plastic explosive from the burlap sack, stuck it under the rail into the hole, shaped it to the rail like it was a piece of modeling clay. He poked a hole into the middle and carefully pulled the shunt which held apart the two wires of the blasting cap.

The wind was picking up. He worried that in this brief time when the shunt was off, the long wires hanging down, without a safety shunt between, the explosive would be an antenna detonated by a German radio transmission.

His hands were sweating. He twisted each wire on the coil to the explosive detonator cap ends. He jumped up, leapt over the rail, the wire from the 500-foot coil trailing behind.

His concentration was so total he felt a trancelike serenity, as absorbed in the task as any artist or writer.

The way down was thrilling. He swung down, hand over hand, enjoying the supreme satisfaction. When his feet reached the ground, Francois reached for the end of the coil and connected the wires to the detonator. Within minutes, the train arrived. The tracks exploded just as the engine reached the bridge's midsection.

The twenty cars carting off Villepente's and other village possessions, pet furs, a flatcar with the kommandant's black Mercedes, a passenger car with several German soldiers and the double agent, followed the engine and careened off the tracks, crashing through the steel railing.

The train twisted in the air like a black whip. It cracked apart and smashed to the ground.

Leon and Francois felt a warm sense of accomplishment, a deep joy. They had destroyed the double agent. There was not the slightest chance he could live through such a crash. However, the Germans would retaliate.

Chapter Thirty-Nine

*T*he eight little tables on the first level of the Poulet Cafe were crowded. A group of travelers who had gotten off the local two o'clock train were discussing the possibility that the four-thirty-one would be late again. Monsieur Roberte, the poet, was suffering over the last line of his new poem. The butcher and his wife were celebrating their twenty-sixth anniversary at the table by the front window. At the rear, Major Hurst and his officers were drinking rounds at one table, a group of enlisted men at another.

"Madame Zonek, more wine," beckoned Karl Walther. As the proprietor of the cafe approached with four one-liter jugs, the kommandant said, "Your big green umbrella out front is falling down. No. It is true. My engineer says so. Go see for yourself."

Madame the saw overturned glasses and the wine stains on the tablecloths. Bad manners. But, what could she say? There was so little soap with which to launder. It must be time to turn the cloths over again. How could it be Saturday so soon? She was so tired. Only two people to help. She liked to keep up standards so every Wednesday and Saturday she pushed patrons out at four o'clock, threw off the stained table linen and made ready for the cafe's two biggest nights. She loved the satisfied feeling of throwing on the sparkling white crisp tablecloths, setting the red lanterns out, and positioning the heavy silverware. Appearance meant everything when food was so scare. It was around three o'clock when she stepped outside into the Place de la Madeline to study the cafe's green canopy. She held the evening menu she'd just hand lettered. She would look now to see if her "green umbrella" was really falling. She heard a loud noise in the distance. Then another.

She screamed. The sounds coming from the distance were loud and strange, and combined with her screams, sent patrons rushing out the door.

Karl knew immediately the sounds what the sounds were. He knew the cargo they'd just supervised loading had been destroyed.

The cafe emptied.

Major Hurst yelled from the crowded plaza, "Karl, get Henri. I'll meet you back here after we've had a look." An enlisted man ran off toward the town hall to retrieve a vehicle.

As Karl Walther walked past Danielle's house enroute to summon the mayor, he thought how easy it would have been for her to have been a victim of the retaliation. How fortunate he had rushed her off on the earlier train.

He thought back to the beginning of the day. He had pounded upon the door of Danielle's house. Madame Ramine as always was polite and courteous when he asked, "Is Danielle ready?"

"Lieutenant, she is having difficulty trying to decide just what to take. Her room is upside down. As if her grandmamere in Marseille will care what she wears. I just hope, after all the trouble you've gone to for her travel papers and buying the ticket, she doesn't miss the train. They have become so irregular, it might even be early."

"I know this is highly irregular, madame, but may I request permission to see her alone in her room for a few minutes."

"Karl, of course. Her room is up those stairs, second from the left."

Resisting the urge to take the steps two at a time, though Karl hurried, each step seemed endless. He had so few minutes.

He burst through the door and saw the empty suitcase open upon the huge bed. Clothes were strewn about the room in little piles. He closed the door and said abruptly, "I had to see you one last time."

Danielle felt a shiver run through her. *'One last time. What did he mean?'*

"Karl. You're leaving Villepente." Her voice trembled.

"No, you're the only one traveling today. I'm not leaving just yet. I've just come for another goodbye." He wouldn't tell her that he was being sent to the front.

They clung to each other. Ticking of the porcelain clock, the only sound in the room, was a painful reminder.

They fell onto a pile of clothes on the bed. He untied her shoes and gently caressed each foot as if to fasten their image into memory. He slipped the skirt from her hips, stroked her thighs, the flatness of her stomach. Unbuttoning her shirt, he cupped her breasts, gently outlined each feature of her face, ears, nose, cheeks, wiping away the tears running down her cheeks.

He felt the erect nipples, the round and firm breasts, felt the smoothness of her stomach which rolled into the navel surrounded by the slightest hint of peach fuzz. His eyes lowered to the triangle of black hair. He seemed to inhale her body, its form and lines. He began to take off his uniform. He detached the shoulder strap and caught the Luger. He hung the gun and holster on the bedpost. After sliding the knot of the black tie down, he slipped it over his head and hung it on top the gun belt.

He smiled and held her gaze as he unfastened the silver buttons with Nazi eagles on the olive shirt. He pulled off the olive shirt, with the embroidered Nazi eagle on the right breast pocket, and stepped out of the field gray pants.

Sliding out of the white boxer shorts, he spread wide her legs to open the lips. He put his body on top of hers and tenderly entered her, and as he did he looked deeply into her eyes to communicate the intensity of his feeling for her. Someday they would be together again. The war would be over.

While Danielle and Karl bid each other goodbye, Henri Gauthier was hiding the family treasures in the cellar next door. Unaware of the crisis, he did sense a foreboding, a gut-level premonition, of impending disaster. He remembered feeling the same inner warning before he had been shot in WWI.

Nerves tense, he had just returned to the house. He was in the kitchen when Lieutenant Walther split open the front door. "Monsieur Gauthier."

"Lieutenant Walther?" Henri noticed his urgency.

"You're needed immediately at the cafe. There's been a disaster of some sort. Didn't you hear the noise?"

Neither spoke as they hurried in and out the rows to the plaza.

As they neared the cafe, a cluster of villagers watched from a distance. As Henri and the Lieutenant drew closer, the people turned away.

Inside the cafe, the butcher and his wife were the only patrons. Lieutenant Walther, who wished to avoid a scene when Major Hurst arrived, went to them at the front table said to Anna, "It might be wiser to drink your wine at home, madame."

To which she replied, "I'll do with my ass as I please."

Henri and the lieutenant went to a rear table and took seats. Lieutenant Walther offered Henri a glass of wine, but he indicated he wasn't interested, and the lieutenant said, "Why can't they listen when we try to help?"

Two convoy trucks drove up to the front of the cafe. Soldiers leapt out and positioned themselves outside the cafe and about the plaza.

Major Hurst got out of one of the trucks and flew into the cafe. He saw the butcher's wife smoking a cigarette, a practice forbidden to women in public places.

She saw him coming and jumped up.

"There is no excuse for your behavior," Major Hurst yelled when he was a few feet away.

"None for yours either." She pulled a knife from her jacket, lunged for him and stabbed his chest several times, thrusting hard to penetrate the thick fabric. Drops of blood began to flow down the front of the black jacket, making a dark stain.

The major was so filled with rage that he did not give his knife wounds more than passing notice. Stabs by the blade had not gone through the thick woolen fabric that deep. He was more irritated by the rips and staining of his uniform than by any pain.

He whipped out a pistol from the holster and shot four times. Anna crumpled to the floor. Her husband rushed to her and heard her last breaths of life. Then, in anger the butcher yelled, "You brute! You monster!"

The major emptied the last five shots from the Luger into him, then calmly walked back to sit with the lieutenant and Henri.

Two soldiers upon hearing the shots came running into the cafe, and seeing the bodies dragged them outside and laid them near the fountain. Villagers watched from a distance.

Inside the cafe, the major, furious about the destruction of the train and its cargo, was now pacing. "I will not tolerate such sabotage. I will not tolerate loss of such a vital cargo or personnel. You," he yelled at Henri, "collect the captains and ward men, have them bring everyone in this village to the plaza. Everyone. Invalids. Old. Young. The priest. Nuns. Children. Within the hour. You hear?"

Major Hurst barked at Henri, "Tell the priest to begin ringing the bells. Tell him I'm sending Schneider over to relive him so he can be in this lineup with everyone else. Immediately. Get a move on."

The bells soon began their clamorous peals.

In the clear autumn air, the sounds reached the Gautheir farm. Helene was in the barnyard tossing feed to the chickens and paused in the task to wonder why the bells of the village were ringing. She began to recall the many happy occasions when the bells had tolled for weddings, baptisms, holidays. Then, her heart stopped. The continuous peel of the bells was unlike anything she'd ever heard. She must get the bicycle and head for the village. Who had died? Or, was this something to do with the thunderous noises she had heard?

Night began to fall. Villagers were being lined up behind their captains and ward men in groups of ten, the ward men and captains at the front, two lines of four behind them. Thirty tight clusters ringed the fountain. The fountain and the knots of people gave the suggestion that a ghoulish net had fallen over them.

Two street lamps cast their eerie shadows across the figures standing in V-formations. All eyes tried to not to look at the bodies of the butcher and his wife thrown beside the fountain.

Karl Walther was going over the list of residents with their captains, and felt the fear spewing from the groups. He glanced over and saw that Father Molterine's people seemed to be standing a little taller than the others and thought the father must be holding them together better than the other groups which seemed to have persons in them who were crying, fussing or sniffling.

No one was talking. The kommadant commanded that there be no talking.

Henri stood at the front of the town hall with Major Hurst. He pounded the fist of one hand into the palm of the other.

Karl came up, saluted the major. "All accounted for but two, a Madame Ramine and Sister Louise."

"Where are they?" commanded Major Hurst, slapping the pistol in his holster. "It's their captains' responsibility to get them here."

"A little boy says Sister Louise must be trying to get Madame to come."

"Lieutenants Lutjemeir and Larsen—you there—get her captain and go to her house and drag them here immediately. Everyone will witness this night—everyone. Now get going—fast. I want this over as soon as possible. It's giving me a headache."

Then addressing Henri, he bellowed, "Tell the ward men to keep those snivelers quiet. Then, tell the captains to choose one person from their group—and have those chosen to report to me right here immediately."

Seeing the frown appear on Henri's face, Hurst added, "I don't care who the person chosen is—just get them over here. If they can't choose one from each group, then I'll choose two. Get that, two!"

The villagers, paralyzed with fright, intently watched Henri express the kommandant's command to the nearest group. The news passed quickly. Each group came up with their person differently: in some, the captain chose, in others, there were those who volunteered, or, the group drew straws. No one was exempt from selection by age, sex, health, or occupation.

Dr. Renet volunteered first. He walked over to the steps of town hall before anyone in his group could protest. "I'll go," he said quietly without a moment's hesitation after he heard the order.

Monique, another of Hurst's romantic conquests, had fallen by draw of the short straw. When she appeared before the kommandant, she was dismissed and told to go home. Said the kommandant, "Madame Ramine will take your place. Run along now. Don't you forget me."

The trauma of the decisions taking place did not stop several villagers from seeing that Monique had run off from the plaza.

The lieutenants approached with the wiggling lady between them, and Sister Louise following. Father Molterine separated from his group and headed to the steps of the town hall. "Heil Hitler," he said with a weak salute before Major Hurst, "I wish to take Sister Louise's place."

"Do whatever you like. You're making all the choices here, not me."

"But, Father," Sister Louise began to protest.

"Sister, the children need you. Their futures are at stake, not mine. Don't you agree? Go back to Monsieur Ricco, your block captain, and lend the comfort of your presence to the children."

Gerald raced up to the steps. "Dr. Renet, please, you can't. Too many need you. Let me. Father Molterine, the village needs him. But, they won't miss someone like me."

From his position on the town hall steps, Henri overheard the conversation and came down the steps as Major Hurst was screaming, "You're all going to pay for what's been destroyed . . . whoever the traitor is does not matter."

Before Dr. Renet could reply, Henri came down the steps into the little circle of the chosen, and said to Gerald, "Run back to your group. Dr. Renet, my good friend, go along, too. Too many lives will be lost without you. No argument now. Just go along quickly before it's too late."

"Think of your wife, your children," replied Dr. Renet.

"I have been ever since the day the Nazis came." Henri was well aware of the Phantams' activities and the stiff human penalty that could be exacted. The kommandant was a man of his word when it came to following up statements of disciplinary action, although he might be lenient with other values, such as he displayed by releasing Monique and sending Antoinette to a Lebensborn.

Gerald clasped one of Henri's hands, then said with a look of explicit trust and respect, "I shall never, never forget you. Never."

"Nor I," replied Dr. Renet as the two sadly parted from the collection of villagers increasing before the town hall steps.

"Line them up around the fountain - facing the fountain," ordered the kommandant. "Count and see there are thirty."

Lieutenant Walther clicked his heels, "Heil Hitler." He walked slowly about the fountain and began the count. "One, two, three . . ." His footsteps could be heard on the cobblestones. He thought—*'What a relief Danielle is in Marseilles.'*

Father Molterine began humming the Marseillaise. His low hum was overheard and another of the chosen joined in. The humming grew louder. Then, a magnificent male voice, pure and clear, began to sing the words above the humming which by now had grown quite loud.

Oblivious to the voice and the background humming, Major Hurst swelled up his blood-stained chest and began to walk around the fountain. Lt. Walther followed him holding a large box of Lugers.

The kommandant shot the first villager, the sound muted by the tolling church bells. One by one they fell upon the cobblestones, the major shooting them in the back of the head.

The kommandant planned the last to be Henri Gauthier.

Major Hurst yelled, "Turn around, Henri. Look at me."

Hurst looked Henri direct in the eye. "Too bad she was your daughter. I never believed for a minute she was having *my* child. Ellen and I would never raise a dark-haired, dark-eyed child. But, you see how good I am. I've sent her to Germany to a Lebensborn," he laughed. "Your grandchild will be born a German." His laughter rang out over the shot.

Helene reached the Plaza just as Henri was shot. Her screams rang out and joined the sobbing of the villagers. The church bells continued pealing.

As the terrible killing was taking place around the plaza, Antoinette was on a bus bound for Germany. As she tried to calculate how difficult it might be to escape from Germany to London, the figure of her father wove in and out, sharp and distressing.

Germany

Chapter One

The SS House next door to the Lebensborn had sinister allure and ghoulish appeal. It was 'verboten.'

Sentries patrolled before the fence surrounding the estate; an ornate double-iron black gate, with double lightning SS insignia etched in gold, stood out so boldly that passersby knew the power of those hidden behind the fence. From the street, all anyone could see through the fence was a tree-lined lane.

In the middle of the night Antoinette was awakened by haunting piano music coming from the SS House. She got up and stepped by her roommate, Clara, who appeared to be soundly sleeping under thick blankets on a narrow iron bed.

She parted the drapery. Those at the mysterious house were also drawn back and she had never noticed them open before. From the third floor of the Lebensborn, Antoinette looked into the SS House and saw the party taking place.

Nazi officers, formally attired in the black uniforms, had loosened or removed their black ties; the women with them wore long, clinging, form-fitted gowns in yellow, red or black silken colored fabrics. They were clustered about a piano and pianist.

When Antoinette saw the women, she knew they had mastered the art of simplicity, suggesting with richness of material in their slender evening gowns, the sensuousness curves of breasts and bottoms. Even their hair, clustered in woven nests or gathered into chignons, seemed natural, casual; yet, Antoinette realized these women knew what they were doing when it came to the art of allure.

She sighed. They had perfect bodies, those beautiful women. Could she wear such a gown now? It was the fourth month of her pregnancy. She ran a hand over her stomach and felt the starched white cotton nightgown and a yet firm tummy.

The music was pensive and rushed her thoughts back to Villepente. The pretty melody's sad ambiance increased in ardor from a quiet, forlorn introduction, like a mountain stream trickling slowly at first, then rushing over the mountain like a waterfall.

It was Beethoven's Sonata, affectionately called the "Moonlight Sonata," a wonderful choice for kind of night it was. She saw clouds wafting across the sky, wrapping about a full moon like soft, torn cotton shreds. Then, the sky grew darker just as the pianist increased the volume and speed of the sonata. Ah, the struggle of learning those stanzas. A smile came over her face as she recalled Leon trying to cover up his fear just before they were to perform a duet for a church night. The golden times, days when they were altogether—mama, papa, Leon, baby Pierre.

The girl slowed the piece as it neared the conclusion, muscles in her slender arms rippling, her shoulders bent toward the keys, spaghetti straps of the golden silk gown taut. An officer, lounging upon the piano, stood back and walked behind the girl. He swept her off the piano bench and into another room.

Antoinette started to pull the drapes closed but a powerful feeling kept her at the window. She looked across; a Nazi officer was staring up at her. Was he one of the officers who had lived with them in Villepente? Did he know her?

She studied him. He was not Major Hurst or any other of the other Waffen SS officers she had known in Villepente. He had a commanding figure just as Major Hurst; however, this man had something else—yes, compassion.

He smiled, in a mysterious way, and reached to her with hands that held up a champagne goblet.

Who was he? In the soft lighting of the room, his hair appeared dark brown; his eyes, even from the distance, intriguing; his arms wanted to hold her. Tears came to her eyes.

There were so many things to guard against at the Lebensborn. Being seen at the window would mean another harsh confrontation with Herr Doktor Krause or Clara. She put one hand to her face in a protective gesture and the officer clasped his arms to his chest.

"Our Lebensborn is two in one," said Frau Muckle when she showed Antoinette around the Lebensborn the day she arrived.

"There are two houses; the section next to this one is reserved for new babies and their mothers. You won't see anything of them. That area is completely cut off and self-sufficient and off limits from this one. You girls, who are waiting to give birth, have your own kitchen and stairway to the outside, just as the new mothers do.

"Incidentally, Herr Hurst has written us about you, and has praised your cooking talents, so much that in addition to the classes you will attend with the others, you will also help Fritz in the kitchen.

"You are the first we've had here from an occupied country. It's to your advantage to participate in our required activities and to do a good job at your work; but, I must warn you, do not become too friendly with anyone, if you understand what I'm saying."

Frau Muckle's thick nose twitched.

"I understand German very well," said Antoinette.

The directoress folded her thin arms about the crisp, white nurse uniform and replied stiffly, "Oh, well, you'll learn. You are too new to appreciate my advice."

Frau Muckle turned around abruptly and Antoinette walked quickly to follow her along a wide hallway leading away from the communal living area. The directoress opened a door and went up a flight of narrow steps to the third floor where she said mothers-to-be slept.

As Antoinette rushed up the stairs, she wondered how long the hair was in the thick, brown braid winding about the directoress' head.

On the top floor of the Lebensborn, Frau Muckle stopped at the door number seven. Each door in the hallway was numbered, the number outlined by a gray Nazi cross encircled in silver. "Your roommate's at class. You have ten minutes to unpack before I take you back to the main floor for your interview with Herr Doktor Krause."

When the door shut, Antoinette got a flash of intuition—there was danger here. But, what? She took her things from the suitcase and placed them in the wood armoire. Then, she sat on the bed wondering what to do.

My beret: I must hide it. Where? In the room? Outside?

She went to the large window over a radiator and with great effort forced the window up, and ran her hands across the brick ledge. The bricks were cold and contained a residue of frost. There was no place on the ledge to hide it. So, she stretched out over the window sill to explore the underside of the ledge. *There's a portion of brick missing. I'll put it there.*

She held the washed-out beret, its color faded under impact of rain and sun, a waterproof signature of France, for decades capping heads of schoolboys and girls. *This is as dear to me as the postcard from Jacques.*

She looked one more time at both sides of the postcard, folded the beret over it, slid the cap into the hole, and quickly pulled the window closed just as she heard Frau Muckle's knock.

The directoress looked tense and did not speak as she escorted Antoinette downstairs. Her hands trembled as she turned the door knob to open the door to Herr Doktor's office.

"Herr Doktor, this is the woman we told you about. She has just arrived." Frau Muckle pointed Antoinette to a stiff-backed chair in front of the huge, square wood desk and left in a hurry, slamming the heavy walnut door behind her.

Heavy wine-colored drapes with dark patterns in them fell to the oak floor like dried puddles of blood. Thick dark books lined one wall up to the ceiling. A desk lamp with mellon-shaped bulbs threw shadows upon the man seated behind the desk. A Nazi flag hung from a standard next to the desk.

The huge desk had rows upon rows of drawers with brass hinge plates and pulls of leather straps plates on all the sides of it. The chair behind the desk was so tall, the back could be seen if someone were seated in it. Herr Doktor had it made special for him when he was in New Orleans by James H. Cohen & Sons on Royal Street and had them ship it to Germany to a camp for upholstering.

Antoinette sat meekly on the chair in front of the desk, clasped her hands together within the folds of the plaid skirt, pressed her shoes together and looked up.

Herr Doktor was studying information in a folder so she could observe him, which she did cautiously, prepared to glance away if he should look up.

He was heavy-set, of middle age with short-cropped hair, and a round face. A long scar started under the left eye and ended under his chin. The scar tissue pulled the eye downward just enough to give an evil cast to a face which otherwise might appear jolly. On the SS doctor's left arm was a black armband with the red Nazi swastika in the white circle.

The stained glass lamp shade on the desk lamp caught her attention. She began to study one of the three countryside scenes depicted on the six-sided bronze piece and elaborately etched tree outlined in the bronze over amber glass.

He pulled a black Meisterstuck pen with three gold-plated rings from an ebony, gold-band pen stand and looked up.

"Your passport?" His gravel-laden voice demanded immediate response.

Antoinette slid the letter-sized passport from her jacket pocket and stood up to lay it on top of the folder. He recoiled. She sat back down and folded her hands together. They were cold. Would he give the passport back? What good was a French passport in Germany anyway?

"It's against the law for you to be here." His words were as frosty as the window ledge in the room above. She looked him in the eye and said in steady voice, "I am having a child for the Führer."

"So you say. If what you say is so, then every attempt will be made to obtain a residence permit for you, an Aufenthatserlaubnis." He thought for a moment, then asked, "Your medical paperwork?"

"Medical papers?"

"Let's get down to facts. Who is the father? How many men were you with prior to the time of conception?"

"No one, only one, the kommandant—of our village—they came and they lived—there were also three other German officers—at my Father, the mayor's, house. The kommandant sent me here because he says he pays for this place and that you take so much from his pay every month for it."

She looked up, saw the doctor violently motioning her to stop talking. He threw quick questions at her like darts, asking about her ancestors, Villepente, the nature of her health, the quality of health of each member of her family and grandparents. She answered them quickly but lied about Leon.

"Your brother, Leon, you say he went to Marseilles. Why?"

"I don't know." Could her lie about Leon be discovered? How much information did he have in that folder? How good was the Waffen SS network? Could he verify her answers?

"Are you taking any medication?"

"Nothing," she said.

"Nurse Jutta will prepare you for our examination. If we find you healthy, and the pregnancy going well, I will write Major Hurst that we have accepted you here for the duration of the pregnancy and for another four months until the baby is placed."

Herr Doktor reached for the buzzer under the lamp. Within moments, the knock came on the door, and Antoinette was ushered off with Nurse Jutta, thankful that Herr Doktor had not touched her.

She left the room with a jumble of questions: place the baby? How did they do that? Would she meet their requirements for Nordic race and healthy mother-to-be? Could she find that out from the nurse? Who was her roommate? Who would be her friend? When could she sleep? What happened in Villepente after she left? How were her loved ones?

But those questions, like unopened books, had to be shelved; she was in enemy land, each moment a test of her endurance.

Chapter Two

*T*he commissary was white, a reddish-colored radiator the only contrast to the bland painted floor, walls and ceiling. In spite of a little heat coming from the radiator, the room was cold.

"Remove all your clothes and shoes," the nurse said and then left the room. Antoinette shivered next to the radiator as she took off her clothing. She was tugging over her head a short white, heavily starched gown when she heard the nurse returning. She had never had a physical examination before. Doctor Renet could tell the state of her health with just a look. The only time she had shown part of her anatomy to a doctor was when Doctor Renet felt her breasts when she had gone to him suspecting she was pregnant.

"Go, sit over there," Nurse Judda said to Antoinette who huddled over the radiator, "the chair there."

The nurse went to the table and took out a form from the top folder on the stack, put it in front of her, picked up a pencil, and said: "I want your full name."

"Antoinette Jacqueline Gauthier."

"Age?"

"Eighteen. I was born September 25, 1923."

"Nationality?"

Antoinette looked puzzled but said, "Why, French, of course."

"Both parents? Grandparents?"

"French."

"Mother's maiden name?"

"Rancenay."

"About your periods. Were they regular? When was the last?" While the nurse waited for Antoinette to answer, she toyed with a short, brown pencil, fanning it between the fingers. Antoinette was thinking: a period. It was hard to remember.

She responded, "Once a month. I never knew. I never kept track."

"Duration?" When Antoinette looked puzzled, Nurse Jutta folded the pencil between her fingers until it snapped. She threw it into a waste can and retrieved another from a drawer.

"If you mean, how long did the menses last—four days, maybe less, a little longer."

"Heavy or light?"

"The first day I might have to change the pad seven or so times, but then things, even like cloth pads, were hard to get, so one had to wash them out . . ."

"I see," the nurse said, "now, was there any unusual pain—any cramping?"

"Slight, but it never kept me in bed or from attending school or church."

"Ever been pregnant before?"

"No, no." What was the nurse getting at? She felt as if she were being interrogated.

"Miscarriages?"

"No."

"How many pregnancies for your mother?"

"Four," said Antoinette.

"All children living?"

"Not all, because the oldest got whopping cough and died before he was one year."

"History of diseases, report if there were any in the family having—" and, she recited a litany of diseases, "diabetes, heart trouble, headaches, mental problems, color blindness." To each, Antoinette shook her head, no.

"We'll test you and we'll make certain. We'll see if you tell the truth."

Antoinette heard, as well as felt, the vibrations of distaste coming from the nurse who watched her with an air of suspicion. Nurse Jutta reached into the drawer in the table and thrust a paper cup to her.

"Go into that bathroom and pee into the cup. Then, leave it there in the room on the shelf and return here."

Behind the door, Antoinette fumbled with the cup, and tried to compose herself. Suddenly the room felt small, crowding in upon her. She felt nauseated.

When Antoinette returned, the nurse said, "Take off that gown and step on the scale." A tall, black scale loomed behind the nurse. Antoinette went to it and stepped up the icy surface of the metal floor. The nurse reached to enlarge the metal stick to measure her height and swatted her in the head with the pole.

Before Antoinette could react, the nurse poked her in the back, "Stand up straight. Five foot seven and a little more."

The nurse slid the weight on the left to the hundred mark and the other balanced at twenty-one.

"I was right," she gloated. "You are underweight for your height and build."

"I've been sick, throwing up. Some things smell funny to me. I've been nauseated. There wasn't much to eat on the way here," Antoinette said, adding, "Madam, I'm cold. Please, may I have a blanket or that gown back, at least."

"In a minute, in a minute." The nurse glared as she looked Antoinette's naked body up and down.

She's trying to prove I'm unfit. Why does she hate me so much?

"Up, up." Nurse Jutta's actions were as crisp as her words as she shoved Antoinette towards a long metal table. Late middle aged, her square face was plain. A slightly different hue in each eye sent chills up Antoinette's spine each time she looked at her so she tried to avoid looking at the nurse's eyes. The spindly woman pushed Antoinette up onto the tall table.

"Doktor wants a blood sample," she said, suddenly appearing with a big needle and vial.

"Oh, please, I'm so cold," said Antoinette.

"Then, here." The nurse threw her a little square of cloth hanging across one of her sleeves, apparently a rag to stop any excess blood flow. She reached roughly for one of Antoinette's hands, pinched each finger, rammed the needle into the tip of the right index finger. Antoinette felt the searing pain and winced. She was thankful for the wee bit of cloth which lay over her lap. *I'm tired, cold, hungry, but I can manage a bit of dignity.* With deliberate footsteps, that sounded thundering, the nurse left. Antoinette heard her talking to someone in the hall. *Please, not that man.* She heard snippets of their conversation and knew they were discussing her.

She sat on the cold table and didn't know what to try to hide. She put the little bit of rough, white fabric over her legs, then crossed her legs and put the cloth over her breasts. Herr Doktor Krause whisked through the door. He had a paper in his hand. He stood next to her and in a commanding voice said, "Lay down. We want to see how you're doing. How many periods have you missed?"

"Two."

She could see one of his hands motioning the nurse to leave. With rough hands, he pushed her down onto the table full length and strapped each hand into a stirrup over her head. She closed her eyes. He grabbed her left breast, squeezed it hard, then the other. As he toyed with each nipple, he told her that the area around each nipple would deepen in color as she progressed in the pregnancy, just Doctor Renet had said.

"Will I be able to nurse the baby?" she asked.

"No one does. It will be fed from a bottle," he said gruffly. "Quiet now, I must concentrate."

He took a stethoscope from inside the brown suit, and as he listened to the heart area, he murmured, "Good, good," then asked, "What blood type are you?"

"I don't know," she said quietly.

"We'll find out. We know the Major's."

He pinched the flesh on both arms. His hands crawled along the arms and thighs until they reached the ankles, which he stroked, then pinched.

"Notice any swelling in this area?" he asked, pulling upon each ankle in turn. "If you ever get any, I must know immediately."

He went to her right hand strapped to the stirrup and felt for the pulse. "Hundred and ten," he said.

He felt her throat and asked, "Many colds? Open wide. I see the throat is a little red."

"I'm okay," she croaked.

"Drink plenty of liquids." He peered into each ear, asked if she had any pain there.

"You're too thin—almost through the first trimester. You need vitamins—calcium, iron, vitamin B. Open wide again. I must see if you have any loose or yellow teeth which would mean a calcium deficiency.

"Now, we must get our measurements and see how that baby is coming along."

He told her to scoot her body down to the end of the table and place each foot in the metal stirrup and placed a strap about her chest, and upon each ankle. The metal table was cold, so cold. He stood at the foot of the table. The little piece of cloth had long before fluttered from her body to the floor. When she twisted her head to avoid seeing Herr Doktor at the end of the table, she saw the cloth laying on the floor like a life raft in the middle of a white ocean.

"Let your knees fall out," he commanded.

She shook.

"This part I particularly like." His voice was ugly. She opened her eyes and saw he was holding a steel instrument which looked like a curling iron, with screws at the bottom.

"What are you doing?" she cried.

"Measuring the inside of the womb." He sat down on a stool beneath the end of the table and snapped on gloves. He spread the labia, looked slowly at the vagina, cervix, and finally put some white petroleum jelly on the ends of the instrument and shoved it up into her.

She groaned. The instrument caused a blazing pain more than the needle thrust into her finger.

"Relax," he said in a stern voice. The instrument felt as if it were pinching her insides.

"This wouldn't hurt if you'd relax." He pulled out the instrument and set it upon a table with others. He slowly drew off the gloves.

"Looks okay. You should have a normal childbirth."

He stood up, put two fingers into the vagina and placed the other hand upon her lower pelvis. She could see all he was doing for there was no protective sheet covering her and she was humiliated. He had not washed his hands or sterilized the instrument he had put into her either.

He walked around to the side of the table and listened to her tummy for the fetal heart beat. She could feel the scratchy fabric of his suit on her thighs and cringed. He pulled a measuring tape from a small table and measured the area below the belly between the pelvic bone. The SS insignia on his huge ring rasped a faint line on her belly.

Finally, he put on a glove, reached back into the rectum with two fingers, one finger touched the pelvic bone, and rubbed and rubbed in the area.

It hurt so much. She felt like peeing.

He drew his fingers out, snapped off the glove and threw it onto the table.

Was this usual? She suspected not. Those suspicions were confirmed when he pinched the part of her anatomy Major Hurst had referred to as the clitoris. Now his fingers were reaching again into the vagina. She felt a blazing, sensation, as if she were on fire, as the fingers reached and pressed the public bone, and massaged the area.

She glanced up, saw that he had his penis out, rubbing it up and down with the other hand.

Finally, he called out for Nurse Jutta, and was gone.

Chapter Three

Frau Muckle knocked briskly on the door of Room Seven. A girl about Antoinette's age opened the door. Frau Muckle marched into the room, followed by Antoinette.

"She has been found fit to bear a child for the Führer. Clara, you will be her official guide until she knows all our rules and can follow them."

"As you command, Directoress." Clara, the epiphany of Nordic blondness and beauty so desired for the Master Race, snapped further to attention and saluted, "Heil Hitler."

Then to Antoinette, Frau Muckle said, "Your privilege is to obey Clara Blocksdorff and to follow her every excellent example."

Frau Muckle clicked her heels, turned about, and made certain the door was completely shut behind her.

Antoinette, with a shy smile, extended her hand to Clara, and said, "Hello, I'm. . . " but, either Clara had not heard her or seen the gesture, for Clara turned her back and went to her side of the room and lay down upon the narrow bed's white quilted bedspread.

"You may as well know immediately—rooming with you was not my desire. They thought we should be together because we're due about the same time—April."

All during the exam, especially the time with the doktor, the small voice within Antoinette had hoped for friendship in this alien place.

Clara continued in a firm voice, staring up at the ceiling, "I have ten minutes in which to explain the way things are done around here. You see, I have the honor of presiding and planning the Naming Ceremony which will take place next week and my time for you is very limited. The ceremony must be just so. We have heard someone of great stature may be attending. If it's our great fortune, it will be Herr Himmler, head of the SS. The Lebensborn are his idea and this being the first of the Lebensborn locations, it is naturally, the best and finest.

"Of course, I should not have to remind you what a privilege it is to be here. We are the chosen ones—the Glorious Mothers-To-Be."

Antoinette turned toward the white wall, her body tense as she lay on top the white quilt.

"When I address you, stand or sit," Clara said. Antoinette did not seem to move so Clara repeated the command more sharply, "Sit up and listen, at once."

When she saw Antoinette wearily raising to sit upon the edge of the bed, Clara said, "Your day starts at six. You are to assist Friz in the kitchen; so, he will knock on this door at five thirty and you will be down to the kitchen by six sharp. Frau Muckle has pointed out the showers and bathroom. Currently, we are six on this floor, so you must be quiet or suffer demerits if anyone complains you make noise.

"We eat at eight, have class until eleven, then the Mittagessen, the big meal at one. We rest after that until three thirty when there's exercise class. It's free time after that, but, you won't have any because you'll go back to work to prepare the last meal, the Abendessen, served around seven. We're the most fortunate women in Germany because we're given the best food, and it's good, too, and all we can eat."

Clara glanced around the room with a look of disdain. "These are spartan quarters, not at all what I'm accustomed to, but we're safe. There *is* a shelter under this building, but no need to see it until. . . or, if ever we need it, which I doubt."

It took all the strength Antoinette could muster to appear interested. Her eyes burned and her body cried out for rest, the muscles tense and stiff from the examination. A headache was beginning.

"Until we are unable, we wear this uniform, the white shirt and black tie and skirt of the Bund Deutscher Mader, the League of German Girls . . . these white sox and shoes," Clara said with disgust, pointing to a flat, black shoe she held up in the air.

"Frau Muckle will put your new clothes outside by the door. In the pile, you will find a regulation watch so you never have reason to be late. No one is tardy here because we hate disorganization."

As Antoinette listened, her eyes took in the girl's golden, shoulder-length, wavy hair clasped back on the left side with a black barrette, the rosy, golden complexion, high cheekbones, perfectly formed nose, jaw and forehead. Clara's coloring and body were the opposite of her dark features.

Clara sat up and directed her blue eyes, the color as silken and muted as a delicate antique Chinese robe, at Antoinette. In a stern voice she said, "Never leave these grounds unless given permission. We do not associate with townspeople, only the staff who have been screened.

"Don't ask questions about the house next to this Lebensborn. It is verboten, verboten to even say anything about that house.

"We have ample area for all that we need. These grounds even go up into the hills and woods." Clara looked bored.

Questions flew through Antoinette's head: Demerit? What was that? When could she sleep? She felt she couldn't sit up another minute. She must lay down.

"When did you leave France? How long were you traveling?"

An eternity, thought Antoinette, replying, "I left Villepente two days ago and have been on a bus ever since."

"You can rest now. If you're hungry, Fritz can prepare a tray." Clara appeared to be fading.

"No, just . . . let me . . . sleep," Antoinette said, as she clawed her way under the covers fully clad, and, with the exception of two mighty nightmares in which she was running through forested hills seeking someone calling to her, she slept to erase the burdens of the journey, the rough introduction to the Lebensborn, and the thought of meeting Herr Doktor Krause again. Her last thought was that she had not thanked God for a safe arrival.

Chapter Four

After Herr Doktor Krause examined Antoinette, he buzzed for Frau Muckle. When she appeared, he said, "You realize what is needed with that one, don't you?"

"Herr Doktor, I believe I do, but, confirm my suspicions."

"Daily reports on her activities, every detail."

"Understood, Herr Doktor."

"Fascinating . . ." he mumbled.

"Herr Doktor?" she said, edging toward the door.

"Major Hurst, why did he get involved with her? I'll have to trust his judgment. He has a fascinating background, don't you think?" The SS doctor patted Hurst's paperwork on his desk.

"Indeed, Herr Doktor, he does have excellent linage, quite complementary for our New Order of the Third Reich."

"Fortunately, he acknowledges his parentage. Did you know that the SS praises his Aryan background. His health certificate is quite commendable. If all goes well with her blood test, she'll stay. She looks healthy enough, barring any unforeseen problem. Quite undernourished; however, I'm prescribing vitamins, double the usual dose. Anything else you'd need to bring to my attention?"

"Have you read the Ministry doctor's letter about the child of Fraulein Volhers? You'll find it in that bunch there, Herr Doktor."

"Oh, incidentally," continued Doktor Krause, "we must make that woman of Major Hurst's a German. I've changed her name to Hannah. Much better, don't you agree?"

"Then, she'll be Hannah. What if she protests?" Frau Muckle asked.

"She's in Germany, what can she expect? She has no choice. Each woman who comes here adjusts differently. She did want to know if she could breast feed." The doctor laughed.

"Herr Doktor, what about the woman Volkers?"

"We must never allow a woman like her to pass crimes along to other generations. I'll review her paperwork closely before deciding exactly what I should do with Fraulein Volkers." His steely eyes stared into space.

"As you see fit, Herr Doktor," Frau Muckle said. "You must excuse me, I have duties to perform."

"Yes, and, one other item. The Gestopo is sending over one of their women; Gesa Buchs will be joining our little family in a few days. You'll need to be cautious with that one, too."

"Of course."

"A good day to you, Directoress. Heil Hitler."

Chapter Five

*A*ntoinette awakened before the wake-up knock came. She opened the door and found a stack of folded garments; but, when she went to put them in the armoire, the items she brought with her had disappeared. She thought immediately of the beret which held the postcard and she hoped it was still under the ledge outside. The person who had taken the clothing had left the family photos within the prayer book. *I must think twice about what I say, too. They may be listening to what goes on in this room.*

She tiptoed through the door, went down the hallway to the communal bathroom and as she stood in one of the four shower stalls, much to her surprise, the water was hot and the soap smelled like gardenias. The white towel she picked up from the basket was large and soft.

In front of the large, horizontal mirror across and above the four sinks, she saw grayish circles under her brown eyes. She pinched her cheeks to bring a little color into them, then held back her shoulders and looked again. The person in the crisp, white shirt and black skirt looked so thin.

Her fingers tangled with the black tie. Was the knot to be little, big, or made into a bow? Perhaps a small knot. She glanced at the silver face of the watch. *Only five minutes to find the kitchen.*

When she located the kitchen, it was a place as white as the health commissary, a room she never wanted to see again. There were black curtains covering the windows on two sides which made it seem like two eyes staring and gave the room a comical appearance. A massive yellow wood cook stove was in the center of the room. A wood counter was constructed about two sides of the large area.

A slightly built man had his back to her and was working at the counter.

"Guten morgen," she said, coming into the room. She repeated it louder and he turned around.

"My, my, my. You must be our Hannah, here at last."

"No, no, my name is Antoinette. You must mean someone else. I'm Antoinette."

"To us," he said firmly, "you are Hannah. It is a wonderful German name, my Grandmother's. Did you know Hannah means, 'She who is with child?' Appropriate, very appropriate. But, come now, we have much to do. I'm glad you arrive safe."

He must be Fritz. The man's once blond hair had yellowed with age. Wide, bushy eyebrows and a beard dominated his small face. A small swastika was in the lapel of his brown suit.

He wiped one hand on the simple white apron he was wearing and reached over to pick up another one just like it from the counter to hand to her.

"I am just turning on the radio for news. It is glorious, isn't it, to hear that our troops are approaching Moscow and Leningrad?" His face lit up and his small faded blue eyes beamed. "See here," he said, pointing to a small round-shaped brown radio, beckoning her to come and read the large red tag hanging from the dial.

"This came yesterday. They think of everything. See, it has a hole punched right in it, so it can slip over the dial."

She read the tag printed in Gothic letters:

Racial Comrades. You are Germans.
It is your duty NOT to listen to
Foreign Stations. Those who do so
WILL be mercilessly punished.

"Music, it comes on any minute," he said with great enthusiasm. "Marches get me moving around. Of course, frequently we hear the Führer or Goering. Listen, now it starts—dum de dum da—listen, the horns." He whirled about, marched some steps, then stopped abruptly. "Now we can also hear about these parades and ceremonies, the Führer's speeches, even the State Funerals."

The elfin man, wound up like a top, stopped moving. "Let's see," he said and put one hand to his head, "yes, today I will show you everything . . . perhaps, tomorrow you can make the porridge. He saw a startled look on her face. "Ah, I see no porridge where you come from. Ah, your specialties, I know them. You make beautiful pastries; so, you will make them for the Naming Ceremony.

"This morning, you watch me. I started water for the boiled eggs for Fruhstruck. That's it—today, you serve the eggs to the Fräuleins. I will tell you 'who' is 'who' and which egg cup is hers."

He pointed to a small white table with painted yellow chairs and shoved her down into one. "Sit, sit, and I get you something to eat. Let Fritz take care of you today."

He went to a large blue pot on the cook stove and dished up porridge into a large white porcelain bowl, carried it to her saying, "Here, here, eat little mother, you must be hungry after the long trip."

He put a pitcher of hot milk and brown sugar on the table and fluttered back and forth refilling the bowl and milk pitcher.

It was strange to eat a mess of lumps; however, she decided it was tasty, especially after she discovered the little bits of apple chunks.

He put a tiny white dish with peculiar looking pellets next to her, and said, "Make you feel good; build you up; good for you and the baby." He waited.

He smiled when she swallowed them with a spoonful of milk. She was putting strawberry jam onto a huge slice of dark bread when he sat down across from her and placed a box in front of him and lifted the lid.

"All of them—beautiful little ladies—excellent backgrounds, from homes of the privileged. Liselotte always jokes. About everything, even her egg cup is joking—the little fairies dancing all over," he said, pulling a painted, wood cup from the box and holding it up to show her.

"Juliane is shy and quiet, always reading, a book by her place. She brought this one." He held up a plain wood cup with fine polished grains showing.

"Gertrude has this fancy porcelain—she's farthest along—wears the navy jumper. This is hers." He held up a white cup with yellow painted daisies.

"Did you bring a cup?"

"It's not our custom."

"Then, I shall bring one for you, perhaps one that belonged to one of my daughters."

He rushed on—"Dora." His eyes brightened as he held out for her to admire, a cup with gold splashes and tiny inset jewels.

"Then, Clara."

Antoinette had been waiting to hear about Clara's signature egg cup.

"Clara has one for every day of the week." He held up the clever cups: Sonntag, Montag, Dienstag, Mittwoch, Donnerstag, Freitag, Samstag, each designed with a flair and artistic strokes.

"Oh," she exclaimed, "what do I call you?"

He motioned that she had a drop of jam on her tie.

"Fritz is fine." he replied.

"Not Herr . . . ?" she asked, wiping off the jam with a cloth napkin.

"No, only top people have such a title. Call me Fritz . . . er . . . when you are angry with me and Fritz . . . L . . . when you are happy with me."

Antoinette suddenly felt a sensation of warmth, a feeling of being at home.

"Come, come, little Hannah, I must show you how to lay the table."

She followed him into the adjacent room, which turned out to be a vast contrast to all the whiteness of the kitchen. Dark paneled walls were lit by wall sconces which gave the room a rich and elegant feeling. A lace cloth overlay a yellow one on the huge table.

Fritz began taking white dishes out of a heavy wood corner cupboard and putting them on the table. She stood by, admiring the scrolling ivy wines and inlaid objects which decorated the huge piece of furniture.

"Take this into the kitchen," he said, and placed a large white porcelain bowl into her hands. "Careful," he warned, just as she discovered with alarm that there was a separate porcelain tray beneath the large dish.

"Guten morgen, Fritz and Hannah."

"Ah, directoress, guten morgen," said Fritz. "I see we are having much needed rain."

"Indeed," Frau Muckle said, a blunt edge to her voice. "Are things proceeding well?"

"Quite, Directoress. We're acquainting Hannah with the way things are. She is going to make a fine assistant."

"Make her acquaintance with the women, too. After Frukstuck, she is to accompany them to class. You may have her back later this afternoon; of course, she'll help you for the Mittagessen."

Chapter Six

Frau Muckle stood at attention in front of Doktor Krause in the dark office.

"I've had news from the head administrator in Munich," he said picking up the fountain pen from its stand. Frau Muckle eyes held a bit of anticipation.

"Concerning the Volker child. SS Colonel Rutters writes:

> 'In case you have not been informed by the Regional Asylum, I hereby inform you that the child Jurgen Volkers died there on the twenty-third of November, 1941.'
>
> Heil Hitler.'"

Frau Muckle felt a bit of sympathy for Fraulein Volkers. Not two weeks before, the letters the Fraulein had written to her soldier had been returned in a bundle, with huge letters stating in red: FALLEN.

"It will be up to you to tell her about the child. I have made plans for her transport to the Lebensborn Ministry in Munich. They have a job for her. Under no circumstances should she attend the Naming Ceremony. I want her gone from here immediately. Do you understand?" The look in his eyes was fierce and the scar on his left cheek enlarged, which let Frau Muckle understand his decision was firm and not to be discussed.

"As you direct, Herr Doktor. It will be carried out before the Abendessen is served. When have you ordered the transport?"

"The house is quiet around eleven. Have her ready then. See that she is isolated away from the others immediately."

He thought for a minute, then said, "By the way, I see Fraulein Hurst is making good progress."

"Clara is a good influence." The Directoress smiled broadly.

"Do not, I repeat, do not allow Faulein Volkers to be here after tonight. She must not attend the ceremony or the new one, Hannah Hurst. Major Hurst has presented us with a special case and I do not know if the ReishsFührer has been appraised of her. There can be no disturbance during his visit."

Frau Muckle puffed up her cheeks. She was horrified by the thought of a disturbance during the ReichsFührer's visit. "I will see that all is taken care of, Herr Doktor."

"I am certain that your feelings will not get in the way of Fraulein Volkers' removal."

"None whatsoever," she said.

Chapter Seven

During the following days, Clara continued to be distant, brusk and reserved. She called Antoinette by the name 'Hannah,' as did all the rest of the women and staff, if they spoke to her, which was rare. Although no explanation other than Fritz's was given, Antoinette was now Hannah. *So what if they give me a German name, if it makes life easier.* But, she longed for familiarity of self, the lovely sound of Antoinette.

Tonight, she sensed Clara might be letting down the barrier between them. If that were so, she wanted to ask Clara who had screamed, then cried so pitifully a few nights ago. The sounds were terrible, the wailing so pitiful.

They had just climbed into bed when Clara asked, "Did you like eating with us?" then got up to tug the drapes tighter.

Antoinette feared Clara would bestow another demerit on her because she had opened the window a little to let in the night air. Each demerit brought a distasteful period of writing, in Gothic script: Henceforth, I will (or, will not) . . .

Her journal in the armoire had pages of demerit writings, each page illuminated in red pencil with Clara, Frau Muckle, or Herr Doktor's signatures.

"It was good—very good," Antoinette said, never saying more than necessary.

"Who do you like best?"

"If you mean among the women who are here, naturally, it's you, Clara. You are a good teacher and guide."

"Stop it. Quit being so polite all the time. Stop it. I want the truth from you . . ."

"Gertrude, then . . . I think she bears such pain for the Führer."

"She does suffer—her soldier at the Russian Front and not had a letter from him for weeks." Clara had a measure of sympathy in her voice. "Fortunately, my beloved is safe behind the lines. He's on Himmler's staff—terribly handsome, a colonel. He wears the silver gray uniform for me. Tell me about your major; tell me everything."

The past came rushing back and Antoinette gave a magnificent picture of Hurst, although behind the details she gave were thoughts of the pain he caused most everyone in the village. Forced to sleep in a hot attic was demeaning, but, giving up their own home and working as a servants in it for the Nazis was even more humiliating. Living under the Nazi proclamations and giving them their possessions was terrible, too; but, the most painful thing he had stolen was her virginity. And, made her pregnant.

"What's the best thing about him?" Clara was insistent.

"The way he swims. He's magnificent, an extremely fine athlete . . . ran track in the Olympics . . . loves to duel. Major Hurst appreciates fine things: good food, lovely set tables with flowers, my cooking, and eats with pleasure and enjoyment."

"His family?" Clark asked, her voice aloof.

"He traces his German ancestry back generations before seventeen hundred and fifty and way beyond, too. His father is a long-time Army career officer, headquartered in Berlin, and he says his mother specializes in creating a wonderful home. He's engaged to Ellen Laudier who lives in Berlin and he carries a photo of her next to his heart. He's much taller than I and has many muscles from swimming. The baby we're making will be wonderful, especially if he takes after him. My Major likes the Waffen SS because he can serve with both officers and enlisted men. He enjoys mens' things—hunting, athletics, weapons—and, he's brilliant, sent to the RSHA School in Hamburg."

Clara interrupted—"RSHA?"

"Hitler's Secret Service School where they teach ways to get information out of people, intelligence training he called it. He came to our village in Villepente, he said, to put out possible resistance fires, part of a 'fire brigade.'"

"What I want to know is how he makes love." Clara's voice was husky.

"I had never made love to anyone before," Antoinette said as she recalled the intensity of the love sessions with the major, feeling again the sultry ambiance of the bedroom, seeing the room which once was hers but then claimed by the Nazi, sensing the deftness of his hands over her body, the nuances of the lovemaking skills he showered upon her night after night until they suddenly stopped.

"He taught me things a woman should know," Antoinette concluded with an unexpected zest that surprised her. "And, your colonel?"

"Wolf-Dieter Suntrop. I love to say his name over and over. I can never hear it enough, for when I hear his name I remember the whispers and things he says to me." Clara breathed deeply and sighed.

"Wolf is tall and lean, and when he comes into a room with me all the women stare. He's older so I always feel safe. We met in Munich when he came to a Bund Deutscher Mader's music festival and his eyes told me, the instant he saw me singing in the front row, that he loved me. I go to parties with him. He has a beautiful suite on the top floor of the Ventzer Hotel and it was there he made the baby I carry."

The room grew silent as Clara thought of those nights with Wolf. "I'm so excited about the Naming Ceremony, I can't sleep," she said. "He might even be there."

"How exciting that your colonel might be at the ceremony," said Antoinette.

"No, no, the ReichsFührer. It would mean everything to me. If he came, it would be a ceremony we would all remember forever, especially the new mothers. This is the most important event in their lives—to have their baby named by the ReichsFührer. Imagine, having the ReichFührer hold your baby in his arms as he gives the baby its name. I have never met him but Wolf speaks about him so much I know I will be overcome with joy."

Antoinette cringed as Clara expounded with passion. She felt Clara's perceptions and passions alarming. What would the ceremony be like? Although she would be working behind the scenes with the food, she might be able to see some of it.

Chapter Eight

*R*esidents of the Lebensborn bustled about excitedly the day before the Naming Ceremony. Antoinette was excused from the geography and biology classes to make delicacies and Fritz supplied the ingredients she requested: real butter, flour, apples, pears, potatoes.

Fritz took her down to the cellar beneath the Lebensborn to show her where potatoes were kept in a bin. When they were in the cellar, his lantern showed another hallway and when she asked where that one led, he only said, "Let's hope we don't find out," then changed the subject. It was almost like Clara had done earlier when Clara mentioned the cellar.

Antoinette was working at a kitchen counter when Clara came into the kitchen and threw on the floor beside her a wool hat, gloves, rubber boots and coat.

"She has to go with me, Fritz."

Antoinette leisurely started to pull on the boots.

Clara snapped, "This isn't a pleasure trip, hurry up; we have to find boughs in the woods. Oh, someone else could be sent, but, I don't trust anyone but myself with something so important."

Clara paced about as Antoinette told Fritz how to continue with the little cakes she was making.

The unexpected venture outside of the Lebensborn lifted Antoinette's spirits. She had only been outside the Lebensborn one other time. During preparations for an evening meal, Fritz had burned a pot of vegetables and he told her to take the burned pot and ingredients outside and dump them into a pile at the edge of the woods.

So, she carried the pot out the back door, up the steps and into the night and stopped to relish the smell of the woods. She was holding the pot, looking up at the stars, when suddenly, out of the night, came a loud scream, followed by horrible wailing. The sounds were coming from the new mothers' quarters. Who was in agony? Then, the dismal cries stopped.

Things are bad for me, but not like that.

She closed her eyes and felt Jacques with her, heard him whisper her name, not 'Hannah' but Antoinette. Her love flamed. *No matter where I go, he's there.*

This afternoon as Clara and Antoinette climbed the hillside behind the Lebensborn they came to a plateau of manicured, conifer trees. Antoinette saw the little village below and snapped a picture in her mind of the roads and buildings.

They climbed further into the woods. Clara, obsessed with finding the perfect greens, shouted, "Get that one," then be upset because the branch she wanted did not meet her expectations.

Antoinette placed the branches on an old blanket. Finally, Clara said there were enough. Antoinette slid the blanket with its cargo back to the Lebensborn and carried armloads of branches into the kitchen and set them on a counter.

"Here's how to make garlands," Clara said, and when Antoinette finished a strand, Clara would take it into the dining room to put it up as a backdrop to the shine she was making. Each baby was to be laid in front of the shrine after it was named.

Clara had covered the dining table, maneuvered into a smaller size, with white linen and then interwove the greenery with fresh asters of burgundy color on the top, positioning a large photo of Hitler in the center. She placed Nazi flags in standards on each side.

Frau Muckle came into the room and said, "Looking lovely, dear." A smile broadened her wide jaw. "I see you have arranged for mothers to sit . . ."

"Here," Clara said, going over to a ring of encircled tall dining chairs, "and, mothers-to-be . . . here . . ." Clara went to the left of the shine. "Dignitaries here," and pointed at two tall chairs on the right side.

"This is the best we've seen," the directoress said.

"Is the ReichsFührer really coming?" Clara asked.

"We're told his schedule will allow a visit—although brief—and, we're to expect him . . . so exciting for all of us."

"Lucky mothers. I wish my baby were part of the ceremony tomorrow, too." Clara had a wishful look on her face when she went to sit in one of the chairs reserved for the mothers.

She began to assess each garland and flower and got up to make an adjustment to the Nazi banner attached on the front of the shrine.

Frau Muckle nodded in agreement with the change. "Directoress, can we go over the ceremony one more time?"

"Clara, you must rest. Everything is just right; the program and your shrine beautiful. I know you and the others have spent many hours scripting the programs. Everything is ready and you can relax and be proud of your efforts."

"Thank you, Frau Muckle, but now I must tell everyone that we'll be taking our next meals in the kitchen."

"You've left no detail untouched, Clara. We're most fortunate to have you here; yes, a real blessing to the Führer."

"Heil Hitler," Clara said, with shining eyes.

Chapter Nine

$\mathcal{T}$he day of the Naming Ceremony was declared an official holiday and classes were suspended. Night clothing could be worn until time to dress for the formal afternoon ceremony at three o'clock and residents could eat whenever they desired. Antoinette brought trays of food that she and Fritz had prepared the day before and set them on the large table in the communal room. No one was about.

Earlier there had been a commotion at the Lebensborn entrance that she heard all the way from the kitchen. A large box had come for Clara and when she opened it, she exclaimed loudly enough for all to hear, "He remembered, my Wolf remembered. He said he'd send something special for me to wear today. Look, everyone, look: don't you think this is beautiful? Wherever did he find this adorable suit? Isn't it wonderful?"

But, Antionette would still be wearing the white shirt and black shirt, while others would be in holiday attire; she had icings to make, cakes to frost, beverages to prepare, fruit to cut. For over a week she and Fritz concentrated on making specialities for the reception.

Antoinette felt the excitement overtake her, too, and she was eager to see the mothers, the babies, and how everyone would be dressed. Would they like the special items she made?

Just before the magical hour, Fritz took a large box from under the counter and told her to turn her back while he changed.

"You can turn around now," he said. "How do you like this?"

He had put an extravagantly embroidered vest over a stiff, starched white shirt and his brown suit. Before she could answer, he went and cracked open the door between the kitchen and dining room, then opened the door a little more to watch the people who were collecting.

There came pounding sounds of boots and Fritz turned to Antoinette and whispered, "It's the ReischFührer, the Führer be praised," and beckoned to her to come and see, too, through the slightly opened door.

Herr Himmler wore a grey SS uniform. Rounded spectacles covered his beady eyes and a small, trimmed moustache shown below a straight, well-shaped nose and thin lips. A slight receding chin fell into his wrinkled neck. The smile on his face looked mechanically set; white teeth glistened between the tight lips. Antoinette shivered as she watched the man whose pale hands, covered with large blue veins, hardly touched the person's hand he was shaking.

Mothers-to-be were singing something that sounded like a lullaby. They were lined up in a row, one arm extended to him while the other held their baby.

They had on their finest garments and all wore an accompanying hat of some sort: Clara wore the white wool suit with big buttons sent by Wolf; Liselotte was in a black dress with a huge amount of silver glitter across the chest; Juliane wore a beige wool dress with large white, pointed collars; Dora, was in a red print dress with a small white, lace collar. Antoinette couldn't see Gertrude for she was hidden from view.

She counted: five Nazi officers and one who carried a large pad of paper and pen. Three went behind the shrine, while the officer with the pad and the ReishsFührer took seats on the tall chairs.

The ReishsFührer stood and everyone was silent.

He said in a loud, clear voice, "Glorious mothers—staff—I greet you.

"Mothers, you are important to Germany, for you ARE Germany. When you give birth, the nation salutes. We stand by your side in the good days and bad, come what may."

He paused. A baby was crying. The mothers, who sat in the circle, looked embarrassed. The mother and the crying baby got up and left the room.

"Germany will soon be home of all the world—of all Germans. You are guarantee of the future. Your child is the future. The world cannot live in constant war. There will be peace. Mothers, you are the guarantee of the peace to come. Germany requires centuries of strong growth and it is our unshakable belief in your racial pureness, healthy bodies and minds which will provide that future.

"Be cheered. There are improvements and new creations springing up all over. Life is active, and so it will remain.

Let the bright flame of your enthusiasm never falter. Forward with Germany to a new era, you soldiers of the home front. It takes great moral fortitude to become a mother when your soldier is going into battle, only fate knowing if he will return or fall for Germany.

"Mothers, you bind together a whole nation. We know you serve Germany by giving the Führer a child with pride. And, so it is for your SS officer who has done his duty and is part of this great Lebensborn movement.

"Today, we experience the love that makes us happy. You bear the youth who will know no class or caste. Always be loyal to the Führer and guide up your child to serve the Führer and all Germany.

"We want one Reich. Educate your child to be peace loving and courageous, but teach him to be hard, not soft. Steel it in your child to accept privation and to never collapse. We will soon pass away, but he will live. Hold firm the flag before him, the flag we tore from nothing.

"In you marches Germany, and behind you follows Germany. Life is worthwhile because of your great mission—

that given to you by God—by the God who created our people. Make it your vow, and that of your child, to think only of Germany and the Reich. Prove your loyalty. You are racially the best, the carrier of the best blood which will keep our leadership rich and strong. We expunge that which is bad blood and what is bad has no place among us.

"Continue to be strong as steel, for this state will endure for a thousand years and your child will carry on the struggle when the old weaken and fall away. Direct all your efforts to those of the Third Reich. Be an indestructible pillar. The traditions of the Third Reich are carried on your shoulders. Be happy, enthusiastic, and joyful for you are creating a Super Race.

"As we know, the Nordic being is the jewel of the earth, the shining example of the joy of creations, not only the most talented but the most beautiful. You have born the royalty among human beings.

"Sacred are you, mothers of pure blood—for you are creating a new kind of man—a Germanic man—the Super Tuton."

A group clapped and cheered. They stood and saluted. The ReishsFührer motioned for silence. The mother whose baby had been crying was returning to her seat, the child pacified and quiet. The mothers ignored her.

Clara walked up to the ReishsFührer and said, "The honor of having you with us is overwhelming." Clara looked at each of the SS officers. "We greet, you, honored guests, and thank you for coming this afternoon. And, now, as our Lebensborn custom, it's time to name the Führer's new babies."

A Nazi officer came from behind the shrine where he had been standing, and, one by one, as each mother came before him, she placed her baby in his arms and told the name. The man was slim and handsome, and Antoinete was fascinated by his smooth way of holding each child. Could this be Wolf-Dieter, the officer with whom Clara was so smitten?

The officer repeated the child's name to the ReishsFührer, who then spoke the baby's name as he placed his hand on the child's forehead and said: "I give you the name—"

After each baby was named, it was placed on a white blanket in front of the shrine.

"Mothers, we're honored," Clara said to the women in the circle. Then to the ReishFührer she said, "Every mother has requested me to ask you to honor her child by signing the program." Clara smiled at him appealingly, then glanced briefly over to the slim, handsome officer who had held the babies.

A smile came across the Reishsfurer's face and he nodded.

Clara went over to the mothers to collect the programs; many were crumpled as they maneuvered the babies so she had to smooth out each program before handing it to the ReishsFührer. He scratched his signature in green ink with a Montblanc pen, the Meisterstuck with the three bands of twenty-four karat gold.

"I now give the program over to our fine SS Doktor, Herr Doktor Krause," said Clara.

After a long speech extolling virtues of the new Nazi Germany, the doktor said, "Mothers, give your babies to the nurses upstairs and to return to enjoy the rest of the program, the fine food and music."

Fritz appeared with a small accordion and his music filled the air. The gay music created a festive air among the participants, including the ReishFührer who was talking to Doktor Krause.

Antoinette slipped in with another tray of food, arranging it on a table away from the main activities. Antoinette thought, *This is so grand—the gold-band dishes—the pastries and fruit cakes on heavy silver platters—the elegant lace cloth over the light blue one.*

She went to watch from a crack in the door, waiting to see a response to her pastries and cakes.

Clara filled a plate for the ReishsFührer who sat as a dignitary, people coming before him one at a time in hopes of hearing him say something personal to them.

The plate on his knee wobbled as the women approached. Finally, he reached down and took up a tiny apple tart and took a bite. A broad smile lit up his face, "Excellent," he said, "I must congratulate the chef."

Frau Muckle stepped forward and motioned to Fritz who had not heard the ReishsFührer's compliment.

Frau Muckle led Fritz over to the ReishsFührer. "All compliments are for this person," she said.

Fritz, accordion in front of him, was dazzled by the compliments.

Antoinette's eyes filled with tears. *I expected no recognition, but not to have Fritz say anything. . .* She rushed to the kitchen and into the chilly outdoors. *I will not stay here. I will find a way to leave. I must get away from this place. God, please help me. Show me a way.*

She heard someone coming up the steps.

Fritz called, "Ah, there you are," he said coming up to her.

"I am so sorry. They loved what you did even though you did not get credit." He saw tears in her eyes and she saw there were tears also in his. He wrapped his thin arms about her and patted her back as if she were a small child.

She turned from him and made her way down the steps, through the kitchen, and back to room seven. The silver cross on the door, the symbol for the glorious Third Reich, a painful reminder that she was carrying one of the Führer's Super Race.

Chapter Ten

*I*t was unlike Herr Professor Pompsel to be late for biology class. His five students stirred nervously in their seats as they waited for him.

Juliane and Gertrude whispered together, then got up and came to Antoinette who sat at the third table in the row where she ordinarily sat with Clara. For some unknown reason, Clara had been excused from class. Antoinette saw them coming and hoped they might feel free to talk to her now that Clara wasn't there.

"Hannah," said the soft-spoken voice of Juliane, "The apple pastries you make yesterday were so different. I wondered sometime if you . . ."

She stopped. The professor had come into the room and with him was a woman of medium height, light brown hair and eyes, dressed in a black and white polka dot dress, black suede shoes and white stockings. Juliane and Gertrude went quickly back to their table and stood at attention.

Herr Professor Pomsel gave the customary hand signal and they were seated. He said, "This is your new classmate, Gesa Buchs." To Gesa, he said, "For today, you may sit there," pointing to Clara's vacant chair next to Antoinette.

The professor took his customary place in front of the classroom and looked down the two rows of long desks. He picked up the official textbook on racial policies laying on the desk in front of Liselotte, and opened it. He glanced at the page, then gazed past the class to look at a large photo on the wall. Everyone turned to see. He stared at Otto von Bismarck, founder of the Second Reich, the most prominent German after Frederick the Great.

"Mothers," he said, in a somber tone, "our discussion today will be of vital importance to you." The middle-aged professor was chubby and when he got excited he looked as if he swelled up and become even more rotund.

"Today we discuss the wiping out of those persons who are less worthy." He paused to dramatize his point. "Why is this important?"

"Yes, Liselotte." He stared hard and directly at the shy girl.

"It is the duty, Herr Professor, of our leaders to be responsible for as large a population as possible. To have many, many people is good, but, they must be just the finest people."

"Very good, Liselotte," he said. "And, so we have important laws which cover this making of a good population. Perhaps, Juliane, you can further inform the class what these laws are."

Juliane's eyes gleamed. She knew the answer. "Herr Professor, we have several such laws . . ." and turned to smile at all the students, especially the new woman, Gesa,—"the law to preserve the hereditary soundness, sometimes called the healthy marriage law."

"And, Hannah, how does this October twenty-sixth law of nineteen thirty-five preserve soundness of we Germans—hummm?"

Quickly Antoinette said, "It prevents increase of hereditary disease, however . . ." She paused to decide whether or not to debate the issue, but if she did, it would mean more demerits.

"However . . . you say. Do you take a different view?" the Professor said in a challenging way.

Juliane waved her arm.

"Herr Professor," Juliane said, "this is an often debated issue, but I think marriage should be forbidden when one of them has a dangerous disease."

Antoinette raised her hand and added quickly, "The law preventing incurable diseases IS good—"

"Then, Hannah, tell us what part of the marriage law you question?" The professor's voice tantalized and encouraged, yet, cajoled.

"Is it right, Herr Professor, to take away a woman or man's freedom to have children? What if they are perfectly healthy and an error is made?" Antoinette folded her hands on the desk.

Liselotte was so eager to join the debate that the professor acknowledged her, and she said, "Only the most serious cases need to be sterilized—just the crazy ones."

The Professor seemed excited by the discussion. He puffed up again and strode up and down the aisle between the two rows of the long desks and stopped in front of Gesa.

"You—you've worked with the Gestapo—you tell us."

Gesa's pretty voice had a melodious quality. "These operations, and I've witnessed several—they aren't dangerous at all. Such an operation wipes out defects. It's better to keep those who have hereditary diseases from transmitting them to others, than to pity the children later and burden us Germans, and the state."

"Gesa, thank you. I'm so pleased you've joined our little group. I can see you will be a valuable addition. You made the point well.

"Now, Mothers, a nation can only be selective with large numbers of people, so you see it all works hand-in-hand. We have lost many good Germans to other countries in mass migrations. We've lost men by selling them as soldiers for other countries' wars. We've weakened our population and must bring our strength to the fore again."

His face grew red. He pounded his fist on the desk in front of Antoinette.

"We must grow—have more births than . . ." His toad-like figure became a wily fox. "Hah, but I digress. Let's go on to explore the law against dangerous criminals.

"Under this law, we can free the criminal from his perversions, prevent serious crimes, bring about security. That's what these important laws are all about—*progress.*"

His pudgy hand pounded upon Gesa's desk.

"Do you know that to teach a child, the government spends one thousand marks a year. To educate a deaf person, it is twenty thousand marks. Every year these afflictions cost millions of marks. Is this right?"

Herr Professor's discussion jumped from dangerous criminals to persons with defects and the mothers-to-be thought, *What if my child isn't normal? What would happen to the child?*

Would I be sterilized?

He continued. "How many sports palaces, homes, kindergartens, hospitals could be built with that money? Do you not feel a sense of guilt for any afflicted person you see? That you are healthy and they are not? Are you not pleased that your leaders have taken this strong responsibility to make these legal steps to prevent—criminals—prevent serious crimes—diseases—to save your child from harm.

"I'm sorry if I frighten you. That is not my intent. You above all have no cause for alarm. You and your partners' histories have been so thoroughly examined that you must feel among the most fortunate not to have this concern. Your children will be perfect—the best—the soon-to-be leaders of our glorious Third Reich.

"So, let us now discuss genetics and the concealed hereditary causes . . ."

They heard knocking at the door. The professor went to open it and Frau Muckle stood outside and whispered something to him.

"You," he pointed to Antoinette, "go immediately to Herr Doktor Krause in his study."

As Antoinette got up to leave the room, she felt someone's eyes on her. She met Juliane's stricken eyes. As she followed the directoress, she thought, *How logical they are. He almost had me believing their marriage law. I know they are wrong.*

If they gain the world, their successors will be these children trained up from childhood that they are superior to all others. Clara says that if a child has not been a good Hitler Youth member, they can't get into the next level of schooling, no matter how smart or talented. The world is doomed if it is to be run by children trained to believe like this.

A problem in the math textbook came flashing to her, the message quite clear:

> In the province of X in the Greater German Reich, there live about forty-five thousand incurably ill mental patients. For their housing, food, medical, and nursing care the state has to provide thirty thousand marks per patient per year. It costs three hundred thousand marks to set up a new farm with land, house, barn, cattle, seed corn, etc.
>
> Question: How many marks does the province X have to spend per year for the care of these patients. How many new farms could be established for the same sum total expenditures?

At the time she read the problem, she saw they were making a unsubtle proposal for mercy killing, stating an official policy for sanctioned murders.

She was in front of Herr Doktor's door and as she waited for his gruff voice to tell her to enter, she felt again the terror the man represented.

"Come in, come in," he said as he held the door open, then took her arm and led her to a twin pair of cozy looking chairs in front of a bookcase wall. A small hexagonal table separated the chairs, a Victorian lamp with a garish pink shade in the middle.

"Don't be afraid," he said in a soothing voice, relaxing into one of the velvet-cushioned chairs. He smiled. The scar widened on his left cheek. He coaxed her into the adjoining chair.

"We have good news. Yes, yes, I know we've had our little sessions, but this morning is going to be different. You won't have any writing to do at all. Now, isn't that nice?"

Her heart beat hard.

"Your services have been requested. Yes, you. By 'Them.' See here, I have this note," and patted his pocket, "from Lieutenant Landruth, counter-signed by Herr ReishsFührer, which requests you, the Fraulein Hannah, henceforth, to assist in their kitchen. He will send someone to escort you later this afternoon. Any questions? I must say you are starting to fill out and look better. How are you feeling?"

"Excellent, Herr Doktor. I look forward to the new assignment, of course."

"Oh, incidentally," he added, "you will no longer be required to help in the Lebensborn kitchen. You will have enough to do there . . ."

"I'm excused now, Herr Doktor?"

"Yes, yes," he waved her out of the room, saying, "go back to class. Herr Professor tells me he's just introducing the racial ideologies. Very important, don't you think, for you as well as for the child?"

She closed the door, but instead of returning to class, she ran to the kitchen to find Fritz to see if he could tell her anything about the place she was going.

Chapter Eleven

The late afternoon sky had colored tiers of blue and gray. It was chilly, the atmosphere blustery, when Antoinette left the Lebensborn accompanied by Nazi officer Von Benner. The heavy, gray wool cardigan thrown over her shoulders like a cape slipped off and fell to the road near the gates of the SS House.

She bent to retrieve the sweater and looked between the branches of the tall hedge. The house was mysterious and she wanted to see more of it than she had last night when she looked into it from her third floor room.

Who was the man in the window? Where was Lieutenant Von Benner taking her? Who wanted her? If they **were** headed for the SS House, it might offer better means of escape. As for where, a plan was forming in her mind.

Instead of victories, might the Germans be losing? She recalled incidents from her trip through Germany, especially the sight of triumphant archways at the beginnings of villages, with names like Polzin, Klosterheide, Hohehorst. The arches, made up of neatly frilled boughs of pine and little bouquets of flowers, were turning brown as they hung from gilded ropes in the center of the arches. Legends across the top read: Rothenburg or Nodlingen or Dillingen, Greets Its Triumphant Heroes. Why were the banners still hanging? When Clara said, "We get all we want," did she mean that others weren't? Then, the sight of forlorn-appearing shop windows came back—they had so few goods in them. There were shops, too, with closed signs in the doors.

Peering through the branches, she saw nothing in the grayness of the day other than the curve in the drive and trees.

The Lieutenant had not spoken to her since Frau Muckle introduced him to her at the Lebensborn. Then he had clicked his boot heels and acknowledged her with a stiff, "Fraulein Hurst." Now he was trying to help her reposition the ungainly sweater. She turned to him and said, "It's cold—are we going far?"

"No, Fraulein, you'll soon be inside where it's warm."

Although he appeared stiff as a person, she thought he was probably as good a person as the other officers who had lived with them in Villepente, with the exception of Major Hurst, of course. Her friend, Danielle, said wonderful things about Nazi officer Lieutenant Walthers. Antoinette especially liked Hans, the farmer who had become an Waffen SS officer, assigned as her bodyguard. When he saw her off at the bus, he pressed into her hand something which might help her escape plans.

Lieutenant Von Benner stopped in front of the closed black gates of the SS House. Close up, she felt the power of the double lightening SS insignia outlined in heavy gold on each gate.

One sentry came to attention before the lieutenant as the other pushed the gates open. They walked up the curving drive toward the house and heard the metal gates clang together. The massive white house of stone came into sight as the drive curved. They walked up three wide, slippery, granite steps, and the lieutenant opened a heavy, wood-carved door. Inside, they came to an indoor staircase of white granite. They went up the steps and came to a large entry hall with large rooms on either side and a hall leading to the rear of the house.

The lieutenant looked into each of the attached rooms. Antoinette recognized the room with the piano, but no one was in either room or the hallway.

There was a loud commotion above them. The elaborate gold ceiling fixture in the entry began to sway.

"Ah, Peter must be in the midst of a boccie game," said the lieutenant. He took her arm and led her into the hallway. The walls were decorated with photos of ranking Nazi officers, and interspersed with photos of Hitler. There was a shot of him greeting a child who held a bouquet of flowers; a photo of him riding in a long car like Major Hurst's; another which caught him with a fist in the air at a rally where thousands watched.

A poster caused her to stop and stare: it depicted a woman with a child at her breast, the words: 'Every German Woman Gives a Child to the Führer.'

The lieutenant paused before he opened a door and said, "Peter was supposed to get you started with this . . . we lost our chef and his helpers several days ago . . . heard screams coming from the kitchen during Abendessen . . . the chef suffered horrible burns, and so did his assistants and we've been in a terrible state ever since.

"Peter's been looking for replacements, but the villagers think we have demons. We've tried to feed ourselves, but we can't do it even with plenty of food. None of our other servants will step foot in the kitchen. Women guests have been no help either."

"How did you hear about me?" she asked.

"Last night ReichsFührer sent over a tray of pastries from your Lebensborn. Everyone got excited . . . especially the little cakes. Clara told us about you and we all said, 'Bravo,' 'Bravo.' So, it's all up to you."

He opened the door. Chaos was apparent: food was strewn about in iron pots and pans on counters and the floor, and dishes leaned everywhere in towering stacks.

"See here," she said, "you must go back to the Lebensborn and tell Frau Muckle that Fritz must send his daughter, Magda, at once. There's nothing I can do until this is cleaned up. Oh, yes, please ask Fritz to give you several loaves of rye bread and a kettle of the potato soup we just made."

"Normally, I don't take orders from females," he said. "However, in this case I'll make an exception." He clicked his heels and said, "It will be as you wish, Fraulein."

On his return to the Lebensborn, he thought, *Whoever she is, she has spunk.*

Antoinette began the laborious task: she found two tin pails in a lower cupboard; discovered soap flakes in a covered tin, and running water at a sink. As she opened and looked behind cupboard doors she realized that the girl playing the piano last night was Clara.

Then she discovered a radio behind a stack of dirty dishes, larger than the one at the Lebensborn, and encased in wood instead of the ugly black covering.

Fritz told her the black "people's receiver" at the Lebensborn, like all radios in Germany, was programmed to receive only government stations. He said, "the new Regime is doing something for the people. Up to a few months ago, even the ordinary household could not afford such luxury. But now, the simple, black box is very low in price and affordable." Antoinette thought, *So Hitler and his government have a captive audience for their Berlin-created programs.*

The same red warning tag hung from the dial. But, this one could tune to foreign signals.

She clicked on the switch and twisted the dial. An English male voice came in faintly over background static. She put her ear close to the mesh of the amplifier and listened and heard him proclaim a series of heroic air battles over London in which the Royal Air Force had taken a disastrous toll of Lufwaffen bombers. Then, he told about heavy snows falling near Moscow.

The ceiling rattled as as if a herd of sheep were tramping overhead.

She switched off the radio and got to work, soon had logs of pine burning in the wood stove, and two buckets filled with water heating on top.

224

Lieutenant Von Benner came in carrying a huge soup pot and several loaves of bread.

"The fire's going," she said. "Please put the pot on the stove. I can take the bread." She reached for the loaves and asked with an impatient tone, "When can Magda come?"

"Tomorrow or day after. She has gone to a sister's, but Fritz says she can come when she gets back."

"How many people will be here tonight for Abendessen?"

"Maybe twenty. It all depends on who has orders. Peter knows." He shifted from one foot to the other. "I shouldn't take up your time when you have so much to do." He shrugged his shoulders, then went to the stove, picked up the lid of the soup pot, sniffed, and said, "This kitchen might become very popular."

At the sink, she turned to him, frustrated by his continued presence, and said, "If you continue to stay, perhaps you'd peel some carrots."

He clicked his heels but still didn't depart.

Frustrated, she said, "Lieutenant, I must talk to Peter."

"Of course. He must agree to whatever you ask. The servants will not step foot in here. They say this kitchen is cursed."

"Lieutenant, please go; but, come back in two hours to return me to the Lebensborn."

"But . . . what will we do when you go?"

"Just fine." She laughed. "In two hours, you can help yourselves to soup, bread, and maybe even a desert. Tomorrow, if Magda comes, we'll be able to serve Abendessen in the dining room."

Finally, the sound of his boots echoed down the hall.

Antoinette thought as she worked, *I might be able to get away in the woods. I'll have time and more possibilities of escape. I will be away from the Lebensborn where I'm watched so closely. Classes are boring, the contents disgusting, the exercise routines with the hoop tiring and difficult. It feels good to be here.*

Chapter Twelve

ReichsFührer Henrich Himmler's guest house in the Bavarian village south of Munich was his gift to deserving SS officers. It was a place for them to step out of the war machinery into a haven of rest and relaxation.

Lieutenant Peter Landruth was an interrogation officer and famous for magical techniques of extracting answers without brutal treatment or torture of those who came before him. His treatment so surprised Russian officers that they would confess to important information without even knowing.

Throughout his life, including his student days at the German University in Leipzig, he was a person without rough edges, someone who immediately drew people to him. He was fascinated by radio equipment and had developed a way of monitoring and interpreting radio transmissions. After his unit was praised for being able to tell when the enemy was taking off in England and where the German planes should meet them, he had been whisked off for interrogation work. He had been assigned to an intelligence unit on the Soviet front.

A resplendent man, he fought without weapons, only with his brains. A curious man, he questioned everyone, everything, and due to his gregarious ways, people always surrounded him. He liked doing magic tricks and was always the center of attraction at parties because of those skills and his humor. He was a master at creating illusions.

The next day, Antoinette was told to wait for Peter in the large room to the right of the huge entry hall. Lieutenant Von Benner pointed to some cushioned arm chairs arranged in a row in front of a massive fieldstone fire place.

The house was quiet. The guests were involved in a scavenger hunt up in the woods. An ornate clock ticked away the minutes in a tall wood case. She stroked the overly polished wood arms of the chair and watched flames flicker, then nervously tugged at the ends of the black tie.

"Oh, there you are," called a deep, resonant voice. She turned towards the voice and her heart beat rapidly.

The handsome Nazi officer, in the light silver uniform of the finest cloth, who came toward her was the one she had seen in the window.

She stood.

"My Angel of the moonlight." He reached for her hands. His brown eyes sparkled with flecks of green in the bright glow of the fire and looked excitedly into hers.

"Fraulein Hurst, how happy—overjoyed, really, we are to have you with us. I have dreamed only of you since the night I saw you standing in the window in the white gown. I knew we had to meet. How truly fortunate it is so soon."

Then he apologized. "Forgive me. I forget to introduce myself. Peter Landruth, a guest here myself, but only another few more days, then back to the Front."

His hands continued to hold hers.

She knew they had never met before, could not have under the circumstances, so why did she feel she knew this tall, slender man with the smiling eyes, the golden, narrow face with the tiny mustache above the full lips with the most captivating smile.

He melted her composure and tears began to flow. He drew her to him, gently stroking her hair, held back by two barrettes.

"Tell me everything, especially how you came to be here all the way from France."

His arms held her. She clung to him, oozing into him, thinking of nothing else other than how pleasurable it was.

Then reality broke the spell and she broke away from him.

They sat side by side and peered into the dying fire. He held one of her hands and a cigarette with the other.

In a brief, straight-forward way, she told him how she had come to be in Germany. In one sentence she summed up the Lebensborn; "The food and shelter are good, but because I am not German, no one likes me."

"That's not so," he clarified immediately. "I am German. I am wild about you. Everyone here will like you."

She protested. "Clara won't. Clara comes to this house and she does not like me."

"People can change." He got up and pulled a bell cord near the fireplace. An elderly gentleman in a black suit with patched trousers came into the room carrying two long pine logs, one under each arm. He wrestled the gigantic pieces of tree onto the ebbing fire, then disappeared.

"It is true that all the women guests are German. Personally I like the idea, as did your Major, of accepting other nationalities for new blood in the Third Reich. An example I use is that of the pure bred species which benefits from additions of different types. I've been trying to explain that to Ellen."

"Ellen . . . Laudier?" she broke in, gasping.

"Do you know Ellen?" he asked.

"No, of course not. I know of her through the Major."

"When she meets you, how will she resist any longer?"

Antoinette said, alarmed, "She comes here . . . to this house? When?"

"Answer to your questions are—yes—and, soon. Perhaps by the time you have shown the village woman how to manage the kitchen, you can be a guest, too. We have great times. You'll see. I want you to be among us."

They heard commotion. Lieutenant Von Benner was arriving with Fritz's youngest daughter, Magda. Antoinette rushed Magda to the kitchen and kept thinking about Peter's remark about Ellen's resistance. What was Ellen resisting? Would Peter tell her what that meant?

Chapter Thirteen

Antoinette worked late into the night so she slept late the next morning at the Lebensborn. She neared the communal bath area and heard sounds of sobbing.

It was the new girl, Gesa Buchs, who was bent over one of the sinks trying to scrub something from her hands. She recalled her being extraordinarily full of self-confidence and pride, obviously from her work with the Gestapo. But, this girl was a different person, she was in trouble.

The girl was sobbing and swearing. "I'll get even with him. I hate him."

"Who is he, Gesa?"

Antoinette wanted to throw her arms about the suffering girl but she dared not.

Gesa threw her hands in the air towards Antoinette. They were stained bright red.

"He made me sit there at his desk and write with red ink, over and over."

"What did you do?"

"Told the truth, that's all. Frau Muckle must have overheard me. *I saw the photos.* He says it is not so. He made me write one thousand times, 'I will not lie.' It is not a lie. I am proud to tell about my work with the Gestapo. I personally have filed photos of infants being shot and other photos of mass executions of Jews. He says it not appropriate to discuss such with mothers-to-be. I told him, it was appropriate. He said I talked back to him so he made me write more lines until my fingers felt as if they would break. I filled the book with lines of 'I will not talk back.'"

"The stain will come off, Gesa. Let me help you. Perhaps Fritz has something which can help. Here, wipe your hands. I'll go with you to the common area and you can wait for me to get dressed and go to the kitchen."

"I've done my share of writing, too, for Herr Doktor Krause," Antoinette confided as she walked with Gesa to the common room. "If I had the time to show you, I'd bring my book full of writing. But, I must hurry for we are getting things ready for a very important occasion."

Antoinette did not say any more for she remembered she could not say anything about what she was doing next door. She threw on her uniform, ran to find Fritz, and returned to Gesa with solvent in a tiny bottle.

She applied the liquid solution with an old cloth and tried to soothe the distraught girl, encouraging her to forget the incident.

The pungent odor of the solution hung in the air.

"Isn't giving birth for the Führer the most wonderful miracle." Antoinette chanted it softly over and over to Gesa like a lullaby.

Chapter Fourteen

*A*ntoinette looked through the window into the gathering darkness outside. Her eyes searched the outdoors. She thought she saw a dark shadow moving between the trees.

"Magda," she said nonchalantly to the young assistant who was placing cups and saucers on the huge silver tea tray, "If anyone comes looking for me, I am out gathering branches for the centerpiece."

Antoinette grabbed the heavy gray sweater hanging on the peg, threw it on and went outside. A light rain had begun. Was it a stray dog? A deer? A person would never dare venture onto these grounds.

A mud-crusted hand clasped itself over her mouth. She felt dirt between her teeth. Another hand clasped her wrists together behind her back.

"I mean no harm," a male voice whispered in halting German with an English accent. The voice had a strange bite, like an acidic orange juice. The assailant gripped her closely, then slowly released his hand from her mouth. She spat out specks of dirt.

He emphasized first in German, then French, finally English, "I am your friend."

She knew he was a big man. She could feel the stiffness of his body behind her. She felt his muscles relax, his rapid breathing slow. She thought she could feel his heart pounding. "Whoever you are," she said, first in German, then French, and finally English, "You are not safe here."

"I have been watching this house. It is the only place I can get food . . ."

"You must believe I am your friend. The house there is filled with the SS." she said.

He released her and without explanation she took one of his dirty hands and lead him across the wide expanse of trees and grounds, down the back steps of the Lebensborn and into the potato bin in the cellar.

She whispered as they moved. "Trust me. I don't know who you are, but I will come back with food and blankets. You can explain later. I am with the French Resistance." She spoke to the man in English. She recognized immediately that between them it was the best of the three languages.

She ran back to the SS house feeling he must be the answer to her prayers with the angels.

RAF Leftenant Douglas, nicknamed Joburg, Knight, a navigator on a Landcaster bomber, positioned his lanky body into corner of the potato bin. He shifted himself about in the piles of lumpy spuds. In the dark, his last minutes in the bomber flashed before him.

Their 321st Squadron had reached Germany inbound in heavy broken clouds with solid overcast below. Ahead had been multiple layers of clouds so the group leader told them to break into sections of eight and to climb to get above the weather. At twenty thousand feet they were still in the clouds and taking on light ice, bouncing around in turbulence. They climbed higher and there was the sun.

"Pipsqueak on," he heard Lenny say through his ear phones. "Hello Woodie? Any trade in sight?"

"Gain altitude, Pipsqueak. Fifty plus. Two o'clock."

"So long then, Golf Course. Right ho. There they are hiding behind a cloud and coming for us out into the sun."

Two Messerschmitt 109's shot out and scored.

Little oil dots blossomed on their windshield. The oil pressure dropped, then shot back up. Lenny turned the fighter towards England. The engine burped and started making funny sounds. RPM's started dropping. Lenny shut off the engine, dropped the nose and began gliding.

"Pipsqueak on—finished on the Golf Course for the day," joked Lenny.

The canopy popped up. The five crew members unfastened seat belts and harnesses. The plane turned upside down. Douglas fell free into the sky, ripping off the oxygen mask and radio plugs. He had forgotten to disconnect them. That smarted.

He could see nothing because he was in a solid cloud. He had no idea how far he had fallen or how close he was to the ground.

He desperately counted—seven, eight, nine—at ten, grabbed for the D ring with his left hand and pulled the rip cord. The chute opened, the cord lines jerked. The fall slowed as he went downwards. It was a rough ride. Anxiously he looked up into the canopy, which he could barely see in the cloud. It seemed to be open. The descent took ages. When he finally broke out of the clouds, he barely had time to get set. The cloud base must have been only four hundred feet about the ground. When he hit, it sounded like garbage being thrown from a moving truck.

He fell into the Rhine, clawing at the parachute harness. The chute canopy was still inflated and dragging him along. He shed the harness fast and began swimming across the river oblivious to the heaviness of the wet uniform. He could see no other chutes in the low haze. What happened to the others?

Swimming across the Rhine was difficult.

On the bank, he was wet, cold and hungry, and began trembling from shock. He knew the Germans would soon be searching the areas where they believed the plane came down. They would keep widening their circle, so maybe he should stay close to the shore just to fool them.

His right leg hurt. He cut a willow stick for a cane and got out the silk map from the gabardine coverall pocket, found the compass and tried orienting himself. All his skills as a navigator were being tested in the cold sleet and drizzle. There was not a sound or a thing to be seen. He scraped together some driftwood, built a small fire and rested. No one was about. When a day or so had passed, he started walking.

He walked it seemed miles and miles, stole milk from quaint villages and speared some fish in a little brook. He slept under bridges during the day and walked at night, marching on using his silk maps. He stole a peasant's jacket and wore it over the jumpsuit. He carried the heavy flying boots; his feet were too swollen to fit into them any longer.

Exhausted, famished, suffering from a major wound to his arm from a nasty dog's bite and cut and swollen feet, he spied the massive SS building from the top of the hill. He watched and occasionally saw a man carrying a bucket come out the back door and dump the contents into a ditch. He stayed on the hilltop and ate the food scraps the man would leave.

One night as he crept toward the scraps, thrown into a ditch for covering over later, the man inside was looking out the window and saw him. The large pan in the man's hands flew up and the contents flung out. Douglas stuffed scraps into his pockets and crawled back to his hideout. He saw the room filling with people.

That night the rains began again. A few days later, with the tiny binoculars he had managed to hang onto, he studied the new form carrying the bucket to the ditch. It was a girl.

Now the girl had led him to this cellar. She apparently had a reason, but, for the moment, being out of the freezing rain felt good.

He heard steps and peered over the mountain of potatoes. He saw a flicker of light out the doorway, quickly rolled into a ball inside a nest of potatoes and began to count to himself, one thousand one, one thousand two, just as he did when he was a boy. Who was it? The steps went by. A few minutes later he heard the person go by again.

He slept, then awakened from a fitful sleep. He heard footsteps which appeared lighter than those he had heard earlier.

The girl came into the bin carrying two wool blankets smelling of mothballs and two tin pails, one which fit inside the other so tightly he had a hard time separating them when he had to use one to relieve himself.

Inside the top bucket had been a delicious rye bread along with chunks of sausage and two apples. It was a feast.

She told him who she was, why she was in Germany, and of how she planned for them to escape together.

"We can't use public transportation—trains or bus—so we either walk or steal a ride. The truck with supplies is due Monday—two days from now, any time during the day or night. If I could help with the unloading—although I barely know or trust the servants—the old man might like help—I might convince him—

"For now you must be quiet and stay here." Their main objective would be to leave the village. For where, she would not say. But she knew. She told him she was a mother-to-be but she acted nothing like any pregnant woman he'd known. He hadn't known many, but those he remembered would not be risk their life to bring food to a downed RAF crewman. She didn't look pregnant. She didn't seem afraid either.

Then the darkness began to claw at him and he let it catch him.

Chapter Fifteen

*E*llen Laudier walked between the tall, elaborately carved doors of the SS House and felt without doubt, that something exciting was going to happen.

She adored coming to this place. The moment she left the House, satiated with the fill of it, as she was on the way back to Berlin, the more she craved to return.

She looked over her shoulder to see how her three trunks were coming. Her glance caught an elderly male servant trying to fit his shoulder to the middle trunk. He gave it a half-hearted shove, but it still stuck out clumsily in the tier of trunks on the wooden cart he was pulling.

'This is crazy. He would be gone but for the war. The war does have its disadvantages.'

She was famous, beautiful and her family for the last four hundred years one of the upper Prussian-German classes. To have a wonderful time for days in a row was laborious, thought-provoking work. "Seeing people" wasn't the world's easiest job. She wanted to look dressy, but not too much so; ravishing, but not too much, and tried for a look of freshness. Being among the same crowd chewed up a wardrobe fast.

Ellen liked skirts which skimmed the hip, making her legs move in and out of view seductively. If she crossed her legs, or even ankle over ankle, the light shift in weight would cause tautness of the fabric.

Her fashion was current, whatever that meant these days. Her dressmakers created clothes inspired by former Paris fashions.

This evening she wore a challis full-sweep wool pleated skirt. As she moved, the pleats revealed red and flame flowers: bright tulips, beige irises, caramel roses with soft green tints, on midnight blue fabric so light it gave warmth without weight. A ribbed sweater with sixteen buttons down the back was the unexpected touch. They'd ask what color it was, for it seemed to change color in various lights and might be brick red or even a deep ruby to match a flower.

Her leather-padded cases were fitted with brass closures, padded leather handles and tiny locks. One trunk held removable, leather-trimmed mirrors with easel backs. Another had secret, pullout drawers for jewelry and journals.

To Ellen, travel was a form of introspection. She always found time to write about her impressions of people and events, at least every other day. Capturing the essence of a moment was important. If you didn't, you lost so much. Who could remember the details of the clothes, the new officers, the feelings, if they weren't caught and written down before they fled from awareness?

Those officers, how lucky they were. Regulation required them to wear a uniform at all times. All they needed was an ample supply of underwear, sox and shirts and to remember on which breast to attach all their medals. *If I were an officer, would I love medals as much as I do my jewelry?*

She caressed the diamond eyes of the SS skull ring, the major's birthday present.

In the trunks were things to comfort: framed pictures, drawers of heavenly scents, linen embroidered sheets and pillow covers, and her childhood feather pillow.

"Peter," she called out.

Lack of an adequate staff here was appalling. Gossip of the kitchen mishap was a joke all over Berlin. Could that be where they assigned the butler? A house without a butler. It was unthinkable. Fortunately, her family through their connections, had been able to maintain their full, well-trained staff.

Ellen's life, like many of the wealthy, was softened by money. The rich never had to worry about the problems of society—the lost wars, the horrendous inflation, the Great Depression.

Ellen would never notice that the long lines of job seekers, the beer hall brawls, or street fighting had disappeared. Nor, would it ever occur to someone in her position that houses were getting painted again, people were dressing better, or that the general mood in families and neighborhoods was optimistic.

Ellen had never known a world of depravation. However, since the events on the new eastern front, Operation Barbarossa had begun, supplies of French cognac, Butch Bols gin and Polish vodka had disappeared and bars no longer had ingredients for cocktails. So far she had not had to drink the stomach-searing alcohol and thick, sweet grenadine syrups she had heard about.

The best entertainers had been drawn off eastward for the entertainment of officers. Potsdamer Strasse, once a busy shopping center, was now a row of closed shops, many of the middle-aged owners called up or no longer able to get things to sell.

Not long ago she had been out walking with a group of friends along the Potsdamer Strasse, which paralleled the railway tracks. On an overpass they stopped to look down and saw on the maze of tracks below, engines and trains with clearly marked red crosses in white circles, obviously hospital trains unloading maimed soldiers from the Eastern Front for hospitals in Berlin.

A drunk passed by and nudged her, pointed down and said, "From France you get silk stockings. From Russia, your returned lovers?"

She spit back. "You're wrong. They are not unloading any of my lovers. Those trains are just painted to look like that to discourage the British from dropping bombs on the Potsdamer Station!"

The image of the hospital trains going and coming in the smoky night stayed with her. Deep down, the war meant little to her until that confrontation. The thought of Major Hurst injured would not go away. It nibbled at the edge of her thoughts.

Reinhard Hurst, her fiancé, was a man so sure of himself, no bullet would dare hit him. His letters from the eastern front assured her he would be home on leave in early April to complete preparations for their marriage on April twentieth. The engagement party was coming up in December; he would no doubt have to ask to be excused and begged her understanding if he had to put country first.

In his last letter, he said he was sending rabbits and geese as well as liquor for the Laudier punch for the engagement party. He said he might also have a surprise for her on her birthday.

The news in the paper today was that a Russian town named Rostov on the mouth of the Don River was being evacuated because of their inhospitable attitude. Were Rostov rabbits and geese now enroute? Why should she concern herself about such minute details? Never before had she bothered. Her life was too full. She came and went according to her whim, which suddenly was more cautious as she ventured out of Berlin due to the increasing number of planes overhead. Just before she left Berlin, servants had come to her mother with the latest instructions. They must carry sand to the attic and have many shovels on hand for any fires which might occur.

Again, she felt thankful for this gathering place, this oasis of pleasure. This SS house of Himmler's was a true joy. She could throw considerations about rightness and wrongness of the cause to one side. There was no question in her mind. Germans needed territory. Germany would win.

However, she did notice the war edging closer.

Gun towers had been built to cover up whole streets. Vast canopies of wire netting and strips of green gauze were placed to make the thoroughfares indistinguishable from trees alongside. Lamp posts were wrapped with green gauze. Monuments with shiny gold angels were painted over so they wouldn't reflect light.

They'd even covered over the big lake in West Berlin. A grey netting was put across so it would like a roadway. But the first winds of winter had ripped holes in the netting and blown the false trees from the lampposts into the tree branches on the thoroughfares. As she left Berlin, she noticed it was all being redone again.

Why was Berlin arming itself? It seemed beyond necessity. But, then she thought, it's all for the sake of keeping up the morale of the people. That was it, of course.

As she maneuvered the big Mercedes past long lines of armored vehicles on the wide Autobahn, she rejoiced that her family had plenty of Berzieheingen, good relations with party big shots. They could still get any item or service they wanted and they were adding to, not subtracting from, their possessions.

Her mother recently had come across a lovely carved antique side table. The shop keeper was on the lookout for matching pieces for their front parlor. Of course, when she was married, they would furnish with antiques and there were plenty available now at little cost.

Why shouldn't they be doing well? After all, hadn't her father, the banker, helped the old families grow rich again producing ammunition and chemicals.

She was unshockable. She had never been one tiny bit innocent past the age of twelve in any area of life.

Tomorrow was her twenty-fifth birthday. Peter promised if she came, he would throw a party of such magnificence that even she might be impressed. She had been intrigued enough to hasten back.

What delights did he have up his magician's sleeve? Her deep-throated laugh harmonized with the half-hour musical notes of the tall clock by the fireplace.

Someone was coming toward her from the end of the hallway.

"Begging your pardon, Fraulein. We have been expecting you for several hours and thought you had given up and were coming tomorrow." The maid, Gerda, curtseyed, the white tails of her apron flew up over the black dress like a bird's tail feathers.

"Never mind. Where is everyone?"

"On the third floor, I believe, watching the American movie, *Gone With the Wind*."

"Anyone in my room?"

"Of course not, Fraulein. The old one should have your trunks up there now. You can tell me where you want things put." The black iron elevator with golden eagles and swastikas slowly came to a halt on the second floor. The women got out and as they neared the corner bedroom on the second floor, they saw the old man pushing a large trunk through the door. Even from twenty feet away, he stank. A heavy stench of acrid sweat surrounded his slight form. He grunted and left when he saw them coming.

Greta maneuvered past the trunk and went into the room. She pushed open the burgundy velvet drapes covering the large windows at both corners, creaked open the windows and released the shutters. She pushed the trunk into the room.

Cool fresh air, with a slight feel of moisture from the light rain, wafted into the spacious room.

Ellen handed a tiny gold trunk key to the maid who opened one of the trunks and began hanging garments behind doors of a huge armoire.

Ellen leaned back upon a burgundy chaise lounge at the end of the huge, wood-carved bed, and stroked the silver ring with the large diamond eyes. "Gerda, tell me about *Gone With the Wind*."

"A beautiful lady—in a time of one of the American wars . . . I took up a tea tray and couldn't help but watch just a little of it. She is at a dance, dressed in black. Lost her husband, is my guess. She wants to dance. I guess she can't because she is in mourning." Gerda spoke with hesitation between phrases, a habit which annoyed those trying to follow her conversation. She'd say a word, the listener would strain until Gerda would to say another.

'War can be horrible—for others, never me.'

"Fraulein, the ladies were saying during the break as I was pouring their tea, they were saying that the movie is about a way of life that is passing. That's what the title means." Ellen knew the maid was puzzled and wanted her to explain.

'Why bother. What difference will it make?' As for a way of life passing—life is such fantasy. What cinematographer could capture even a day of life and get the true essence. Even the female Hitler had commissioned to produce the film everyone was watching, 'Triumph of the Will', showed emotion-provoking scenes, but, she could have done more. I am a skeptic. Nothing ever meets my standards, or hardly ever.

'The Third Reich will go on for a thousand years and I am here to relish it. Tomorrow is my day.'

Ellen took in the busy maid's petite form as she flitted between armoire and trunks. *'She might be pretty if she knew what to do about that frizzy hair. And, if she knew how to move and speak with less of those halting phrases. How can a man stand to be around her?'*

Breeding and class status were so apparent. She could look at someone and know intuitively their station. Even clothing could not disguise a person's background. The maid knows nothing of culture, the arts, entertainers, or music. She has to grub day to day just to survive.

Interests, grace of bearing, the feel for the arts all come

down to you from people who, through the years, have honed themselves. It was charm that counted. Charm. The better a person's grasp of manners, the higher their station and the more charming they were.

'If someone, and I know instantly, doesn't match up to my station in life, they drop from my consideration.'

Ellen's vivaciousness, beauty and family connections drew a wide collection of admirers. She felt there were many layers to friendship, each revealing more of a person's secrets. Peter was the penultimate friend. She wanted to tell him everything. Major Hurst was not as privy to her innermost thoughts as Peter. Reinhard did not understand some of her thoughts and feelings. He tried. He had different ways of viewing the same situation. In some of their recent heated discussions, he always put his way first. On most points, they were in agreement. However, this disagreement over her not wanting children was becoming a real problem. He could not accept the fact that having children around would be so . . . stifling.

Ellen glanced at the tiny, gold watch on a chain about her neck. "I'm starving. I would like a little tea."

Gerda was stroking the pink satin of a dressing gown with ivory lace, satin rosebuds and delicate ribbons. She looked perplexed by Ellen's request. Her eyes were vacant. She was lost in the pleasure of stroking the delicate garment.

"Finish up here, Gerda. I need to move a bit. I've been sitting too much. I'll go to the kitchen myself." Before she left, Ellen held out her hand to retrieve the little golden key and replaced it on the chain about her neck. This would give her the chance to see the kitchen.

In the kitchen, her deep voice startled the village girl who was putting up tea dishes in the cupboard. A teacup fell from her hands and shattered.

Words flew out of Magda's mouth. "Who are you?" She recognized it was not her place to ask and capped her hand over her mouth. She had spoken to an honored guest without being addressed first. "Begging your pardon, Fräulein."

"Fetch a tray with tea and a little snack and I might ignore your impudence."

"Of course, Fräulein . . . in front of the fire in the front drawing room?"

Ellen nodded and looked over the clean and orderly kitchen. "Did you do all this . . .?

"If you mean, get things to rights again, no, it was Hannah."

"And, who is Hannah? Where is the person who created this miracle?" Ellen eyes glanced about the area.

"Fraulein, she out collecting greens for the night's centerpiece. Magda's foot maneuvered pieces of the tea cup together on the floor, trying to hide them.

"When she returns, tell her Ellen Laudier would like to see her in the drawing room."

Magda put the kettle on. When Antoinette came into the kitchen Magda told her that Ellen wanted to see her.

"Whatever does she want? Did she say?"Antoinette saw the girl seemed frightened.

"What happened, Magda?"

"Oh, Hannah, I broke a teacup when she came into the kitchen. She is going to make something terrible happen to me."

"Peter would never allow it. You know that, Magda. They have told you how much you have helped them continue their elegant ways. Do not be concerned. Just get her tea things ready. I must get myself tidied up and go see what she wants." Antoinette knew who Ellen Laudier was, but did Ellen know who she was?

How will I feel when I meet the woman who is to marry the father of my child? Will I be able to disguise my disgust of him? Does she know I am here? What has he told her?

Chapter Sixteen

Antoinette hid beside the large clock beside the fireplace and studied Ellen who basked in one of the cushioned, high-backed chairs before the fire. She presented a lovely picture.

She still wore the sweater with the many buttons which took its color from one of the many flowers in the skirt. Glints from the fire reflected in her shoulder-length, golden hair. Antoinette admired the straight, small nose, the deep-set eyes, the high cheek bones. Ellen was exactly how she had envisioned she would be from Major Hurst's photo of her.

So curious was Antoinette about meeting Ellen, the female counterpart to the woman Himmler referred to in his speech—the ideal of the Third Reich—she felt almost eager, in fact wanted to rush over to her, to hear what Ellen's voice would sound like, to discover what she would say.

Perversely, Antoinette felt, for just a fleeting instant, we are connected. Haven't we both been loved by the same man? I am no longer under his spell. Yet, I know that the woman I am about to meet, isn't either.

Ellen, in repose before the fire, the tea cart nearby with the exquisite china and silver, made such a favorable impression of assurance and completeness, that Antoinette walked slowly to her, full of expectation and exhilaration.

"Fraulein Laudier, you asked to see me?" she said in a voice clear and confident.

Ellen turned her head. "You must be Hannah. Please sit a minute," and indicated then adjacent chair.

Antoinette continued to feel at ease. She felt as if this meeting had taken place before, it flowed so naturally. It was the same strong feeling that she had when she first met Major Hurst.

"Hannah," said Ellen in a tone of respect, in a way she would speak to one of the women in her inner sanctum, "You are extraordinary."

Antoinette tried not to appear overeager to hear Ellen's explanation. She straightened her shoulders to sit as regally as Ellen. However, to Ellen she presented a plain image, decked out in the Bund Madel white blouse, the black skirt, the black shoes with the white sox. The edges of the black tie about the blouse hung placidly which gave Ellen a clue that the girl was not nervous. She disliked jumpy people.

"I have just seen your remarkable ability to get back into order that colossal mess out there. I didn't think it could be done so quickly."

A relieved Antoinette broke in. "It was not pretty. It was as if the staff were uncommonly, if you permit . . . it was . . . Ellen's nodded in sync with Antoinette's assessment as Antoinette continued, "Trashy. Unprofessional. Almost disrespectful. Something happened which even intensified their already great mess.

"I prefer a place where food is created to be well organized. I believe that those who dine can tell immediately, perhaps without knowing why, the care and, yes, the love, which have gone—goes—into the preparation of a meal."

Ellen nodded.

"I like the little bits and collections which make up a kitchen to be in order as I proceed. Disasters and messes, to me, are as unlikely in a sacred place like a kitchen as they would be in a courtroom. Can you image mismarked exhibits, the judge's bench filled with debris, the lawyers and the witnesses having side conversations. At some point, a kitchen may look messy, but, not really for very long, just while the process of creation is going on. Both reverent places, of course, but, I ramble on too much."

"On the contrary. By the way, is that the Bund Maden uniform you wear?"

"It is. It is what I wear every day."

"Can't you wear anything else but that skirt and blouse?" Ellen was appalled by the thought of putting on the same style garments everyday.

"It's the uniform of the Lebensborn. Soon there will be a change because I will be wearing the navy jumper, but until then, maybe another month, this is it." Antoinette ran her hands over the skirt and blouse.

"You're having a baby?"

"In April, perhaps on the very day as the Führer's. She cringed, thinking she might have been too enthusiastic.

"You want the child?" queried Ellen.

"Very much."

"Why?" Ellen bent towards Antoinette. Her eyes met Antoinettes'. "The truth, tell me the truth. Are you happy to be having a child? Giving birth to me would be impossible."

"Is it the pain you fear? Most say that one forgets."

Antoinette wanted to speak from the heart. "I want a child so it can walk in the footsteps of the wonderful people who gone before me. We all die. I heard someone say that life is a journey that concludes with death. I want someone to live after me who will remember even briefly who I was."

Before Ellen could reply, the mansion filled with noise of people pouring out of the elevator and others clamoring down the stairs and coming toward the drawing room.

Antoinette rose quickly. "I must go. The evening meal is soon. Until I see you then, goodbye." She reached over to shake the hand extended by Ellen and caught the fragrance of her perfume, a scent of wild flowers in a sunlit meadow.

Ellen smiled and thought, *Reinhard has better taste than I thought.*

Chapter Seventeen

Near midnight Peter came into the kitchen commanding Antoinette to follow him. "Ellen wants you," was all he would say. He was in a hurry and she had to almost run to keep up with his long strides.

Now, she was in the front drawing room by the piano, surrounded by men and women, some older, a few, younger. Several had the unmistakable sheen of old money. From several, she sensed a hint of primeval excitement rising, similar to that people exhibit before a 'hunt' begins.

At the edge of the gathered crowd an older gentleman bore the easy pose of power and success. Of course, that must be Wolf, Clara's Colonel. Clara must be here, too. Antoinette had not seen her since the day of the Naming Ceremony.

Next to Antoinette squeezed in Gesa who was trying to get a better look at Peter. Gesa crunched her hands together. Faint stains from the ink were still there.

Peter leapt to the top of the piano. He pushed his hands down to gain attention of the group.

"There. That's better. Thank you," he exclaimed. "We are gathered together at this most wonderful time to honor a very dear lady. You all know of whom I speak."

Heads turned towards Ellen. She stood in the center of a group. A slim, black wool garment of full length draped her body, diamonds glittering on bracelets and dangling earrings.

"I've enticed this lovely lady back here with a promise to give her a birthday party of such unforgettable nature, that it will go down in all our memories as the most wonderful of all parties. What do you say to that?"

The crowd let out a cheer of tremendous force and agreement.

"Make way for our lady, Ellen."

Officers and their women thrust Ellen forward. Eager male hands lifted her onto the piano with Peter, who said, "Hand up that chair." He bowed magnificently before Ellen, then asked her to sit upon the straight-back, plain chair.

Ellen's eyes glistened. She awaited Peter's command. Stillness fell over the room. The people were spellbound by Peter, the Master Magician and Illusionist.

His voice was soft and melodious. Warmth radiated from his wide smile. "Unto you, we pledge an evening of splendor." He whispered to her, "Do you trust me?"

Ellen looked deeply into Peter's searching eyes, could only nod her head, so filled was she with emotion.

Everyone held their breath in expectation.

A gasp broke the stillness. Ellen and the chair slowly began to rise, then slowly return to the piano top. Spontaneous cheering erupted. The room grew quiet again.

"Turn off the lights," said Peter. In a few seconds, he snapped his fingers and when the lights came back on, he and Ellen were surrounded by piles of boxes wrapped in gold.

The crowd roared with delight.

Peter took a small box from the top of a stack, ripped off the gold paper, tore it open, looked inside, glanced at his appreciative audience, then placed a hand into the box.

Agony of suspense gripped the viewers. "Oh, Peter," cried a woman's voice. Whispers came from little clusters of people. "Whatever is he up to?"

"I can see this is going to be quite the event," said a male voice.

"I'm thrilled to be here," said another woman.

"Ladies and Gentlemen" continued Peter. "Let us return to another era of glory—the time of Anthony," and when he said, "Cleopatra," he removed his hand from the box and lifted into view a black Egyptian wig trimmed in gold and placed it upon Ellen's head. A huge asp adorned the top.

Again, he asked the that the lights be extinguished.

When they came on again, faces of the audience were as enchanted as Ellen's.

In the time the lights were out, Ellen *had indeed become Cleopatra.* A slinky, white silk fabric with tiny pleats fell from one shoulder, to bare one peach-shaped breast to view. It was a costume as authentic to that period as if it had been showcased in a museum.

"With the help of Gesa—let everyone see where you are, Gesa," the crowd parted so Gesa could be seen, "all women will be part of Cleopatra's royal court. Lovely exquisite garments are here in these . . ." and his hand sweep over the boxes which filled the top of the piano.

"Gesa is trained in the art of theatrical makeup and will help each of you women be transformed into a woman of ancient Egypt. So, disappear ladies—up those stairs to a corner of the ballroom which has been set up as a splendid costume shop. We gentlemen will await your royal procession back to us, say, in two hours . . ."

"Ah, but Our Cleopatra must choose whether to join you ladies or to reign over us while she awaits your return. Which will it be, Our Royal Great One? Your Anthony requests a reply to his eager question.

"Peter," Ellen laughed with glee, "you are wicked. A nasty choice. But, I choose . . ." She paused. The crowd waited, filled with unrealized tension. "I will be among the women of my royal court."

The women in the audience, swept up in the excitement, threw their arms about the boxes, rushed to the stairs, and scrambled for the third floor. Ellen led the way. Gesa and Antoinette brought up the rear.

Ellen was so pleased with the elaborate preparations that she decided to magnanimously be cordial to all the women and to be agreeable to everything Peter planned.

Chapter Eighteen

The exterior and grounds of the SS house were forbidding; whereas, the house within had the atmosphere of a relaxed home. There were the daily parties, the lavish meals, a lot of conversation and music of all sorts, a gradual drift up the stairs for those who chose to go.

No expectation was put upon anyone. Most guests stayed with a regular partner, but many were there to enjoy a discreet intimacy with the opposite sex. Some felt stimulated just watching other couples.

Guests were as independent as the weather and as sexual as their appetites. They might be charismatic, tender, or playful, or their conversations probing due to the high level of intelligence of the officers and their invited guests. Topics ranged from their extensive travels, prior professions, or exotic experiences.

Someone might make a joke about a military objective, a high-ranking official, or a new program, but that person was the exception and once the offensive comment was made, they would feel uncomfortable enough not to continue. This was a house off-limits to war.

A guest was immediately accepted into the group. There were few disagreements, or incidents to disturb the tranquility and languid mood of the house.

Some guests came, passed through with beneficial unwinding experiences, then left refreshed. All seemed to get positive strokes from the collective group and its mellow activities. A guest could chose to participate or not. It was all so easy.

One of the officers was acknowledged officer-of-the-house and would spend a few days of their stay more-or-less leading the activities and attending needs of the house and its guests. Peter had such grand ideas that when he was there, he was pressed into filling the role of chief host.

Coded personnel files of officers and reports of each guest's background were locked in a wood file cabinet in the corner of a secured room on the second floor. Only the chief host had access to the room. Guests would wonder as they passed the room with grey door with its ornate oak leaf what was inside. They knew there was a phone inside because they could hear it ring. Was it a direct line to Waffen SS headquarters?

Every week a large truck pulled up to the gates with food, booze and other items the chief host requested from Himmler's SS headquarters. Servants would come with carts to take the contents into the house.

Earlier that evening, Peter had offered Gesa a unique reward if she would use her talents to do the makeup for the women. A casual remark from Clara had called Peter's attention to her theatrical background.

He wouldn't tell her what the reward would be until she said yes, so, of course, she agreed. Peter showed her the treasure. It was a dagger in a fine grain black leather covered scabbard. The blade was etched with "Meine Ehre Heisst Treue" on one side and Himmler's motto on the other.

Gesa and Antoinette neared the third floor and could hear shrieks of joy coming from the end of the ballroom. Behind those heavy-louvered screens, Gesa knew there was a makeup case.

Antoinette felt a wave of wonder when she saw the women tossing out contents of the boxes and throwing items to each other. Several guests paraded before the large wall-to-wall mirrors on two sides.

Ellen went to a high-backed chair, one of several scattered throughout the room, many now overflowing with clothing.

Gesa spied the case and beckoned to Ellen. Clara saw Antoinette and rushed over to lead Antoinette to Ellen. "Ellen, dear," she laughed, "Here's someone you definitely *must* meet."

"Clara. Clara Blocksdorff," Ellen cried as she embraced Clara. "I haven't seen you for an age. Your mother told mine that you'd gone off somewhere . . ."

Antoinette debated whether to break away from these two long-time acquaintances.

"Ellen," continued Clara, "Do you know who this is?"

"Of course. We met earlier this afternoon. I think Hannah is so extraordinary that I must convince her to come back to Berlin with me." Ellen looked to Antoinette.

Antoinette was thinking, *'Hummm. That's interesting. Leaving here and going to Berlin. Might just be. . .'*

Clara found Ellen's invitation to Antoinette distasteful and made a sour face.

"Ellen, please, please. I'm ready for you," Gesa called.

Two women came up to Clara and pranced before her. Ellen said to one of the them, whom Antoinette had not seen before, a brunette with buxom hips and a warm smile, "Trudy, I'd like you and Hannah to be my number one hand maidens. Won't you please look for matching garments and have Gesa make you up soon as possible. We must join the gentlemen. We can't leave the dear men alone, too long, can we?"

Someone shouted, "Men. Aren't they like fires—go out if left unattended?" Gleeful laughter filled the area.

Gesa filled a tiny brush with the bright royal blue powder she called lapislazuli, and asked Ellen, "What do you think love is? It's different for men than women, don't you think."

"But, of course. To men, having sex is just being a man. They fall in love when they make a commitment," returned Ellen.

Trudy had been listening and said, "That's it. When a man makes a commitment and says to himself that he is in love—

he is. Myself, I make commitments all the time." She giggled. "Being in love is so much fun."

"What do you think love is, Hannah?" Antoinette was nearby applying nail polish to Trudy's fingers, painting red on the outside of the nails and blue in the center as Gesa had instructed.

"Love is the glue that holds a man and a woman together," she answered as she focused on making neat paths on Trudy's long nails. She did not look up.

Gesa finished putting the blue powder over Ellen's eyes and was drawing the huge lines under and above her eyes up to the heavy black wig with a heavy Kohl pencil. The huge golden circlet on the wig bounced and the asp looked menacing as Ellen moved her head with Gesa's pencil work.

The women paraded about in the ivory or white silky, pleated Egyptian garments made of see-through fabrics and heavy wig headdresses bound with gold. Heavy jeweled necklaces graced their necks and golden sandals their feet. They traded heavy earrings with long, jewels back and forth.

They paired up to work on each others' nails while awaiting their turn before Gesa.

Ellen wanted lipstick, but Gesa said, "No lipstick— eyebrows either. See, I must wax yours over."

Vibrant sounds of the men who were singing floated up from downstairs.

Trudy said, "I love it when they drink beer from steins and sing. The power of their voices if magnificent."

From a way off Clara said, "Wolf doesn't drink beer out of a stein. He sips sherry. "

Antoinette concentrated on the fine lines she was making on Trudy's nails. Her mind was busy thinking about the man she had hidden in the cellar in the Lebensborn. Who was he? He was English, of course. But, why was he in Germany? He is probably wondering about me, too.

Ellen prodded Hannah with the golden sepulcher she had just been handed. "What do you mean, Hannah, when you say love is like glue?"

"When things aren't going well between a man and woman, it's love that keeps them together."

Clara said from a distance, "Love has no strings. You don't have to do anything. You just know when it's love. At least that's what Wolf says."

Antoinette asked cautiously, "What about Peter? Who does he love?"

Ellen laughed. "Every woman who meets Peter asks that question. He has a wife back home and two or three children. Are you disappointed?"

Antoinette shook her head.

"Love. Men are hungry for conquest, power, achievement. A woman wants to be held, comforted, hear words of love," emphasized Ellen. "I want it all. I want what a woman wants. I want the same things a man does, too."

Clara said, "Ellen, you do have it all. All the men love you. How do you do it?"

"As a woman you don't have to say much, just let them talk."

Trudy looked up and said, "Every time I tell a man that I want to hear his point of view and I take time to really listen to what he's saying, he falls in love with me and what he does with me is extremely wonderful." Trudy's face bore a seductive smile.

Clara marched over to them. "Love to me is . . . someone who loves me just as I am."

"Ah, not the men I know," proclaimed Ellen. "For them, it's different. They want other things from me. They want me to be home all the time . . . have children . . . care for their homes and them. Why have children? Men are like children. They are all the children I need in my life. I tell Reinhard how smart he is, how brilliant. You won't believe how sexy he becomes.

"A women must know certain things that tempt a man—letting a man know she wants him—suggestively sitting without crossing the legs—tossing your hair behind your shoulder—peering sideways at him—taking his hand to the bedroom and throwing off one garment—but stopping and letting him take it from there . ."

"Oh, Ellen," sighed Clara, "I can learn so much from you."

Ellen continued. "Lovemaking is an art. When we're young we practice with our dolls, but men aren't dolls. They have their own thoughts which are far different than ours. Did you know that a man doesn't know what he wants and we have to tell him. Oh, they have emotions but don't know how to explain what they feel. We do. We talk about what we want and need constantly. They never do. It is not man-like. They must always look powerful. Sometimes they feel like little boys but can't say so. Men like to talk to me because I can make them feel powerful. I lay naked on the fur rug in front of the fire—I'm wild in bed . . . I wear the clothes that make him want to touch me all over. Or, I wear just part of a garment and that, too, drives a man crazy.

"A new man to me is a lovely tree full of fruit. I want to taste him, see his fruit. But, then the leaves begin to fall when he wants things I don't want. One of us gets bruised. That's when you see the reality—the real person when what we wish doesn't coincide with what he does."

Trudy exclaimed, "That's why I quit seeing Hermann. He was wonderful in the beginning but was always saying things which hurt me. Once he said he could not sleep next to me because my body had so much heat coming off when I'm asleep. What can I do about something like that?"

"Maybe it was just the sex he wanted," said Ellen. "Was there anything deeper between you?"

Ellen rushed on. "A woman must tell a man he is the best you've ever been in bed with. Listen for the things he feels are important and tell him how proud you are of those. One of the most important is his male organ. Tell him how wonderful that is and he will see you as warm and understanding and infinitely desirable.

"Most men will be unfaithful. We are at war. These are not normal times. There are so many obliging females. Maybe he has just been amazing and brave in battle, won a medal, wants to celebrate with a woman. He may be worrying about going into action, or the next phase of action. A man has much different things to face than we do. But, this is too dismal. Let's discuss more exciting things, Trudy, name three things your lover likes to do when you make love?"

Antoinette froze. She felt sexually naive.

Clara asked impatiently, "How can I find out?"

"You ask questions. 'Do you like this better than this? Does this feel good? How does this feel? Ask 'yes' or 'no' questions because it makes it easy for a man to answer."

"Feel good? How does this feel?" puzzled Clara.

Trudy said, "Ellen means things like positions, places you put your hands on them, how hard you press. Isn't that so, Ellen?"

Ellen laughed. "Making love does not come naturally. Trudy is right. You need the right strokes. If you don't know, ask a man innocently, 'Oh, please show me how,' and you'll end up having a wonderful time.

"The big difference between a man and a woman is that he wants hands upon him that are strong and firm on his entire body, everywhere. We like a touch, light and longer, and just on our more delicate places."

The conversation of the women clustered near Ellen was building in sexual tension and excitement. In their costumes of antiquity, the women felt exceedingly beautiful. A glow of anticipation had arisen from their discussions of love.

Gerda came to Ellen and handed her a note folded like a bird in flight. The women wanted to continue their discussion and were disappointed by Gerda's interruption.

Ellen quickly unfolded the little bird, read the message inside, and announced, "Clara, Gesa and Hannah, come with me downstairs." To the others, she said, "Please come down together when Gerda is sent for you."

"Away we go, my beautiful Egyptian maidens. But, a drink before we go."

Gerda had also brought little golden goblets on a tray and from an exotic pitcher with Egyptian hierogliphs and etched in gold, she filled them.

Antoinette felt the thick, yellow fluid slide down her throat and within seconds, felt waves of uneasiness and became a bit of dizzy. However, she thought nothing more about the brief nausea; the few months of pregnancy had brought strange sensations ranging from nausea to fatigue to energetic highs.

Clara jostled Antoinette and gave her a dirty look. As they left the room, Clara cut over as if to go to the elevator. Ellen gave Clara a poke with the long sepulcher to steer her towards the stairs. The regal procession began going down the steps.

Ellen glowed with a feeling of power, but in the role of Cleopatra her sensations of majesty were magnified.

"We must chant," she related gaily to the women in gauze trailing behind. "Let's try singing this—Anth–tho–ney." She sang it out and was soon joined by the others. The chanting resonated within their bodies like another hypnotic aphrodisiac.

They neared the front drawing room and heard the men singing. Ellen beckoned for them to be quiet. They heard:

"When I get home, I'm going to build a house!"
Chorus: BOOOO!!!
"A Whore House!"
Chorus: HOOORAY?!"

"No women!"
Chorus: BOOOO!
"Just 18-year-old girls."
Chorus: HOORRAYYY!
"Going to fence it in."
Chorus: BOOOOOO."
"A fence three inches high."
Chorus: Hoorraayyy!!

The men stood about in front of the fire or were lounging in the chairs. Ellen came into the drawing room and paraded the women about the admiring officers. Without words, these women were objects of beauty and pleasure. They paraded with shoulders held back and heads held high.

The men admired the slender bodies weaving about them in the see-through gowns. The men cheered. Ellen stopped beside Peter.

She spoke. "So, only 18-year-olds?"

"You just heard the first verse," he laughed. "Wait until you hear the second. We composed it especially for your twenty-fifth birthday!"

There was much laughter. In the soft glow of the fire and the subdued lighting, the women seemed exceptionally enchanting, exotic beings.

Peter spoke to the women: "How lovely, lovely you are." The officers cheered. His warm smile enchanted the women.

"Are you ready, Ellen, for the second verse?"

They sang:

"When Cleopatra asks for me tonight"
Chorus: HOORRAAY!
"She can't love you."
Chorus: BOOOO!
"Just the Three she chooses."

Chorus: HOORRAAY!
"It's me. It's me. . . . Not him. . . ."
Chorus: BOOOO.

Peter whispered to Ellen, "Only three, my dear. There are four."

Ellen went to Gesa. "Peter reminds me. I should not have taken you away from your work upstairs. Return to the ladies. Soon you can come back down with the others."

Ellen smiled. The men watched appreciatively as the tall brunette, Gesa, glided out of the room.

Peter then commanded their attention. "Ladies and Gentlemen. It is time for our contest, an event, heretofore, after this night to be remembered as 'Cleo's Contest.'

"Gentlemen—if you haven't already, find a comfortable place to sit. Ladies, you see, while you were dressing, we choose the officers who would compete in 'Cleo's Contest.' And, now, here come the props."

Two officers carried into the room a large plain table made of wood on which were piled several logs. They solemnly set the table in front of the fire. One of the officers laid two of the logs upon the bed of coals while the other officer stacked the remaining logs beside the opening. The blaze kindled.

"To be a man," continued Peter, "Is not all swagger, boasting, swearing, or mountain climbing. To be a male is also to be tender, gentle, considerate. So, our contest is most unique in that those male characteristics will be those which make points.

"You men think you can decide who is a man, but only a woman really knows. These loveliest of the creatures will be the judge. Life's beauty is to be expressed for us.

"Ladies," he said, his smile lighting up the room, "Trust that you will experience joys unknown before; you will reach plateaus never before reached; discover emotions never touched.

"No woman will achieve what you will tonight. No man will ever see again what takes place here. No woman will ever feel as you. Take the gift we bring you. Fill as vessels drop by drop with the honey of their gift. Feel the glory."

He was so profound. Antoinette tried to understand, then grew lost in what he was saying. She found she had no desire to make plans for the future, to be concerned about the strange man hiding in the potato bin next door, or to feel anything except be lost in the moment.

Clara's friend, Wolf, came to Peter and whipped three long pieces of cloth out of the inside of his silver jacket. They were silken scarves of a light gray color.

The scarves slid through Peter's fingers, joined up, sped about, turned red in color and were tied together, then magically came apart as Peter covered the eyes of each woman with a red scarf.

Someone was playing the piano in the next room. Classical music, perhaps Liszt.

Antoinette felt herself being lifted and sat upon the table. The grain of the wood beneath the gauze fabric of the gown was not exactly smooth and little bits of the fabric got caught by a sliver or two of the wood. She became one with the beautiful music.

"I have one more thing to add, before we begin. Ellen," Peter said sternly, "There may one part of you that is twenty-five, but, another, you'll discover is only twenty, and, yet another has not yet been born. We in this room are not afraid to die. Nor, for that matter are you. You must not be afraid to live. Life is for living. Experience everything. Don't be concerned about what is to take place. Go as far as you can, and then, when you are there, go farther."

It seemed so mysterious. Currents of an electrical quality buzzed about the room. While Antoinette waited primly for what was to take place, she recalled that this was the same dream-like circumstance she had experienced the first night she had been with Major Hurst. There were many nights with Hurst but she could recall only the passion and allure of the first.

Ellen wanted her to go to Berlin. There was attraction to Ellen's world. What was Ellen's reason? If going to Berlin meant seeing Hurst again, she wouldn't do it. She was through with him.

What was this contest all about? What were the rules?

Antoinette thought she was sitting at one end of the table, that Ellen was in the middle, and Clara at the other end. She was tempted, so tempted to pull down the scarf from her eyes. She heard noise of chairs scraping along the wood floor. Her heart began to beat fast.

She sensed someone in front of her, perhaps seated in a chair. She stained to hear the music. Fingers began caressing her toes, ever so gently, without attempting to tickle, touching softly, then increasing the tempo, releasing the touch. One by one, each toe explored; the edges of the sole manipulated with pressure, massaged.

Antoinette tried imagining who doing this to her. Which officer was it? Were the others watching or had they left the room? She did not know. She thought she could hear breathing. She heard the clock ticking.

Without words through touch, he seemed to know what she was feeling. His touch felt wonderful.

After each foot, a hand slowly slid up one leg to the thigh and down the other side of it, the touch bringing satisfaction to the skin so powerful the other leg cried out for the same.

A dreamlike state came over her. She no longer heard the clock ticking.

The dream-like state was interrupted by Ellen's laugh, a male voice from afar which said, "A point lost."

The creative hand began its journey again, exploring the other foot, the toes, the leg, the thigh. The touch was light, intoxicating.

She felt a bit drowsy. A fragrance of the aftershave he wore floated up, just enough musk to be sultry, not cloying.

A hand was on each leg, velvet, yet rough, the strokes coming higher, pushing the gown into her lap.

The hand ventured further, into the crevices between her thigh, near the parts of her anatomy which were ablaze with desire.

She felt consumed by intense desire.

A hand cupped her right breast, contained it all, a whisper of unspoken enchantment by the creative artist. Both hands glided to the taut nipples. She had a crazy feeling.

Her insides throbbed. The nipples grew tall against the filmy fabric.

She felt connected to the artist, overwhelmed by his tenderness.

The fingers began another dance, frisking in the hairs of her womanly masterpiece. Fingers reached inside flirting and tantalizing.

She groaned, intoxicated with ecstasy and no longer cared to remove the scarf. The languid feelings were now all that mattered.

The hands now were holding a foot and showering it with kisses. The kisses started up the leg, soon creating unbelievable varieties of pleasure.

The steamy contest was interrupted by loud noises in the room.

BRRR–ittt . . . BRRR–ittt . . . BRRR–ittt . . .

The room felt as if it had exploded. Had a bomb fallen?

She snatched the scarf from her eyes and looked into those of Major Hurst.

"No," she cried out.

Then things happened. Lieutenant Von Benner snatched her from the table and began running down the hall carrying her. Officers and women were running down the hall, some being carried over shoulders, others frantic in their haste to leave the house.

She saw Ellen and Major Hurst heading to the elevator.

The crowd rushed through the kitchen and out the door. A stream of people ran into the drizzle of the night toward a lantern being swung back and forth.

Young lads in Hitler Youth uniforms pumped huge levers up and down of pipes going into the hillside.

There was an opening in the hillside, something she had never noticed before. She had walked directly in front of the opening and had never seen it.

Lieutenant Von Benner ran with her into the cave-like bunker had a low, musky smell. It was cold and damp. He saw blankets piled in a corner, and pulled one off to throw over her. She huddled next to him on a low bench along the grey, concrete wall.

Was it an air raid? If it were, it would mean another means of escape, for who in the midst of such confusion would look for her?

Suddenly a realization came. Difficult as it might be, she realized she respected people with money so much that she deferred to Hurst simply because he was rich in background, manners, class, and, of course, to his appearance in the uniform. With Ellen, she had felt the same.

Her mind was a jumble, her breathing anxious. One voice inside seemed to pled—'Go. Go with Ellen. See more of that life. Think of how good it might be for the baby. You owe it to the baby to accept Ellen's offer.'

At the same time, the another voice shouted, 'How could you? Face up to the past. Pleasure is deceptive, the devil's tool. Clear your name. What would your father and mother think if you became more and more swallowed up by the Third Reich? What would Jacques say? He'd say you were selling yourself, *again*. One mistake, perhaps. The second, no.

Was Ellen the devil, like Hurst? What was right?

In her mind she saw Ellen and the Major. She knew with the utmost clarity what she had to do. She felt indescribable joy.

Lt. Von Benner put his arm about her. "Don't worry," he said quietly, "This is just a practice alert. I'll be hearing the real thing soon enough though," and sighed.

She buried her head in his shoulder.

He continued to speak quietly to her above the racket of conversations going on about them.

There seemed something he wanted to say. She was so tired.

"I was on a train coming here when a strange officer came into my compartment. He was amiable and polite and told me he was on his way back from Latvia. We talked about sports, weather, everyday things. Until, he told me he helped shoot Jews somewhere in the Baltic, more than three thousand. That they had to first dig their own grave as big as a soccer field.

"I asked stupid questions like, 'Is what you say really true? Who led the operation?' It was true, he said, anyone could check it. There were twelve men with machine pistols and one machine gun. All very official.

"This just does not fit into the picture of me, of my country, of the war. So, I asked if I could check his identification. I wanted to report him . . . to someone. I told one of the officers here and he said, 'Son,' just as if he were my father. 'Forget the incident. It never happened.'

"Either what he told me is true, and in that case I can't wear this uniform any longer, or he was lying, in which he shouldn't wear the uniform any longer."

"Lieutenant," she said softly, "my father told me of similar injustices from his experience in the first world war. He told me the same thing I tell you, *survive*. Just hope you are never in such a compromising position. I wish you well as you go into battle. I know there will be peace in the world someday. I certainly hope that with all my heart for this child I carry."

The alert over, after she had changed back into her uniform, the Lieutenant walked her back to the Lebensborn, clicked his heels, took one of her hands in his and said, "Fraulein, it has been an unforgettable pleasure."

Chapter Nineteen

Doktor Krause was enraged, his anger fueled by the passing hours. In the middle the night, he was awakened by the defense alarm and rushed to the bunker in the depths of the Lebensborn and discovered several expectant mothers missing. The directoress was absent, too.

No, they were not in their rooms, according to the terrified women who had checked all rooms according to policy and said that no one remained upstairs.

He sat up the rest of the night in the chair in his bedroom thinking about what would happen to him if the French woman were missing, or, the other ones, too, for that matter. *Security must be tightened*, he said over and over.

When morning came, he dressed hastily and rushed to his office to summon Frau Muckle. Where was she? His heart could not stand this pressure.

Frau Muckle came in, saluted and said, "You—you think you're so smart. How can I keep order when you countermand my orders?"

"Hah," he asked, "where were you last night?"

"If Herr Doktor would recall, I do have a life away from this place. If you looked at the official register, you would see that I was taking a day off. I just checked in. I do my job well and you know it." She muttered under her breath, "Better than you."

"I was shocked last night when I didn't see you or several of the women at the shelter," he said. "Fortunately, there were no planes, but the alert pointed out we have some problems."

She glared at him. "You gave them permission to be over there, what do you expect?"

"What I expect?—I expect the expectant mothers to be in bed and asleep by ten o'clock, getting a full eight hours rest. The alert last night occurred at one o'clock in the morning. We are both responsible to headquarters for the health of each one of those women. Have you made certain every woman is here now?"

"No, Herr Doktor, not yet." Frau Muckle then straightened her shoulders and said, "I'll go immediately."

"Send the French woman, that queen bee, Clara, and that little Gestapo lady, Gesa, here immediately." He waved her from his office.

Frau Muckle roughly awakened the three women and rushed them into their uniforms. They looked as if they had been up for days: their hair hung limp from the heaviness of the wigs they had worn; their eyes were puffy, and their complexions shallow.

By the look on the directoress' face, they knew they were in trouble. Frau Muckle wouldn't explain why Herr Doktor wanted to see them. There was no hope of sympathy from her. What did Herr Doktor know about what went on last night at the SS House?

The directoress hurried them downstairs. Outside his office, she knocked loudly.

"It's open," he said in a harsh voice. They came in and saw him sitting behind his big desk. He told Frau Muckle to leave. "I'll buzz you when I'm through with them."

The three women stood in front of his desk. His cheeks puffed up and swelled the scar on his face. Antoinette stifled a snicker. She looked at Clara whose face was ashen. Gesa was trembling.

"What do you have to say for yourselves?" He looked sternly at each woman.

After a few awkward moments, Clara said, "Herr Doktor, what is all about? Why has Frau Muckle snatched us from bed?"

"Yes," meekly put in Gesa, "What have we done?"

He pushed himself up from the desk chair, "Plenty, so much that I could send you all to a work camp, that's what."

"You wouldn't do that," Clara said. "Colonel Sentrop would not be happy." Clara's confident voice referring to the Doktor's superior officer brought sighs of relief from Gesa and Antoinette. Muscles in the doktor's face fought for control. Finally, he said, "We have a curfew at this Lebensborn and for good reason. I do not have to ask you why that is so. It is my responsibility to watch over you and I will. Beginning immediately, you are confined to your rooms."

"Just like that," Antoinette said, "but. . . "

"And, to whom little French girl now a German, would I need to be explaining?" Herr Doktor's voice was steely.

"Why, I have a responsibility over there. I've been doing what I've been asked." Antoinette was angry.

"For now, that is all. Remain in your rooms until further notice."

Gesa asked, "May I take a shower?"

"Is there a shower in your room?" he asked, with sarcasm.

"Understood, Herr Doktor." Gesa reply was tight, her voice constricted.

Herr Doktor buzzed for Frau Muckle.

Antoinette felt prospects for escape dwindling.

Chapter Twenty

The door to number seven slammed shut. A key turned in the lock.

"How dare he!" exclaimed Clara. "Did you hear him? He's treating us like prisoners in some work camp. He can't do that to me. Just wait until Wolf finds out. He'll get me out of here."

Antoinette sat on the edge of her bed and watched Clara march back and forth across the small room.

"You—you've got a way out, too. I heard Ellen say she'd take you to Berlin. Oh, just wait until Wolf hears. He won't stand for my being treated like this. Who does Herr Doktor think he is—ReischFührer Krause? He's hiding at this Lebensborn away from the war. In a month, I guarantee, he'll be up to his neck in snow."

A button burst from Clara's blouse and landed in front of Antoinette. Clara wrestled off the rest of the Lebensborn uniform and threw them into a heap and put on a nightgown.

"Nothing requires me to be here. There are other Lebensborn houses, other places I can go. I will be treated with the respect I deserve." Clara fumed and continued pacing. Antoinette sought refuge under the covers.

A knock was heard. The key turned.

"Colonel Sentrop here for you," Frau Muckle announced pleasantly, sticking her head into the room.

"Not a minute too soon," said Clara with glee. "Tell him I will be down immediately."

Chapter Twenty-One

Ellen came into Doktor Krause's office without knocking. The Doktor was reading papers in a folder as he sat wedged into one of the arm chairs. He looked up. *Who dare intrude in such a manner?*

"There you are," Ellen said. "I want words with you."

He thought twice before answering. The woman was obviously someone of wealth. The simple eloquence of the black suit, fur jacket and smart pillbox hat told volumes about her.

He rose and said in a cloying way, "Do me the honor?"

"No, I prefer to stand."

He took his time getting up and heading for his large desk; a barrier between him and the world. This afternoon, obviously to protect himself from this angry woman. Was she to become a resident? She seemed far too young to be one of the resident's mothers. What was she so angry about?

"I am so upset with you, I can't put into words the unladylike things that come to my mind. I told the ReischFührer I intended to see into the matter immediately." Ellen swatted her black leather gloves on the desk.

"To what are you referring?" he managed to get out. The woman's intimate referral to the ReischFührer was too familiar for comfort.

"I've heard of your ways here—things you do—liberties you take. You can be replaced—easily. There are many who'd— but that's not my point."

"Then, by all means, get to the point," he insisted.

"Peter told me you put them in their rooms like criminals. I told ReischFührer he must come back again unannounced to really look into this operation you're running. This was supposed to be the best, the most conducive environment for new mothers. But, this action of your, plus the others I've heard about, I want no part of this place for her any longer. She has to leave. I'm leaving for Berlin now—my car will be sent for her."

Ellen retrieved a silver cigarette case from the pocket of her jacket, choose a long cigarette, lit it with a tiny gold lighter, then blew smoke in his face.

"Tomorrow be certain she has all the necessary papers and is ready to leave this place."

He put a pudgy hand to his head, "You are not making yourself clear. Who is the person you want to leave?"

"Hannah Hurst—you know her. I see her file right there in front of you. I can just imagine all the gory details you've written. I might just have a look."

He pushed the folder into the top drawer.

"Her official paperwork is not back yet. You know as well as I do how long these things take," he said.

"Then, make some papers up. Make her into a Pole. I see them working everywhere in the fields. She'll be working at my home in Berlin. My Father, of course, is on the inside with ReischFührer. In a few weeks, ReischFührer Himmler will be a guest in our home—for the celebration of my engagement to the major."

Ellen took a long drag and blew a stream of smoke into his face.

"Whatever do you want with that woman from France?"

"None of your business, and neither is this visit of mine. Pretend I was never here. You will never dare mention anything about me or Hannah Hurst in any of your documents. It will be as if she never were here. After I leave, burn those documents in that folder of hers. Do you understand?"

Ellen crushed the cigarette into his prized antique wood desk.

"Tomorrow night, have Hannah packed and ready to leave, travel and ID papers and all. Expect my car around seven."

Ellen stared down at the Nazi doktor.

She turned. Before she closed the heavy door behind her, she stated clearly, "Release her from that room immediately. I want no further upsets for the mother of my child."

Herr Doktor instantly buzzed the ReischFührer's direct line and was told the ReischFührer was not accepting calls. Suddenly he felt the same nasty sensations that had come to him the first time he heard a mother-to-be was coming to the Lebensborn from France. Now that woman had put him in an awkward spot. Just in case, he had better get the new identity papers. Perhaps the ReischFührer had given his permission for Hannah to leave. He was responsible to Major Hurst for her well-being. This was all so difficult.

If he had known the problems inherent in a medical director's job at a Lebensborn, he might not have been so eager to take the position.

Chapter Twenty-Two

After Clara left, the third floor was unnaturally quiet. Although exhausted, Antoinette did not think of sleeping. She looked up and down the hall again. No one was on the floor and that was odd because it was free time and the women were usually in and out of each others rooms, the bathroom and common area.

An uneasy feeling came. She ran to the draped window, thrust open the drapes and shoved the shutters apart and reached over the ledge. Her left hand held to the sill while her right hand roved across the icy bricks to find the place where she had put the beret. Tips of her fingers touched the woolen material and carefully she tugged at the fabric and drew it to her. It was soggy but safe. She picked it up and held it to her cheek.

Her heart thumped. She could do so much now that there were no eyes to see. She scooped up the pile of dirty clothes from the floor and raced to the bathroom where she threw off the clothes she was wearing and began to wash them all. She showered and watched all the hot, sultry feelings of last night go down the drain and turned on cold water of resolve.

She returned to room seven to wait in the dark. A gleam of dull light from the hall came under the door.

A timid knock came.

The door opened into the darkness and she heard Fritz's familiar voice whisper, "I've brought you a tray of good food, just the thing."

"Oh, Fritz-LLLL, I'm so glad to see you. Just a minute and I'll turn on the light. Where is everyone?"

"Out. Cars came for all of them and they left. A reception for a big whig. But, oh, what's this I've heard about you?" Fritz had such sadness in his voice, she felt undeserving.

"You don't know. Didn't she tell you? Everyone knows but you?"

Fritz frowned.

"Didn't Frau Muckle tell you why I'm leaving?"

He said, "All the staff is talking about the rich woman who came today. No one ever upset the doktor like she did. Nurse Jutta heard the woman say that she was sending her car for you tomorrow night and that you had better be ready. So, you're leaving. Clara left. Everyone is leaving. If everyone goes, I won't be needed here anymore and then, what will I do?"

Fritz looked like a bent twig. His mustache quivered like a leaf. "Herr Doktor is so angry, we don't know what's going to happen to us. If there are no women left, there will be no job for old Fritz."

"Oh, Fritz, you're in trouble because we broke curfew." The twig bounced back. A breath of hope seemed to lift his spirits. He said, "Now, now, little mother, don't you go worrying, you've got happiness ahead. The rich lady can take care of you and you won't have to work so hard and it will be good for the baby."

"Oh, Fritz, Wolf came for Clara and I'm glad for her. She wants to be with him so much."

"The people here have not been good to you. No good for a future mother to be so sad. I am not happy to witness such things. The days we worked together were good, weren't they?"

Antoinette smiled.

"You will be happier away from this place. Herr Doktor will make it even more difficult as more women leave."

She asked, "What did Doktor Krause do? I know how nasty he can be. What did he do to you?" she asked again.

"He lined us up in the front hall—had a horse whip

behind his back—lashed us with his tongue first, then we had to turn our backs."

She cringed.

"He said, one more slip and we would be 'reassigned.' He smiled real big when he said 'reassigned.' And, we all know what that means. We are at war he said and reminded us we are all soldiers, even us on the home front. Every one is a soldier with our duty to the Führer."

"I know," she sighed, "it's very hard to be a soldier of any kind for the Führer. Oh, Fritz, if I am to go to Ellen's, I have nothing but this uniform to wear. What will I do? Frau Muckle and Herr Doktor hate me so much they'll never give me anything else to wear."

"Now, now, don't you go worrying. Fritz has lots of daughters, some your size. We'll find a nice outfit, a coat, some gloves and boots."

Her hand reached over the tray on the bed between them and she found his hand and squeezed it tightly.

"There, there, Hannah girl, eat and get some rest. Look forward to tomorrow and your new life."

"Oh, but a question before you go? Tell me again where all the others are? I can't seem to remember what you said?"

"All were invited to a big party in the next town, the whole works."

As soon as Fritz left, she put most of the cooked cabbage and potatoes, sausage, and bread into a large handkerchief and stuffed it all under the wet clothes in the washbowl. She had eaten a bit of the food Fritz brought but she wanted to save most of it for the English man.

She had to move quickly before the others returned. If she were caught out of the room, her reason would be that she was hanging up laundry in the room next to the potato bin.

Was he still there? Her plan depended upon an accomplice. They'd be looking for a single woman, not a couple. She clutched the washbowl and ran down the hall and down the steps and along the path to the dark cellar.

When she breathed the damp air of the cellar, she lit a candle. She passed the potato bin and threw the clothes over the line in the room next to the potato bin. There were no sounds coming from the bin.

"Are you still here?"

She shone the tiny candle about the bin but saw no one and a sinking feeling came over her. He must have gone. Distressed, she turned to go.

"Wait." It was the voice with the odd English accent. Some potatoes moved. She pointed the candle toward the voice.

"Thought you'd never come," he said, peeking over a heap of potatoes in a corner.

He looked to be in his early twenties, husky and broad-shouldered, dark hair, perhaps gray eyes. His cheeks were wide and when he smiled and parted his lips he was quite handsome. He had bushy eyebrows and his hair was parted nearly mid-center, locks falling across the forehead in two directions. His ears were big and held to the head, not flapping about. He had a short neck, a stout, stubby noise, and altogether presented a most pleasant appearance.

Antoinette spoke slowly. "I brought food. We leave tomorrow night. A car is coming for me. You must be wait outside and somehow sneak into the back seat. I'll convince the driver I must ride in the front seat. He'll believe me. Most pregnant woman get ill riding in the back."

She passed him the washbowl with the messy clump of food in the handkerchief.

"We'll get as close to Berlin as possible. I know of a place—a farm—in the North, near the Danish border, a haven. My friends in the Resistance say it is easier to cross the Danish border than Switzerland which is now turning back refugees."

She passed him a candle, matches, and another lump.

"I say, what's this?"

"It's my beret. Wear it if you like, otherwise, please just keep it for me. There's a map inside. Memorize it, then destroy it. If something happens before tomorrow night and we get separated, the map shows where to meet. Otherwise, when we leave the car, we'll still go separately and meet at the place indicated on the map.

"Wait outside tomorrow night. I'll distract the driver somehow. Get in back of the car. Just before Berlin, I'll find a reason to have the driver stop. Then, we'll both disappear."

She removed her watch and handed it to him. "It's dark outside now, late in the afternoon, about four o'clock. Hope you're feeling better. If you decide not to come withe me, that's okay, but, I hope you will. Be safe."

She put two fingers to her lips as if to seal the bargain and passed the tiny candle to him.

She closed the door of room seven seconds before she heard the cars returning with the women. "God," she prayed, "I've done my part, now it's up to you."

Chapter Twenty-Three

Speedometer of the touring car neared one hundred twenty meters. Douglas huddled in back and strained to hear the conversation going on up front.

The driver spoke in a loud, course voice. "Ellen is looking for a new place to live. Most of us will follow her. Her father has lists and lists of vacancies so she has lots of choices. She's awfully particular. I like the way that lady operates.

"When it comes to Ellen, there's never a gray area. She's someone way beyond her time, terribly independent, don't you think? She does what no one else has the courage or can even conceive."

"Like having a woman driver?"

"Oh, I do more than drive for her." The driver was a tough-looking, burly person, who had dancing blue eyes. A black cap covered blonde curls and she wore a black suit with a white shirt underneath. Antoinette didn't realize she was a woman until she spoke, and even now, it was hard for her to believe because of the woman's deep voice.

"It's my first time to drive for her, but I didn't want to tell you in case you'd get nervous. I usually—um—do other things for Ellen. You might say that I'm a finder and seeker." She laughed. "But, I didn't find you. Ellen did all by herself. She likes you and she didn't think she would. But, you surprised her and Ellen's not easily surprised."

"My name's Helga," she said, and during the long ride she told Antoinette about her life. "Ellen heard me sing in a Berlin cabaret and put me on her staff.

"Ellen likes the way I sing—lusty and feisty. I'd sing something for you but I want to hear you talk about that place I picked you up. What's it like? They're a big buzz because they're so secret and snotty. Oh, go on, tell me, there are no secrets where we're going."

"Lebensborn," said Antoinette. "One of the women said it means 'Fountain of Life' and told me they were organized by ReischFührer Himmler who wants to make Germany into a super race by selective breeding. It's our duty as women to bear racially sound children for the Führer. It's unimportant whether we're married or not; for that I am glad, of course, but I don't want to marry anyone."

Miles sped by quickly as Antoinette told Helga about the quarters, the clothes the women wore, the classes she attended, the naming ceremony. She said nothing about the SS House next door and tried not to be concerned whether or not the man was in the back seat.

She had waited outside for the car near the entrance to the Lebensborn and when the sleek Mercedes drove up, the driver stepped out and took her little suitcase. She looked as if she might put it into the back seat, but instead unleashed the trunk straps on the rear and put it on the back of the car.

Antinette turned to see through the window into the backseat but saw nothing. The touring car was designed with two hoods which made the detection of someone in the back less likely.

Antoinette listened to Helga recite the woes of nightclub life as the car traveled at great speed along the Autobahn.

Chapter Twenty-Four

*I*n the backseat, Douglas grew more and more uncomfortable. His limbs ached being in the same position and the back of his shoulders began to throb. How long had they been traveling?

To keep his mind occupied and still the pains of his body, he began recalling one of the major triumphs of his life. He was twelve years old and had been playing the bagpipes for six months with the Lorena Scott Bag Pipe Band in South Africa. On St. Patrick's Day, they were to march in a parade. Being a piper was quite difficult: you needed desire, to be half deaf, and work extremely hard, doing four or five things at the same time.

First, there were the fingerings to learn, then the grace notes, and how to make the reed play, keep the drones playing with pressure from your arm, play in tune and walk in formation with eleven others, all at the same time.

In the beginning, he had difficulty learning how to turn around without killing the person behind with the three-foot drone off his left shoulder.

On that early morning, the Senior Piper called for them to form the tuning circle. The Piper finished his rounds, had listened to each piper, and, with a thumb up, for sharp, or down, for flat, for their tuning.

The Senior Piper began giving hand singles for position.

The woman who held the "piper's post", the person marching directly behind the Senior Piper, the position of honor, who gave the visual cues to the other pipers when the

Senior was out of position, shook her head. She refused to accept the position.

The Senior Piper was amazed. This had never happened before. He stepped into the center of the circle, his swirling kilts coming to a halt.

As all this was going on, the bagpipers continued to play the Scottish traditional piece, "Scotland the Brave." Douglas could feel the vibrations from that tune tonight these many years later as the car roared along the Autobahn.

In the six months he played with the group, the woman in the "piper's post" had never refused the assignment.

The Senior Piper pointed to an old, crotchety gentleman, the oldest in the group. The old piper took three steps back from the circle and stopped his pipes.

One by one, the others stepped back and stopped their pipes until Douglas was the only one left playing. That was the rule. When you were in position, you played until you were told not to play, either by the end of the piece, by hand assignment or by drum cadence.

He learned later that night, after they'd played in the long parade and for nine parties, that the pipers had made a decision among themselves to honor him in that way.

When his father told him, he cried. Until then, he had not realized the significance of the honor. From time to time in the parade and at the parties, he overheard people ask, "Who's the young piper? Who's his teacher? Where did he get such pluck?"

When the night was over, he had no pucker left, any more than now ten years later laying bunched up in a Mercedes.

He heard drone of planes in the distance.

Antoinette clutched her stomach and bent her head between her legs. "I feel sick," she said, and moved close to the door.

"Hang onto those britches. I see a place to turn off," said Helga.

Antoinette breathed heavily and clutched at her mouth.

"I've held the head of many a drunk . . ." Helga said.

"Please don't feel you have to," begged Antoinette, now beginning to feel genuine nausea arising from her stomach. "It's something I have to do by myself."

Helga rolled down the car window and poked her head out. Planes were coming.

The car clipped off the autobahn and began slowing down on a country road. There were thick hedges on both sides and a slight opening on the right, an entrance for a hay cart, perhaps.

The car slowed and stopped.

Antoinette, who already had tried the door latch, pushed down the handle, jumped out of the car and made her way between the bushes and ran out into a field. She stopped, bent down and waited. The planes were closer, almost overhead.

She ran again, stumbling over the ground, saw a wooded thicket and ran toward it.

Helga jumped out of the car and yelled, "You, girl, you okay?"

There was no response from the girl. Helga felt waves of anxiety. She thought the girl may have passed out. She unleashed the straps of the trunk on the rear of the car, fished out a flashlight and ran to the spot where Antoinette had gone through the bushes.

Douglas counted: two doors had opened so he counted to ten, threw off the blanket, and looked out the window and saw the beam of a flashlight in the field on the right side of the car. He opened the door on the left, closed the door, and slipped into the dark.

The night was cold, dark and misty and he stumbled across a field, stepped into puddles, bumped into rows of dirt and thought about an earlier conversation with Antoinette.

"Yes," she had told him when he had questioned about her plan. "I trust Hans. Just because he's German, doesn't mean he's not a good man. He was my friend. He is good in spite of being an SS officer. At heart he is just a farmer like my uncle."

"Do you honestly believe that his father will help a French woman?" he had asked.

"I put my safety in his hands in Villepente," she said, remembering Big Hans, whose hands were as huge as his heart, and as frustrated by happenings in her French village as she was. It was Hans who consoled her during the horrible hours of the pet turn in, after ugly words were discovered on her doorstep, the day she confirmed her pregnancy and Major Hurst questioned that he was the father of the child she carried.

Hans was last person she saw in Villepente. He had tears in his eyes when he said goodbye as she boarded the bus which began her journey to the Lebensborn in Germany.

Hans always looked uncomfortable in the black Waffen SS uniform. It hung on his thick body so sloppily that he looked liked a sack of potatoes. That morning in Villepente, he tried to be cheerful.

"I will think about you," he said. He was a man of few words or one to make physical contact. But, that morning he took one of her hands and said that he would miss her.

"I . . ."

"I will miss you, too, Hans."

"Take this," he said, and took out a piece of paper from his pocket. "It's a note to my father and a map to his morgans where he raises potatoes. Should you need a friend in Germany, go to him."

"Hans," she cried, ashamed because she wanted to give him a goodbye kiss but could not because villagers might see and talk all the more. People in the village shunned her after she had been seen so often in the company of SS officer Hurst. Anna, the butcher's wife, seemed the most hateful. There were others, too, mostly after the turn in of their pets.

The major had openly entertained other women in the village, but, Antoinette felt she was the one at whom their anger was directed. Was it because they thought she was a collaborator? They wouldn't know the truth until the war was over.

No one seemed to be upset with her friend, Danielle, who was often seen around the village in the company of the Nazi officer Lieutenant Walthers. Antoinette had been so busy with the cooking and cleaning chores for the Nazis that she rarely went out, but when she did she had often seen them together.

Those days in Villepente were ugly, all caused by Waffen officer, Major Reinhard Hurst. The thought of him was disgusting. It was hard to believe that once she had felt lust and passion for him. Or, that just a few nights ago, his hands had been upon her again.

A low branch snapped her foot as she ran into the thicket. She clutched at a tiny sapling and fell and lay sweating in the heavy wool coat which came down to her ankles. She stuffed the woolen cap into the coat pocket, wondering if she should get up and continue running. The planes groaned off into the distance.

The motor of the Mercedes started up. The car skid on the dirt, then zoomed off.

Antoinette continued running through the dark night until she bumped into an object, looked up and saw that it was a statue. She felt the stone up and down and discerned that it was an angel. *Where am I?* She moved cautiously. A square object met her hand. *I'm in a cemetery.*

She discovered a bunch of bushes and created a nest for herself, throwing off the black coat and wrapping it over her head and body. Her legs, covered by thick stockings, lay on the damp ground.

The last moments before she dozed off, she reflected again upon her resolve to get to England. *I will do it. I will find Jacques.*

Chapter Twenty-Five

It was the middle of the night and very black when she shot up, alarmed by a dream. She was in a car which moved as if on tracks, slowly and methodically. The car on the tracks passed many scenes, but the one which roused her up from sleep was a vivid picture of her father standing by a roadside next to a fence, staring at her as she went by.

It was a simple dream, yet in reality, the starkness of the dark surrounding his figure, his vacant stare, the odd way his eyes followed her, sent chills through her.

"Father," she cried, "are you alright?" Utterly dejected, she felt distressed not knowing the health or status of any of her family in Villepente. *I must get news of them somehow. Something terrible has happened.*

She finally slept a fitful few hours and was awakened by daylight and the feeling that she wasn't alone. She heard something. What was it? Such strange sounds. It was people crying. Cautiously, she parted the frost-laden branches of the bushes and saw a group of mourners clustered around an opening in the ground.

The sight brought back the dream with such impact, she covered her head with the coat and began crying. Her body shook and moved the bushes.

Someone in the cluster of mourners must have seen the bushes move for soon a minister and a few persons were looking down at her. She stared back at them, tears streaming down her face. Someone asked, "Who is she? Do you know her?" The mourners shook their heads and wondered why a young woman was in the bushes crying.

Antoinette said in German. "Air raid . . . lost." She took out her identity papers which said she was a Pole on a work assignment.

The papers passed hand to hand. There was much shaking of heads.

Antoinette spoke again in broken German, "I go here," and held up the piece of paper with the map.

A big woman stepped up. "I know the people," she said as she held a hand to Antoinette who soon found herself in the back of a cart.

The ride along the rutty dirt road made her nauseous from jarring. She threw up over the side.

The woman yelled often at the old horse pulling the cart. The back of the horse was swayed, its eyes rummy.

The woman stopped the cart beside a walled enclosure and motioned her to get out. A small wood door was in the grey stones. Antoinette climbed over the rough boards and jumped down. She clutched her stomach and ran over to throw up beside the wall.

The woman yelled at the horse. Antoinette thought she might be cursing her so she tried to kick dirt over the mess but it was frozen and wouldn't move. Antoinette saw a large rock nearby, kicked it with her foot until it moved, then lifted it and covered the mess.

She turned the rusty handle on the door and saw the cart start off. The driver didn't look back.

Slowly, she walked into the farmyard. A large looking wood building ringed three sides of the enclosure. A two-story building of stone stood in between, bales of straw in one of the buildings.

She stood on the wide, stone steps to the house looking for a door knocker but there was none. Wood shutters covered over the windows. Quietness of the late morning hung in the air as the sun shone feebly through the clouds.

She sat the icy steps, feeling very alone, more so than in

the cemetery when she thought she had reached the bottom of abject loneliness. In Villepente, even though there were times she felt utterly deserted and alone, there was the uplifting thought of seeing her father or her mother. Now there was no one. Even the man was gone.

She thought about the child. Then, she felt the new life twitter within. Her eyes flickered, her heart fluttered in recognition. She bundled the coat closer to her body and saw a man coming out one of the out building carrying a heavy, iron-looking object. He looked familiar. Of course, he was an older Hans, the same wide cheeks, the broad lips, the deep-set eyes, the dark, blonde hair, a light band of color above the bushy brows. He wore no cap and she looked to see his hands. Yes, the same big hands: the huge hands that always looked out of place splaying from of the sleeves of the SS uniform. The father wore baggy, black pants held up with a rope and a coarse white undershirt beneath a heavy knit sweater.

As he drew near, she carefully removed the note Hans had written, opened the folds of the many-folded paper, and creased open the tiny four-by-four square:

'Receive the bearer of this note as you would . . . Your Hans.'

The farmer's tired eyes read and re-read the paper over and over. His faded blue eyes looked down into hers. She passed the bundle of identity papers to him and noticed that his eyes blinked when he saw there was no accompanying photo.

"Temporary papers," she qualified. She thought, *They must be different than any he's seen. He's suspicious.*

She asked, "When did you last hear from Hans?"

He shook his head. His eyes were sad. "Nothing, we have heard nothing for weeks."

"Herr Lutejemeier, I have come to work for you." She stood up and waited for him to say or do something.

"Tomorrow, that will be soon enough. Come, I will show you the quarters. Work tomorrow when it is light."

Chapter Twenty-Six

She followed him past the house, to the large "L" of the single story barn-like building. They entered a door and came into an area with several low beds lined up along the wall. The only light came through the door. There were no windows. The area appeared orderly. She thought, *They must keep their things in those wood boxes.*

Herr Lutejemeier went to a box in front of the last bed and swung open the top. "Your things in here, then." Inside the box was a dark, gray woolen blanket and white-covered pillow.

She sat on the bed and heard the straw crackle under the course linen covering and watched him go out. He turned and said, "The others will be in soon. You will get food then. They will tell you where."

He beckoned her to come to the door. Wearily she arose to see where he pointed into the field to little wood buildings.

She nodded.

After he was gone, she walked along the dirt path to the out houses. Edges of the long wool coat brushed against the wet brown weeds along the path as she weaved her way.

She looked at the sky. It would be a few hours until the sun set. Small figures moved along slowly in the distance. She felt exhausted and made her way back to the building, removed the coat, took out the blanket and was sleeping when the workers trudged in.

She opened her eyes. Someone had lit candles. No one appeared surprised to see her.

A woman in baggy tweedlike trousers, work boots, and a vest made up of scraggly fur pieces sewn together like a quilt, came and squatted beside her. Her dark eyes searched Antoinette's face and a slow smile spread across her face. She spoke rapidly in Polish.

"No kapish."

"Ah," exclaimed the woman, "parlez vois Francais, eh?" The woman saw Antoinette's eyes light up and announced to the persons in the room, "Bien, bien, attendez vous." The others whispered, "She is French," with amazement.

In the group there were, besides the husky lady, two men, one who was quite young, and they sauntered over.

In French, Antoinette told them that she had escaped from a German place for expectant mothers having babies for SS officers. She had been treated so poorly that she fled and ended up at this farm offering to help with the harvest.

Heads nodded. The older man of nondescript age stretched out his hand to Antoinette. "Bon Soir, mademoiselle, vous avec vous Monsieur Roggue."

Antoinette looked at a younger man, a skinny fellow with ancient eyes sunk into dark sockets, who appeared perhaps fifteen or sixteen years old.

"He can't speak," said the woman. "They cut out his tongue in prison. They let us out to help in the fields."

The woman stroked Antoinette's hair. "I am Maeva. May-Vah. Old Polish Name. No wonder you never heard it before."

They said it was time to go for food. They walked to the back door of the stone house and Maeva looked serious as she confided, "Watch out for the young German boy, the son. He is Hitler Youth with passion. If he can turn someone in to the Gestapo, he can be a hero."

Antoinette bent her head into the dark coat and followed the group into the square-box of a kitchen.

Maeva pushed Antoinette into the back corner of a double bench seat. She brought back to the table a wide porcelain bowl of steaming vegetables in a broth and set it in front of Antoinette who devoured the cabbage soup without waiting for the others to be seated. She was famished and chasing the last morsels of cabbage around the bottom of the bowl when a lad in a Hitler Youth uniform marched in and stood before them.

"Heil Hitler," he commanded. Their arms shot up above his outstretched arm.

The lad directed his conversation to Maeva who sat on outside of the other side of the bench from Antoinette.

"After work in the 123 field, you begin immediately the number 131."

There was an adult directness in the young boy's eyes as he spoke. It was as if he didn't see her at all but was envisioning the field and the work digging the potatoes for shipment to Russia.

The boy was gone as quickly as he had come. The group no longer spoke. They filed out of the kitchen and returned to their building.

Maeva sighed, "It's better than prison."

Monsieur Rocco kicked the wood support of his bed. The young boy they called Sergio fell face down on his bed, his arms to his sides.

Maeva whispered, "Do you have news?"

"Three days ago the Japanese bombed Pearl Harbor. America has joined the war," said Antoinette.

"How do you know that! Can it be so?"

"Yes, it is. There was a radio in the kitchen where I worked and I listened—in secret. The broadcasts came from London."

"We had no idea. These Germans show no emotion at anything," said Maeva, who sat on the wood box by the bed Antoinette had claimed. "What are your plans?"

Antoinette knew that how she answered might have an effect upon Maeva's own plans, so she replied, "I understand your concerns about me. I am an unknown and show up unannounced. Can you trust me? Can you believe my story?"

The certainty of positive response was reflected in Maeva's dark eyes.

"My being here should not jeopardize you."

Monsieur Rocco listened to conversation of the two women and smiled and when he did, Antoinette gasped. His open mouth confirmed what she thought: jagged, brown-black teeth. *They must be so painful. How does he eat?*

Antoinette told them about the physical exam by the Nazi Doktor, of his office with the chair made of human skin, his brutal abuse of Fritz and the rest of the staff.

Maeva and Monsieur Rocco exchanged knowing glances, then the professor said, "Nothing which happens to us is the fault of just one person. In prison, we had time to ponder why things happen, why we were being afflicted by the unkind strokes of these inhumane creatures.

"I thought many times, over and over, of an old story told to me by a Rebbi, a Jewish mentor, a teacher. He told it to show that suffering can be a miracle brought by God, so that God's words can be in the heart instead of setting on top the heart. Suffering, the story told, causes a crack so that the words can fall into the heart.

"Suffering can open you up and bring wisdom. The only question to ask God is: What can I make of this?

"I see you have suffered. What you have borne can bring great blessings."

Maeva said, "he taught philosophy at the University of Warsaw so watch out for him. Every question you ask, he'll counter with a thousand more.

"I was one of his graduate assistants. I typed and ran off the political papers we circulated; that's how we came to be rounded up and sent to prison."

"How long were you there?" asked Antoinette.

"Three years. Iodine in the water made his teeth rot. I was saved for the guards' pleasure. The professor has helped me resolve those horrors. Oh, but, we have interrupted you."

Antoinette then related how the Naming Ceremony brought her to the Nazi SS house and told them about Ellen and Douglas, the RAF flyer she had hidden.

"There's a guy out there somewhere who's coming here." The Professor clasped his hand over Maeva's mouth.

Antoinette said, "he knows the way and is coming, unless he's been captured. We're going by foot across the Danish border, contact the Resistance, and get over to England."

"Take me with you," exclaimed Maeva.

"Ladies, ladies," begged the Professor, "let's consider all the parameters: we have one pregnant woman who has escaped from a highly secret place; one Pole with a known political background; and, one escaped RAF officer. Now who do you think will be looking for all these different persons?

"Of course, recall if you will, my analogy of the picnic," continued the Professor, rubbing his stubby chin whiskers.

"Yes, yes, but, of course," smiled Maeva who explained the Professor's analogy of a picnic. "When we discuss a big issue like this in a group, we can get that bigger wisdom, because we put in all the little bits and pieces of insight from everyone. It's like going on a picnic. You bring the bread," she pointed to Antoinette. "You bring the cheese," she pointed a finger at the Professor. "I'll bring the wine," she said, touching her chest.

"None of us has the answer alone," said the Professor. "No one person can, but, we hope that if we listen and exchange with each other, we can better face problems together. And, this is one grand fellow of a problem, this RAF officer. When he shows up, the boy must not see him. Now that we are out of prison, we must take all precautions not to trip the cage again."

He rose wearily from the box beside Maeva and went to his bed. "I must say goodnight."

For some time the women whispered together as they sat on Antoinette's bed. Maeva wanted to hear more about the RAF officer, about the campaigns going on in Russia and Africa.

"So, you didn't want the baby to born a German." Maeva plucked out a piece of straw and picked her teeth.

"No, they'd take him from me and fill his head with propaganda. He'd be a machine, just like that boy, a fanatic, unthinking, unfeeling human being."

"Why do you want to go to England, Maeva?"

"I have this strong feeling that I must."

"I, too, must go to London to find Jacques. I would know if something has happened to him." Then, she told Maeva about the frightening dream about her father. "He was trying to tell me something. Such a cold feeling came over me when I saw him."

Before saying goodnight, the women concluded that they had the same thing in common: they knew nothing about their families' whereabouts.

Finally, sleep came over them. A loud cry in the night awakened everyone. The Professor was up pacing. He bumped into boxes. Someone lit a candle. He had a pair of pliers in one hand and the other pointed inside his mouth to one of the few rotting teeth.

Like a dazed mosquito, he lit upon the wood box by his bed. Maeva went to him and shouted to Antoinette, "Hold his shoulders." Maeve stood by his side holding his head. Sergio grasped the pliers and pushed them into the Professor's mouth.

When Sergio touched the affected area, they felt him quake. The pliers jockeyed into position. Sergio tugged and yanked.

With much exertion, the lad was victorious. He grinned and held up the stub of the tooth. Antoinette handed the wash-up rag to the Professor whose eyes sought each of theirs in thanksgiving.

They crept back to bed, dawn was not far off and the best hour of sleep yet to come.

When morning broke, Sergio was first up and jostled the others awake. He took the bucket out to fill with water for wash up, then stood waiting while they wiped their faces with the drab rag.

Antoinette threw the heavy coat over the clothes she slept in and followed the group to the back door of the main house. Sergio went into the kitchen and filled an old tin bucket with bread and cheese. They picked up heavy shovels and burlap bags and walked through the big fields which had already been picked until they reached the one designated for the day. The work began.

The field was flat and unappealing but the sky changed colors as cloud formations soared over. Shovels went into the hard ground. Soil was lifted out and five or six potatoes heaved out from the hole. It was exhausting to bend, shovel, and pick up the potatoes.

Antoinette still felt the chill of the morning and worked in the big coat. The others worked in shirt sleeves. She began sweating and threw off the coat.

Maeva looked at her as she came by to leave a filled sack and said, "You don't look good. Maybe you should eat something."

Antoinette sat down.

"How are you feeling, little mother?" called the professor.

"Fine," she managed to say, then fainted.

Chapter Twenty-Seven

When she came to, she was back in the narrow wood bed, a bit of straw tickling her back. She tried to get up but a headache of monstrous proportions sent her flat again.

A large hand clamped over her mouth.

"It's me," said a male voice. She reached up and pulled his hand away.

"What's happened?" he asked. He put his hand on her forehead and frowned. It was hot.

"I passed out in the field."

He sighed. "You're sick. You can't come with me . . ."

She managed to sit up. "You must forget about me. Go with Maeva, the Polish woman, as soon as they come back from the fields. It is not safe for you here either," and told him about the overly-zealous Hitler Youth.

He put the sour cloth, still damp from the morning's washing up, on her head. "I owe so much to you. There must be a way to help you."

"You can go to the art dealer in London where Jacques took the painting. Ask him to tell Jacques I'll be coming. But, please don't say anything about the baby. It's been months since he left."

"I have a better idea. Once you get to London," he said the words slowly thinking about what they could do, "find me and together we'll find that dealer and Jacques." He gave her his parents' address: 1941 St. Michaels' Lane. "Now, that should be an easy number to remember—today's year, plus the name of a saint.

"My family—" They heard the others coming in. Antoinette said, "He's here."

The three workers went to the house for food and when they came back the women switched clothing.

Douglas whispered to Antoinette, "Hawka gashle. The words are Zulu," he said, "and mean 'Go in Peace.' It's for good luck." "Salla gashle," he continued, "that's what you say back to me. Salla gashle. Say it back to me for good luck."

When he said, "Hawka gashle," as he and Maeve were slipping out into the shadows of the night, she called, "Salla gashle."

"When we meet again, little lady, remember 'Salla gashle. Stay in Peace.'"

"Salla gashle," she repeated after they were gone, the words remaining with her, like a sweet bird singing.

The professor and Sergio brought food but she could not eat. The next day she had fever, chills, aches and a gigantic headache and did not go to the field.

"We told the boy Maeva was ill," the Professor said the next night after the two men returned from dinner at the house.

"Let us help you up so you can get in her bed. The lad might come here."

Indeed, there he was. "You're not the same woman," he said, his voice incensed.

The professor said under his breath, but loud enough for them all to hear, "One Polish woman is just like another."

"You," declared the boy, "are up to something. I don't know what, but I will find out." He shook his finger at them.

"Stay here. By order of the Führer, I put you all under house arrest."

He ran out.

Chapter Twenty-Eight

Antoinette sought her work papers which appeared to be stamped with authentic-looking signatures. No one knew about the Lebensborn facilities. The operation was a secret. The Gestapo could tell she was French. They would conclude she was a spy, no matter what she said about why she was sent to Germany.

They heard noises outside. The Professor looked through the doorway and said there were two old soldiers in ill-fitting World War One uniforms coming across the barnyard.

A cart with an old horse, which looked to be the same weary one as before, was outside barely standing upright. The boy stood beside the cart, his right hand gripping the splintered wood rail. His lips curled in relish.

The cart stopped in a village and they were taken to a dark stone building. The Professor and Sergio were thrown into a cell and she was put into another. It was so cold that chills came to the marrow of her bones.

She fumbled around in the dark and thumped something. She reached down and felt the straw and thought, *Oh, maybe a blanket.* Her hands touched a rough piece of bunched up cloth. She lay down upon the pallet of straw and tugged the pieces of the crazy-quilt fur vest together, and tried to unravel the unruly blanket and throw it over her legs.

Her thoughts were upon the Jungfolk boy whose angry eyes burnt through her during the cart ride to the dank military prison. She grew angry, not so much now about the Jungfolk boy, but those who had taken him from his family and turned him into a monster.

She remembered what the professor said about the Nazi programming of youth. "They go into the Jungfolk at the age of ten for four years, then into Hitler Youth for another four. After that they don't give them back to their old ways but take them straight into the party, the Labour Front, the SA or SS, or so on.

"After another two or so years, they are completely National Socialists. Any pride or individuality by then is wormed out. If there is the slighted trace of any weakness, back they go for further treatment. Hitler says, 'They'll never be free again as long as they live.'"

She thought about Gerald, the lad about the same age. *They'd have to spend years and years with Gerald. He could never be so cruel.*

She felt the eyes of the guard outside the cell looking at her. From time to time she heard the Professor talking to Sergio. She sat up and drew her knees to her chest to repel the cold air.

She saw that the guard had been replaced by an old man who was not in uniform. He was looking at her.

Two men walked into the cell and yanked her to her feet. One of them spat on the straw showing his contempt. She was jerked to a small, sparsely furnished office thick with cigarette smoke.

A thin man sat at a square table going over some papers. There was an empty chair at one end. Three men were sitting on wood chairs along a wall. They were smoking and talking with each other and didn't seem to notice her.

The room was rather warm but she still felt chilly.

One of the men got up. "Sit down you dirty swine." He pushed her toward the chair.

She was still too cold to be warmed by fear. The thin man pushed papers towards her.

"These yours?" he asked rather nonchalantly. His eyes were pale and dangerous. What should she say?

"You don't want to talk to us—not good enough for you?"

The men on the chairs laughed. Another man leapt up and squeezed her neck.

"Answer the man's question," he demanded. His fingers squeezed blood up and down her spine. She put up her hands to unloosen his fingers.

"Don't touch me!" he bellowed but released his hands.

Weakly she admitted, "Yes, those are mine."

"Thank you," replied the inspector who nodded his head up and down. "You are so gracious to give my question an answer. As long as you feel you can answer questions, how about telling me the truth about your connections with the underground."

In German she replied, "I am a Pole working the fields."

He barked, "How long have you been a Pole working the fields? One month? Two months? If I knew more Polish, I'd have you speak it to me, but you're lucky that I don't. So, we'll continue to discuss this in German."

The men laughed. Another came and yanked her hair and pulled her head back.

"Tell me, Pole, have you lived all your life in Danzig?"

"Yes," she struggled to say.

"Beautiful city, that Danzig. Nice river you have there."

"Yes," she gurgled, her head still being held back.

"Some day you would like to see it again, wouldn't you? Maybe take a boat ride. Visit the casinos. Go dancing. I see you can't decide. I'll have to decide for you. Yes, you want to go back. Tell me, why did you leave?"

The last question in the string of questions was asked so gently she replied, "I wanted to help the Germans. I was afraid of the Russians who might be coming. My father didn't want me to stay in Danzig if the Russians came."

"Your father doesn't like the Russians but you do."

"No, I didn't say that. I don't like them either."

The thin man motioned that her head should be released. Then he asked, "You seem to like Germans better." He was being sarcastic.

"We—I trust you more."

He roared, "More? You trust us more. But, not now. How terrible."

"Why don't you believe me."

He looked at her with disbelief. "You tell me you like us but you wish to leave us." The inspector tilted his chair back and closed his eyes.

"Even if I told you the truth, you would not believe me."

The inspector urged, "Yes, yes, go on. You are starting to become a little more intriguing." He motioned to a man with a pad of paper on his lap to bring his chair in closer.

Antoinette decided to tell the story of how she, a French woman, was sent to Germany to a Lebensborn to have a child for the Führer and how she met the beautiful woman from Berlin who wanted her to come to live with her there.

"Let's see if I completely understand you," the inspector put in. "Some nasty planes kept you from going to Berlin so you went instead to a farm to work in the fields. How very unfortunate."

His eyes opened slowly. He had a weird smile when he said to the man taking notes, "Did you get all that? I don't want a word changed. I don't want you to say a word more. Tomorrow someone else will have the pleasure of hearing your story again."

Then he growled, "Get this lying bitch back to her cell."

The men yanked her up from the chair and violently pushed her back to the cell. When she reached the door, one of them put his hands on her back and flung her through it.

Her legs felt weak. She collapsed upon the pallet. Who could believe my story? Who is the man coming tomorrow? A dim light shone from the hall to show a slop bucket in the corner.

A few hours later a scowling man, different from those the day before, came and called her out of the cell. He escorted her back to the room where the first interrogation had taken place.

A small table now had been added. On it was a typewriter, paper, and pencils. A fat man in a black SS uniform sat in a tall-padded chair drumming his fingers on the table.

Two men dressed in brown uniforms held rubber hoses.

"Sit down," commanded the man. "If you tell the truth you won't be harmed. You must answer all my questions at once—no time to think. It must be the same story as before."

It grew chilly and quiet in the room. He leaned toward her. "Keep your eyes on my eyes. Do not look away. We're going to get to know each other quite well, aren't we?"

Antoinette nodded.

"Do not nod. I told you to answer. We must hear the sound of your sweet voice. I am a Gestapo inspector and you won't crawl out of here without my hearing the truth. I can, however, give you this reassurance. You may soon be begging me to let you die. I won't give a damn if you die or not. I don't have any regard for a hero—male or female. In my opinion, you females are the worst, so soft and appealing, but so hard inside.

"We'll get to know each other, you and I. Now I'm going to start asking some questions—remember the rules, no hesitating or you'll get help from the guards. Are you with the Polish underground?"

'No," Antoinette quickly replied.

"Why were you traveling?"

"I was on my way to Berlin."

"Then, why were you supposedly working in the fields."

She didn't answer quickly enough so he gave a signal to one of the men behind her who rapped her behind the ear with the rubber stick. She felt a flash of pain as extreme as when a dentist hits a nerve. She cried out, "You'll kill the baby."

"Then, we'll give you another chance, won't we. Can you be honest with me now?" he asked.

"You won't believe me. Why should you?" she mumbled. Pain of another blow came. The lack of food and sleep, the bitter cold in the cell and the ride to the prison made her nauseous. She began to vomit.

"Get her out of here," screamed the inspector. "Or, run to get a basin before she throws up all over the place."

In the hall they thrust a bucket under her nose and held her over it while her stomach rolled. She put her head up and when they saw she was through, they dragged her back to the chair. The inspector held a handkerchief over his mouth.

He pulled down the handkerchief and said sternly, "Are you still going to insist on telling me your fairy tale—of the handsome SS prince in love with an enemy girl."

"She's a Goddamn liar!" shouted one of the guards and crashed his stick over her ear.

The inspector waved the guard away as Antoinette held her hands over her ears. He continued, "Do you expect us to believe a woman like Ellen Laudier, an intimate of Himmler's, would be so dumb as to take a spy into our very midst?"

"It's the truth," she pled with all her strength.

"You're lying," he screamed.

This time she said nothing. The rubber truncheon landed behind the other ear. She slid forward and crumpled to the floor.

The inspector's voice seemed to drone above her like an engine.

"That fainting act won't get you anywhere. Those little touches behind your ears, I know they're painful, but you won't lose consciousness from them." The inspector got up from his chair and went to the door.

"You can work on her. Just leave enough for me for later," he said before departing.

The guards pulled Antoinette up and propped her upon the wall. As the blows thudded and crashed, she sagged but they held her beneath the armpits.

Her face was bruised and puffing up. One of the guards kicked her in the stomach several times. Every muscle cried

.

out in pain. When the guards were finally through with her, they threw her back into the cell.

The guard outside the cell brought some food and water but she was too weak to swallow.

The next day the old guard led her to a lavatory and tried to wash away the dried blood from her face and arms. Blood began to gush out of her body and pool on the floor. Then the world stopped. She was in the bottom of a deep pit. More blood gushed out and a horrible cramping began.

Chapter Twenty-Nine

When she came to her senses, blurred impressions started to seep through a dull and steady pain. There was a bitter taste in her mouth. A motor seemed to be running in her ears. She felt the urge to let go and fall into darkness but something forced her into awareness.

She wasn't in the cell because she could sense some light. Her hands touched something starchy beneath her. She forced her eyes open. A powerful glare came from a lamp dangling from a high ceiling.

A gentle voice whispered, "Don't be afraid. You are in a hospital. We will make you well. In a moment you will have a blood transfusion."

"No," Antoinette cried. "I don't want a transfusion."

"Everything will be alright," continued the gentle female voice.

When she came to again, she found herself in a different room. It was late at night. A bright moon illuminated the room so she could see three other beds with occupants, many who were snoring loudly. One was groaning.

She felt little hope. Even if there were a chance to escape, she doubted that she could muster the strength to flee. She feared being back again with the Gestapo inspector.

When morning came, the same cheerful voice awakened her. A nun in white robes stood beside the bed holding a thermometer. She put it through Antoinette's cracked lips, leaned over closely and whispered, "Do you understand German?"

Antoinette nodded.

"Listen carefully," said the soft-spoken sister. "It is bad for you in prison. We will try to keep you here in the hospital as long as possible. Do you understand?"

When Antoinette tried to say something, the sister shook her head, "Don't talk. Just trust that we're trying to help you."

One night the sister in white came into the room when the guard was not there.

"What's happening?" Antoinette was asking for news of the war but the sister responded, "You've lost the child."

Each day a doctor came. She begged him for news. He managed to whisper, "England is being bombed. Morale of the Brits is low. No doubt England will surrender in a few days."

On the tenth day, two familiar Gestapo men came into the room. One shoved a bundle of clothes on the bed and called for a sister. When one arrived he said in an angry voice, "Get her dressed and do it in a hurry."

The doctor heard the loud voice and rushed in saying, "What do you mean trying to get her up. She's very sick. She can't be moved."

"Oh, can't she?" one said while the other quipped, "You take care of your business and we'll take care of ours. And she's our business."

"I tell you, you take her out and she'll be gone." He jerked the shirt out of the agent's hand.

"I'll help her dress," the doctor continued. While the doctor was buttoning the shirt over bandages," he whispered, "Act sick as can be. I'm going to try something. It may or may not work." The doctor rushed past the agents and out of the room.

Antoinette fell back onto the bed. One of the agents said "Where'd he go. You go find out," he said to the other man.

When the agent came back he said to the other, "Looks like she can stay a while longer. Then to Antoinette, he said, "You can't go home yet, darling, back to the place you miss so much."

The future looked as black as ever. A guard was posted in the room.

The next day a young girl came into the room. She was smartly dressed in street clothes and wore a grey suit, red shirt, and fashionable chunky shoes. She held a bunch of red roses. The guard eyed her with curiosity.

"You must be in the wrong room," said Antoinette as the girl came closer to her bed.

"No, I've just had an operation myself for appendicitis and we've heard you lost a baby. We took up a collection for these and we wanted you to know there are people who care."

She put the flowers by Antoinette on the bed. The guard rushed over and seized her arm and forced her back from the bed. He tore apart the flowers apparently looking for a hidden message. The girl began to cry and left the room.

Shortly one of the Gestapo agents returned shouting through the doorway to Antoinette, "Hey, you. You're going to be leaving in a few hours. Bet you can't wait."

The doctor rushed in after he left and said to the guard sitting by the wall, "You don't do any good when you crowd me like that. Can't you watch from the door." The guard got up and left the room.

The doctor bent over Antoinette and began unwinding some clotted bandages on one of her arms. He called out for a sister and when she came he asked her to bring more ointment and bandages.

To Antoinette, he said, "Courage. Have courage. Then shout that you are dying and want to make your confession. You got that?"

Antoinette nodded. To the sister the doctor said, " Change these dressings every hour. If I'm needed, I'll be near by."

Antoinette wailed, "I'm dying. I want to give my confession. Please, please, find a priest. You're a Catholic. You know I can't die a sinner."

The sister returned with a different doctor. "If you're

determined to die," the doctor said sternly, "There's nothing more we can do. Bring the wheelchair, sister."

Then he yelled loudly, "You'll get to make your confession so stop all this moaning."

The sister tucked Antoinette into a bathrobe and helped her into a highbacked wheelchair. She wheeled her out the door with the guard following. The procession led to a chapel.

Antoinette sat in the wheelchair. She heard the sister's faint clicks on rosary beads as they slipped between her fingers.

It was quiet in the chapel and there was the faint smell of incense. The sister at her side said, "Don't worry. Everything has been arranged. When the priest comes, he's bringing clothes for you. Get in the confessional but go out the back of it. Behind the altar you'll find a hallway. Look for a window. On one of the sills will be a rose. Jump from that window. There will be men below."

Antoinette felt her heart pounding.

The sister pushed the wheelchair to the front of the confessional and helped Antoinette into the cubicle. A pile of clothes lay on the bench. Quickly she dressed in the skirt, blouse, shoes and sox and coat.

She pushed upon the wood panels and found one that was loose. She slipped between the boards and went along a corridor until she spied the altar. Behind the altar she felt a draft of air and realized the air was coming from windows.

She found the hall and went down it seeing many windows but no rose on any of the sills. Finally, she spied a rose on the floor by one of the open windows. It was dark below.

She drew a deep breath, climbed up onto the rough and wide sill and jumped.

As she hit the ground, a pair of strong arms caught her. For a moment she feared they might be the arms of the Gestapo.

"Hurry—run like the wind," urged a voice. The man took her hand and they ran over a field, across a road and into some trees. Her ribs ached and she fell down.

"Go on. I can't run any more."

The man flung her over his shoulder and ran with her to a marshy area laying along a river. She painfully stepped into a small boat.

A man with oars said softly, "Congratulations on your divorce from the Gestapo. We're so sorry we're not making the wedding either."

Then, members of the Polish underground, alerted by the escaping Maeva and Douglas, carried Antoinette to safety along a vast and far-reaching underground network.

Epilogue

$\mathcal{V}$illagers and tourists were gathering on a hot August afternoon at the Plaza in Villepente for a big event in the history of the village.

Dr. Gille, master of ceremonies, was chatting with two village council members. He saw Karl and Danielle Walthers arriving and that completed the cast of dignitaries, except for special guests of honor who were to arrive later.

Danielle uncrossed her legs. She tried to listen to Dr. Gille's opening remarks but she was so anxious to see Antoinette, it was hard to pay attention.

Dear, dear Antoinette. To see you after forty-five years. When I left Villepente so long ago, I never dreamed it would be this long until I see you again. Danielle could hardly bear waiting much longer.

One day a few months ago, Dr. Gille, now mayor of Villepente, had received a letter from a South African law firm. To his astonishment, a check fell out. To the village's good fortune. a statue would be commissioned by a former resident, if the village approved the idea.

The unknown person's attorney sought permission of the village council to commission the statue. The beneficent person wished to remain anonymous. However, Dr. Gille finally persuaded the contact that the council must know the identity of the benefactor before they could accept either the statue, or money for a dedication ceremony.

Insiders learned that the person was a former resident, a girl who left the village during the early years of the second world war under a cloud of suspicion.

As time elapsed between receipt of the original letter to the day of dedication, a lot of missing details were filled in for the village leaders. The person wanted to acknowledge the bravery of those persons who died at the Plaza long ago. Any one who was there remembered that night and spent a lifetime trying to forget, she said. The new villagers heard the stories.

Why should the village accept a painful reminder of its past?

Dr. Gille called a meeting of town leaders. As it often occurred when he faced challenges, he thought how good doctor Jean-Claude Renet or Henri Gauthier would present the idea.

They'd tell me to face the tiger.

It was an angry session. Long past and pent up feelings were expressed. Dr. Gille returned to the proposal. "Can't you see, it doesn't matter if anyone still thinks of Antoinette Gautheir as a Nazi consort. You've heard otherwise. Does it matter if you think she is giving the statue to redeem her past, or, whether it's her father she is especially honoring? Who cares?"

Yes, a nod of heads showed that those were a few of the things the leaders were thinking.

"Let us start with this premise, and, go from there," said Dr. Gille. "That she wants the statue to reconcile those things that happened beyond anyone's control. It's a way Villepente can bury its past. Finally. Don't we agree that we need to do so?"

"Humph," snorted one woman. "A statue will never make me accept or like Karl Walther."

"Maybe you wanted Karl but Danielle got him," countered another.

"Ladies and Gentlemen," insisted Dr. Gille, "these hurts and slights are important, but, can't we agree, so that the past can finally be put behind us. Villepente can be revitalized and move into the new century."

A council man's thinking must have been changed by Dr. Gille's remarks for he said, "Yes, we are pursuing several new manufacturing plants . . ."

Another added, "And, we do want the tourist trade to increase."

The group finally agreed it would be good public relations for the village and decided to accept the statue and the money for its dedication.

The news was announced. There would be a big village celebration to dedicate the statue and it would take place at the end of August. What the statue depicted would not be known until the moment of its unveiling. After the ceremony, it would be installed as part of the fountain at the Plaza.

Antoinette, until today, had never returned to the village. *Oh, what will she be like?* thought Danielle. That morning when she came into their bedroom, Karl was looking out the window. He was lost in the past. She went to him and wrapped her arms about his waist.

"My Karl," she said, "what courage you had to come back here."

Karl was watching the people walking along the cobblestones below.

"Oh," he replied. "It must be time and I haven't finished dressing." The former SS officer put on clothes which helped hide his wounds from the war. The wide trouser legs hid his mangled legs and the cut of suit jacket his scared chest, but no surgeon would ever completely mend the side of his face torn away.

For many months after being so severely wounded, he had not written to Danielle. Then, one day he wrote, taking great pains to simply express the fact that he was alive. "There's not much of me left but all that remains is yours if you still feel the same for me as I continue to do for you."

Danielle sobbed and sobbed when she read the letter and her tears covered his words on the thin transparent paper. She had thought him dead.

The love between them was strengthened by the challenges they faced when Karl came back to Villepente.

On the platform, Danielle was thinking about what Karl had told her just before they left the house for the ceremony. "Danny, you are as wonderful as the first day we met." Their lives had been hard, but good. His father built another of his canning factories outside Villepente and Karl managed the factory. They bought the Gauthier house.

A few years after WWII was over, Karl heard that Major Hurst owned a motorcycle business. On a cycling trip in the walled town of Rothenburg, he stumbled across his former snooty fiancé who owned an antique store. In its back room, she lived in the past as she presided over a hidden trove of Nazi uniforms, medals, weapons and other memorabilia.

Helene Gauthier did not live long after the tragic night at the Plaza. One after another of the family followed her beloved Henri. The shock of seeing him sprawled on top the other bodies at the fountain caused recurrent migraines that weakened her heart.

Leon, who set the explosives which detonated the bridge, had gone to the village after the Nazi train crashed. Francois begged him not to, "You know there will be reprisals. I beg you, don't go. You must not." But, his friend had not been able to persuade him otherwise.

Leon found his mother prostrate over the body of Henri. A grief so intense brought Leon to his knees crying, "Mother, I'm sorry. It was me who caused this."

A soldier overheard what Leon said and rushed to tell Major Hurst who hastened back to the plaza and shot him.

After the war, Helen tried her best to raise the youngest son, Pierre. She found herself so financially destitute that she had to sell the generations-old family home in Villepente. The only one to come forward with any money for it was Karl Walther. Yes, she would sell to him. Although he had been one of them, she felt he had been upright.

She told him life in Villepente would not be easy, that some would accept him and that others would never forgive.

Terrible events would not stop happening to Helene. Just before the war ended, Pierre was hunting with a friend, tripped over a rock and was killed by a blow to the head.

Dr. Renet grieved that he was unable to do anything to help the wife of his oldest and dearest friend. Even when American trucks loaded with bags of deceased American soldiers were parked at the Gauthier farm, it made no difference to Helene that the war was over.

The village deeded a plot of ground for burial of the Americans and promised that the village would keep up the grounds. Following the war, several Americans came to Villepente to spend time on the hillside looking for a familiar name on the tiny white crosses.

The crosses were good neighbors for the rows of headstones which all bore the same August 1941 date.

Danielle caught a few of the words of the priest at the microphone. He was telling the crowd about Father Molterine's sermon after the death of the pets. But she couldn't pay attention. Her eyes stared into the crowd. Was Antoinette out there?

She saw a few tourists near the Poulot Cafe. She recognized Nanette, the former Gauthier maid, who was very ancient, in a wheelchair near the PTT.

Where was Antoinette?

A few letters had passed between them over the years so she knew that Antoinette had married and that her biggest disappointment in life was not being able to have children.

Karl poked Danielle. The band was playing a march and everyone on the platform was standing up. They began the Marseilles.

A stocky man was being led to the platform by Dr. Gille.

Where was Antoinette?

At the microphone, Dr. Gille announced, "I take great pride to present Douglas Knight of Johannesburg, South Africa." Dr. Gille smiled and continued to smile as he shook the hand of Douglas Knight and then took a seat at the right of the podium.

"Thank you all for being here today," said Douglas. "It is a great honor to be here. And, you're probably wondering who I am and what I'm doing here all the way from South America.

"Actually, the world grows smaller every day through technology. But, years ago, when I met a young woman from this village, Villepente felt a planet's distance away.

"That girl saved my life and I've spent the best part of my life admiring her courage, her zest for life in spite of dire circumstances, and her love for creatures great and small.

"I promised her that I would come here to dedicate this memorial to the memory of an era in Villepente. Before she died, which happened a few weeks ago, through agreement with leaders of your village, she commissioned a statute to commemorate the tragic culmination of the event which took place but a few feet from where I'm standing.

"She wanted to be here to pull the cord to reveal the statue which might reconcile the past, but, it was not to be.

"I hope you'll consider me, her husband of many years, the next best candidate. No others remain in the Gauthier family, nor does her beloved friend, Jacques Duval, a member of the French Resistance who also left Villepente in August 1941 never to return.

"There was one bit of communication that we know about, a postcard sent from Marseilles so we know he got that far. Later, we learned that the merchant ship he was on was sunk. He was never heard from again. If he is alive anywhere, she has mentioned him in her will.

"The years were kind to us, and, although we were never to be parents, she became very active in charitable works in Johannesburg where she'll continue to be missed by all who knew her.

"Antoinette was a person who found treasure hidden in difficulty. Compassion was her heart's response to sorrow. She felt the sorrows of life connect each of us to one another by bringing tenderness, mercy and the all-embracing kindness that make a difference.

"Antoinette thought life was like dancing or listening to music. That we don't do any of them to reach the end as fast as possible. She knew that you can't love in the past, or the future, but only today.

"It is what she would tell you if she were here. Live and love and forgive."

"So, Dr. Gille, I defer to you."

Karl handed Danielle a handkerchief.

The doctor exchanged places with the husband of Antoinette.

"I was only ten years old when this village took me to its heart," said Dr. Gille. "I, too, owe my life and livelihood to persons from Villepente.

"Those who were here in August 1941 know they played a role in the world-wide struggle for freedom, the Gauthier family perhaps making greater sacrifices than anyone ever realized.

"Henri was your mayor then. I sat with him that day of the turn in of the pets. Together we felt the agony of those giving up those animals. His great gift to me was my life and I vowed when he traded his life for mine that I would never forget him.

"I never have. Everyday I attempt to treat others the way Henri might have, with tender love, infinite wisdom, and lack of judgment.

"If anyone here, or if anyone knows of anyone who harbors hateful thoughts stemming from those years, please, please put them behind you.

"If seeing the memorial state helps you put things back together so your life can go on and you can be at peace in your heart, the legacy of the entire Gauthier family will be fulfilled."

The crowd was very quiet.

Dr. Gille gave a signal to the band.

Douglas and the doctor started down the wood steps of the platform. They were followed by the other guests on the platform who began to collect by a canvas-covered object by the fountain.

People craned for better views. Dr. Gille motioned to a gaggle of children that they could go up on the platform where they could see better.

Douglas announced in a loud voice—"We dedicate this to the people of Villepente, past, present, and future."

He tugged at a cord and the canvas fell away.

A tall man, easily recognizable as Henri Gauthier, held the hand of a small boy. In each of their hands they held a small animal. A tear could be seen on each of their cheeks.

Etched within the base which held the statue of the man and boy were names of the people whose lives had ended the night of reprisal. And, so too were the names of the pets who gave their lives earlier.

The End